Crane

The Legends Saga

Book 1

Written by Stacey Rourke

Anchor Group Publishing
PO Box 225
Flushing, MI 48433

Dedication;

Sandra, thank you for sharing my love for the legends and for joining me in my giddiness when I mentioned Sleepy Hollow.

1

If his wife hadn't let her ass grow to the size of a sofa, Vic wouldn't have to cheat. Shrugging his navy blue sport coat over his shoulders, he stepped forward, allowing the hotel room door to shut behind him with a soft thump. A smug smile curled across his face, his chest puffing with pride at his own prowess—thanks in part to those spiffy little blue pills his doctor prescribed. The heels of his wing-tipped loafers clicked against the cement stairs, one impeccably manicured hand running along the handrail as he descended. The rusted metal rail squeaked its protest under the faint touch. Taking its suggestion, he retracted his hand.

Why he humored Karma by letting her drag him to this dive every week, he had no idea.

Her firm little apple bottom isn't that great, he mused to himself, snorting a quick, dry laugh.

Of *course* it was. She made good money with it at the Sugar Shack down by the airport. Grinding to R&B's raunchiest hits, while clad only in a sequin thong. She was a sweet, albeit naïve, girl that believed if she stroked Vic's ... *ahem*, ego just the way he liked, she would someday find a fat rock on her finger and the title of Van Tassel behind her name. Hence her insistence on the flea bag hotel. She had flipped her bleached blonde waves, batted those ridiculous fake eyelashes, and pouted that she couldn't be seen as the "other woman" by the same crowd she would soon be rubbing elbows with. As if he would *ever* let that happen. Karma's airbrushed nails and hooker heels would *never* fit into his world. After all, in Tarrytown the Van Tassel name meant something, and not because of the stupid legend the residents of the small glen of Sleepy Hollow mercilessly clung to. No, as one of the founding families they helped build this town. Meaning, here, he might as well be a Rockefeller. A fact he reveled in and would *never* tarnish with outward displays of his cheap conquests ... no matter how well she could wiggle.

Vic crossed the parking lot, lit only by one humming street lamp, with a wide, jovial stride. As he shook his keys from the pocket of his slacks, thumbing the button to unlock the doors, his phone buzzed from the breast pocket of his Armani shirt.

Snatching it from its resting place, he tapped to answer. "Yello?"

"Don't you sound chipper for someone working late?" Yvonne slurred, the only hint he needed that she'd already cracked open tonight's bottle of wine.

"Why shouldn't I be chipper?" he playfully asked, turning to glance back up toward the room Karma had rented. A flash of her blonde locks appeared from behind the stained drapes. He raised his hand in a casual wave, but couldn't tell from this distance if she returned the gesture. "I just finished showing a multi-million dollar estate that the buyers are *very* interested in, and now I get to head home to my loving wife."

"Yeah, right," Yvonne openly scoffed, her voice muffled by her glass as she took another sip. "We're the friggin' Cleavers. Hey, Cassidy is at the mall. I need you pick her up on your—"

Vic jerked his head to the right, in the direction of the neighboring gas station. Between the normal ebb and flow of rushing traffic, he heard the distinct snap of hoof beats pounding over pavement. "What kind of idiot would bring a horse out this close to the highway?"

"The highway? Where the hell *are* you, Victor?"

A moment ago the drum of the approaching rider had been coming from the south of him, Vic was sure of it. Yet somehow, without so much as a faltered step, it shifted to the north. "Stopped for gas, that's all." Vic paid little attention to the lie rolling off his tongue as he rose up on tiptoe and craned his neck to peer into the darkness.

"Oh!" Her momentary flash of accusation was all but forgotten at the exciting prospect of fresh booze. "Are you near Gordon Bleau's? I need a bottle of Amaretto."

Vic stifled a cringe at the thought of his wife's mixed drink induced wandering hands. If he wanted to fend off an overly Botoxed hag that reeked of booze, he'd go visit Nana at the home. Her old biddy friends loved him, and putting in his time there helped secure his spot in her will. "I'd love to, pet, but I'd hate to keep Cass waiting."

A hot, snorted breath heated the exposed skin of Vic's neck, tickling down the collar of his shirt. He spun, his heart pounding painfully in his chest, and pressed his back to the car door. Chills raced up and down his spine, electrifying his entire body. *Nothing.* There was nothing before him but that lone buzzing light and the seedy motel. "Damn it! Punk kids!"

"And they have a horse?" Yvonne's giggle morphed into a hiccup. "You better watch out, Vic. It could be one of those lesser known equestrian gangs."

The lightning that flashed on the otherwise calm night was the only omen Vic needed to spur him into action. Throwing himself off the car, his trembling fingers fumbled with the door handle. Behind him, metal hissed free from leather. Slowly—with a cold, hard fist of dread clenching his gut—his head swiveled.

"Oh," he said with a nervous lilt of laughter to the ominous symphony of black before him. "That's ... good. You got me. I really believed for a sec—"

Vic's anxious, cracking plea morphed into a scream as the figure pulled back. The blade of their arched sword gleaming gold under the yellow-hued light.

Victor's hands raised in the only defense he could offer. "*No! Noooo!*"

He sucked in one last gasp as metal winged through the air.

"Vic? Victor!" Yvonne screamed, panic clearing her alcohol induced haze. "*What's happening?*"

The only response she received came in the form of a ghostly whinny ... followed by a soft thump. Her shrieks were muted as the phone tumbled to the ground—right next to Vic's still rolling head.

2

Ichabod
Shortly after the Revolutionary War

"I feel we should have been more specific on the terms of our wager, gentlemen." The carriage rocked under his weight as Rip Van Winkle climbed down, a smirk curling across his chiseled features. He flipped a lock of caramel colored hair from his eyes and straightened his royal blue suit coat, allowing the gold embroidered lapels to lay in symmetrical lines. "When we declared that we three bold, daring bucks would venture to the first town in which one of us secured a job, we should have added the disclaimer that a town is defined as one inhabited by *people*."

Washington Irving, Irv to his friends, pushed past the still lamenting Rip. There was no telling how long his ramble would last, and Irv needed to retrieve his satchel from the trunk at the back of the carriage.

"You, sir," Irv interrupted, his satchel thumping to the ground at his feet, "are just bothered you were not the first to find acceptable employ. Mostly because, as the women that keep company with you can attest, the only services you provide pay in salves and a burning sensation over the chamber pot."

Rip's brow rose in mock shock. "How lewd a claim! Lewd ... with the faintest hint of accuracy."

Ichabod Crane was the last to exit the carriage. Some may have called him a handsome man, with his deep mahogany hair that fell to his strong jawline in waves and his almond-shaped eyes framed by lashes his sisters openly envied. Yet, for anyone to make such a claim they would have to actually notice the painfully shy educator. He was more than content to spend his days blending with the background.

Ichabod forced his gaze up in an apologetic nod to the driver on his friend's behalf. The driver snorted in contempt before flicking the reins and spurring the horses onward.

"Without so much as a good-bye?" Rip *tsk*ed. "And I'd grown so found of staring at the back of his head over these past two days. I fear there will be a nameless driver shaped hole in my heart."

Irv removed his glasses and cleaned them on the handkerchief from his breast pocket, his hair puffing around his head in an unruly mess from the nap he'd taken during the last leg of their journey. "You never get the least bit tired of listening to your own voice, do you?"

"Have you heard the hypnotic symphony of it?" Rip asked, throwing an arm around his friend's shoulders, much to Irv's visible annoyance. "Like a divine tune from an angel's lips."

Irv rolled his eyes and shoved Rip off of him. "Exactly where are we headed, Crane?"

Ichabod fumbled through his satchel. The spastic quaking of his right hand caused his pocket watch and Bible to jump from the bag, tumbling to the ground before he could locate their travel papers. Rip and Irv bent to retrieve the fallen items, careful not to acknowledge the ailment that caused their friend to lose hold of them.

"The school house that hired me is in the middle of town." Ichabod crinkled his nose to scoot his glasses further up its bridge. Shifting his gaze, he squinted over the top of the paper, attempting to match the directions to the structures. "The Hollow Inn, which I believe is that building there, has been kind enough to offer us stay."

Three sets of eyes stared for the first time at their new home. A narrow, cobblestone street led into the tiny village of modest dwellings. Most were quaint, plank-board homes whose chimneys puffed thick clouds of grey into a dreary sky that matched their hue. Modern architecture seeped its way into the tiny burg in the form of the occasional brick store front. A river cut through the town, made crossable by an enclosed bridge, which silhouetted the steepled white church that lay beyond it.

"One needn't remove one's shoes to count the business prospects in this glen." Irv stated and adjusted the strap of his satchel to get a better hold. "Yet even in the midst of a select few, there are sure to be those in need of legal aid. Come, let's find our rooms and get settled."

The dismal pallor of the sky was set against the deep brown foliage of late fall, of those last clinging leaves that had yet to join the corpses of their fallen brethren that covered the ground and crunched underfoot. Add to that the fog hanging low across the ground and the town seemed to possess an almost ethereal feel. Perhaps that was to blame for the beads of sweat suddenly dampening Ichabod's upper lip. He patted them away with his handkerchief before hiding the cloth in his pocket and offering a nod of greeting to an elderly man and woman who had watched their approach from the porch of their cottage. Instead of returning his greeting, the man seized the woman, which Ichabod assumed to be his wife, by her upper arm and ushered her quickly into the house. The door slammed and latched behind them. The further into town they ventured, the more of the same odd behavior they found. As the cloak of night settled in, and the newcomers paraded down the street, any townspeople they happened upon scurried into their home, pulling the shutters and bolting the doors.

"Where have you brought us, Ichabod Crane?" Rip attempted a tone of nonchalance, yet the nervous quake in his chuckle gave away the truth.

"Perhaps they know of your reputation," the soft-spoken schoolmaster jabbed, "And have busied themselves locking away their daughter's virtues."

Irv and Rip stopped walking and exchanged looks that resembled maternal pride.

"Not only have we managed to get him to speak, but also to jest." Irv beamed.

"If that *is* the case, then *we* should have been the ones awarded the Badge of Military Merit." Rip's eyes widened to goose eggs the second the words slipped from his lips.

Ichabod's shoulders instantly curled inward, his gaze drifting to the ground. "The inn is right up here." He shuffled on without glancing back to see if his friends were following.

Irv's lips disappeared in a thin, white line as he smacked Rip in the shoulder with the back of his hand. Rip rubbed his shoulder and nodded, accepting his just punishment for the huge faux pas.

The remainder of their hike was made in an uncomfortable silence, until their journey reached its conclusion in the foyer of The Hollow Inn. The Colonial style two-story was decorated by humble means. Even so, it radiated with warmth and the smell of fresh cinnamon loaf. While the lamps still burned within, the mahogany desk in the foyer was empty. The only sign of life came from the great room to their right where a rocking chair in front of the fireplace swayed. Back and forth it creaked, yet all they could see of its inhabitant was a thin pair of bony ankles that disappeared into tattered house shoes.

"Dark grows near, sense the fear," a voice, possessing the deep rasp of death, croaked in the sing-song tempo of a nursery rhyme.

"Cloak of night,

brings Horseman's plight.

His pricy toll,

will be a soul.

Run and hide,

before his ride.

Or the dead—" The face of a haggard old woman peeked around the back of the chair, her mouth open in a wide, toothless grin. A shock of white hair framed her ghastly face, falling to gaunt shoulders in wiry wisps. "—Shall claim ye head."

"Mother! That's enough! You'll scare our guests away!" The interruption came from a robust woman with a welcoming smile as she sauntered in from the kitchen, the floorboards creaking beneath her feet. "You'll have to forgive her. She hasn't been the same since Papa died, and that was thirty *long* years ago. Now, I suppose you would be Mr. Crane, Mr. Irving, and Mr. Van Winkle?" Before the three men could even nod in agreement, she pushed on in a long winded ramble that left no opportunity for interruption. "Well, my name is Roselynn Tremaine, however around here everyone calls me Mama Rosa. Don't know why, I have never had any littles of my own, but I find it charming so I do not ask. Let me be the first to welcome you to Sleepy Hollow and to thank you three for serving our country. I was able to get you each rooms of your own, just as you requested." She swiveled to retrieve three bronze keys from the three separate pegs and splayed them on the counter between them. "Was not much of an act of luck, we only get the occasional merchants come to town to sell their wares. Availability is seldom a concern, which only means we will be happy to house you as long as you like! Breakfast is at seven, lunch at noon, and we sup at five. Even so, if you ever need a little something to tide you over in between, do not be afraid to ask! No one goes hungry under my roof."

Ichabod directed his smile to the floorboards, the mystery of how she got the nickname "Mama" revealed.

"Oh," she continued, "I suppose I should mention the curfew."

Irv's head snapped back as if she'd slapped him. "Curfew? Surely as a business owner you cannot expect paying guests—"

"Oh, it is not *my* curfew, sir." Mama Rosa's second chin wobbled with the adamant shake of her head. "Not even a governed matter, far as I know. More a ... precaution, taken and adhered to by all the residents not to go out after dark. Just how we do things around here, I am sure you can appreciate that?"

While Irv and Rip exchanged dubious glances, it was Ichabod that shrugged and offered Mama Rosa a timid smile. "Who are we to judge the ways of a town we have yet to properly meet?"

The sincerity of his smile wavered, interrupted by a loud cackle from the next room. Ichabod didn't want to look. Yet, with a gulp, he let his gaze slide slowly to the frightening old woman. Air slipped over her gums in a steady hiss. Her stare was directed at Ichabod alone as she dragged the tip of her index finger across her throat.

3

Ireland

Present time

"If this is some sort of sick Sleepy Hollow hazing ritual, it is *just* twisted enough for me to totally dig it."

"No, ma'am. We make it a rule never to be less than one hundred percent serious when questioning someone about a brutal homicide." Curly black tufts of hair winged out from beneath the stern-faced officer's hat as he adjusted the holster that hung below his thick paunch.

"No, of course you don't. Because that would be wildly inappropriate," Ireland Crane tipped her head before murmuring to the cement porch beneath her feet, "not unlike what I just said."

"You claimed you last saw Mr. Van Tassel the day you signed your lease and he gave you the keys?" the still scowling officer asked.

Ireland raked a hand through her newly sheered locks, her eyebrows practically disappearing into her hairline. "Yeah, that was the one and only time I ever even saw the guy. Which makes it all the more confusing why you boys are knocking on *my* door about this."

13

"We're just looking for answers, Miss Crane," the slightly meatier officer—with a kind, easy smile and thick mustache—reassured her. "Do you mind if we come inside to discuss this matter further?"

Ireland's gaze flicked down to read their badges before she pushed herself off the door frame and wandered inside, leaving the door open in invitation. "By all means, Officers Potter and Granger, sit if you can find a place." She waved an arm at the mountains of moving boxes that cluttered the living room, her face an open apology for the mess.

The duo followed her inside, Officer Potter—who appeared about as happy as a thumb smashed by a hammer—shutting the door behind them. He stood ramrod straight at attention while Granger perched casually on the arm of Ireland's hand-me-down couch.

"I'm sure you can understand with a crime of this magnitude we really need to get to the bottom of it quickly." Granger crinkled his nose, his head bobbing like they were buddies in this together.

Ireland cleared off a spot on the coffee table and plopped down. With her elbows rested on her knees, she thumped her thumbs against each other as a means of distraction. What she really wanted to do was scratch the hell out of the new tattoo on her forearm that had reached that maddeningly itchy phase. Since that was a *huge* no-no, she thumped. "I completely understand that. It's just a bit off-putting since I've been in Sleepy Hollow less than a week. It kinda sounds like the plot of a cheesy B movie."

Officer Potter tipped his head back and glared down his nose at her. "A man was decapitated outside a local motel. There is no script here, or director to yell cut. What we have is a twisted perp that needs to be brought to justice *immediately*."

"Then you tell me," Ireland replied in a tone she hoped resembled sincerity, "what can I do to help this process along?"

Granger's quizzical gaze wandered to his partner. Even he seemed taken aback by his abrasiveness. "I'm sure you're aware of the implications of the Crane name in Sleepy Hollow?" he asked, forcing his attentions back to Ireland.

"I've heard the stories, read the book, and even seen the Johnny Depp movie," Ireland answered with a tight-lipped smile.

"Hey!" Potter jabbed a finger in Ireland's direction, his face reddening in his snit. "In no way can a motion picture measure up to the mastery of storytelling in the book! No matter how 'dreamy' Mr. Depp might be!"

Granger and Ireland stared for an awkwardly, silent beat.

"Well ..." Ireland flicked her tongue over her lips to wet them. "There really is no comparison to the wonders of the written word, is there?"

Granger cocked his head in a clear 'oh, you sweet girl' expression. "*Anyway*," he stated, attempting to steer around the odd conversational detour. "Your name sets off certain ... red flags around here. I'm sure you understand that. Do you happen to know if you have any blood ties to the Hollow?"

Ireland shook her head, her long bangs falling into her eyes. "Not even the foggiest idea. However, Crane is an *incredibly* common name. I bet I'm not even the only one with it in Tarrytown. That can't be the only reason why you're here? It seems like quite a stretch."

Officer Granger rubbed the side of his index finger over his mustache, back and forth, searching for the right words. "Actually, ma'am, you *are* the only Crane within city lines. And it's a crucial detail regarding that which brought us here. You see, the vic ... Charles Van Tassel, had ... uh—"

"He had *your* last name carved into his chest," Officer Potter finished for him in a flat, emotionless tone.

Bile rose in Ireland's throat; the pizza she'd scarfed down earlier threatening a second coming. "Oh. That's," suddenly all of the adjectives in her vocabulary seemed inadequate, so she settled for a meager word that didn't even begin to describe it, "awful."

Potter nodded to the ground, shifting from one foot to the other. "We think we're dealing with a copycat that has decided to act out his fantasies inspired by the legends." Meadow green eyes, ringed by deep emerald, suddenly locked on her with a drilling intensity. "Unless you know of another reason why your name would be carved into a man you claim you barely know?"

Ireland's spine straightened, drove up by a hot indignant flare from his unspoken accusation. "I didn't *claim* anything. I found this house online, exchanged a few emails with the guy, and met him once to get the keys. End of story. Don't believe me? I can show you the emails."

"That won't be necessary." Granger let slip an involuntary groan as he eased himself off the couch arm. Ireland couldn't help but notice he'd positioned himself between her and his partner, and wondered whose benefit that was for. "But you keep a firm look out, you hear? Your name being what it is, you could wind up a target. If it *is* a copycat, they'll want to act it out with the most realism possible. What better way than with an actual Crane?"

Ireland couldn't have stifled that nervous gulp if she wanted to. "As far as welcome wagon greetings go, this one is lousy."

Officer Granger clapped a sweaty hand on to her shoulder, a blend of apology and regret etched in the lines of his face. "Sorry to drop all of this on you. Truly we are. This really is a great town. I have no doubt you'll do well here." His icy blue eyes brightened with a fresh idea. "Hey! Have you checked out the tour of the Old Dutch Church and cemetery? You can see the actual route of the Horseman! That's sure to be a treat for a town newbie!"

"Perhaps *you* should exercise *your* right to remain silent," Potter muttered out of the corner of his mouth. "You just informed the girl that someone posing as the Headless Horseman may want to kill her, then suggested she explore the cemetery he was rumored to frequent. Should I draw you a diagram of why that's a bad idea?"

Granger chewed on the inside of his cheek, mulling that over. "Yeah, probably shouldn't go to the cemetery."

Potter tipped his hat, then yanked open the front door. "We appreciate your time, miss. I'm sure there's no cause for concern, just be sure to keep your doors locked and stay in after dark if you can manage it."

"I'll cancel any raves on my schedule," Ireland deadpanned. "Can't find my hot pink fishnet top anyway."

"If you have any problems at all, just give us a call," Officer Granger said, kindly ignoring her sorry attempt at a joke.

"Mm-hmm," she automatically answered, following him to the door. For a moment she stared outside, lost in the looming darkness. An undeniable sense of dread bloomed in her chest, goose bumps sprouting up and down her arms. What if they were right? What if out there, right then, someone was watching her ... waiting for their moment to strike? Ireland ran her hands over her arms, trying to shake off her self-inflicted chill.

Midway down the sidewalk, Granger paused, casting one final glance back. Plucking his hat from his head, he held it loosely in front of him, what resembled hope building in his gaze and earnest smile. "Sleepy Hollow welcomes you, Miss Crane."

Replacing his hat, he strode to the waiting cruiser without another look back.

Ireland sucked in her cheeks, turning her head one way then the other. According to the bathroom mirror and the 1970's retro-chic light fixture, her new 'do had an unforeseen benefit. The spikey, chin-length bob, colored a deep cherry cola red, gave her a confident—slightly punk—air. Combine that with a little eyeliner and a coat of lipstick, and even *she* had to look hard to find the quaking ball of nerves that lay beneath the effective costuming.

Puffing her cheeks, she blew air out through slightly pursed lips. She *couldn't* mess this up. There had been too many life-altering, ground-shaking screw-ups over the last year. This was her new start, and more than anything she needed it to pan out so she could finally shake off the stagnate funk of bad decisions that haunted her.

Fearing the doubts plaguing her would seep in and taint the self-assured doppelganger reflected back at her, she forced herself to click off the light and step away from the tell-tale mirror. Her low-heeled ankle boots clicked across the wood floors as Ireland hurried out of the bathroom, through the living room, and around the corner to the quaint kitchen/dining room combo. She yanked the rolled sleeve of her blouse down while she walked, buttoning it around her wrist. Sure, the principal at Sleepy Hollow High, who had hired her as the new guidance counselor, *claimed* the new sugar skull tattoo on her forearm was completely okay. She'd even complimented her on the beautifully colored flowers and delicate scrolls that added a touch of femininity to an otherwise harsh image. Ireland covered it for herself. Because this particular piece of artwork wasn't to show off. It was a self-reminder of the pledge she'd made to reinvent herself into someone she was proud to be.

Grabbing an untoasted bagel from the counter, she crammed it between her teeth, freeing her hands up to pour the last of the coffee into one of the few travel mugs she'd unpacked. Coffee in tow, she snatched her supple new briefcase from its resting place on the floor and hurried to the door. With the bagel lodged between her teeth, she fumbled in her pants pocket for the keys, all the while saying a silent prayer not to drop everything else.

"Need a hand?" a deep, gravelly voice murmured from the sidewalk in front of her.

19

Having been born and raised in Manhattan, Ireland was used to a stream of people surging around her in a relentless flow. However, this was not Manhattan. Here, quiet reigned and human interaction, in the week she'd been here, had been shockingly sparse. Therefore, she handled the surprise with all the cool reserve she could muster. Spitting out the bagel in a rain of crumbs, she screamed and threw her coffee at the intruder. Thick-treaded work boots jumped back as the scalding java sloshed across the front stoop, narrowly missing him.

"Why do I feel I just committed a cardinal sin?" her guest asked.

"You did. There's no coming back from that." Ireland shook her head with genuine sadness as she wiped bagel crumbs from her lips.

As the last of the burnished brown liquid seeped through a crack in the cement stair, Ireland brought her gaze up.

Short, sandy brown hair blended into skin kissed golden by the sun. A shadow of stubble darkened the chiseled cut of his jawline. Hazel eyes hinted at cobalt blue to match the sky. Pulling his hands from the pockets of his *Carhartt* coat, he bent to retrieve her mug. This man was salt of the earth sexy—a fact that instantly caused Ireland to bristle and hate him.

"Lucky for you there's a *Starbucks* in Sleepy Hollow, I'll even buy," he said with the kind of smile guys like him probably thought was panty-dropping charming.

Ireland ran her tongue over her teeth before forcing a tight smile in return. "I've found the candy from strangers rule also applies to caffeinated beverages."

"Let me remedy that." Stepping forward, he offered her his hand, rough and calloused from many a hard day's labor. "I'm Noah, the ... *uh* ... handy man for the Van Tassel properties."

"You sure about that answer? There's still time to change it." Ireland was well aware her tone was sharp and biting. That fact was quite deliberate. As was dropping Mr. Bedroom-Eyes's hand like it scalded her.

As a teen, when she still believed in the notion of romance, Ireland had read many contrite love stories in which the girl sees a boy for the first time and feels an uncontrollable draw to him. Somehow she just *knows* he's the one. This was nothing like that. If it was, Ireland probably would've thrown herself into traffic as a public service to mankind. The feeling *she* had was more of a chill, like ghostly hands pushing between her shoulder blades, encouraging her to step closer. To allow herself to breathe in the spicy sweetness of his scent that the morning breeze teased her way. Ireland physically shook off that reverie and fought against the feeling to take a needed step back.

Noah's gaze shifted to the sidewalk to hide the smirk that threatened, while he kicked a pebble with the toe of his boot. "Sorry, usually when I knock on the door of rental properties, I find single moms, crazy cat ladies, or newly divorced guys with stacks of porn that boggle the mind. The porch theatrics was a fun surprise."

"Is that why you're here, Noah?" Ireland adjusted the strap of her briefcase on her shoulder and forced a judgmental sneer she truly wasn't feeling. "To investigate my porn collection? Let me save you the trouble. A biography DVD that shows Janis Joplin's boobs is the closest thing to kink you'll find in there."

Oblivious to the vibe she was trying so hard to lay down, Noah threw his head back and laughed. "As inclined as I am to ask if they're nice, I think I'll get to the actual point of the visit. I live next door and saw the cops here yesterday. I just wanted to stop by and make sure everything was okay."

Ireland momentarily forgot she'd chopped off her hair, and flipped her head in a way that *would've* made her long locks sway across the small of her back. Instead it made her look like she had a twitch. "For me? Yes. For the unfortunate fella that lost his head? Not so much. Apparently some sick SOB carved *my* last name in his chest. Hence the impromptu night time visit."

Noah's features sharpened, a storm cloud of sorrow rolling and chasing away any traces of humor. "Yeah, I've heard all about that. The whole thing is ... horrible." He jerked his chin toward the door. "If it makes you feel any better, this house has an alarm system. All you have to do is type 1-2-1-5 into the keypad just inside the door to arm it."

Ireland hitched one eyebrow. "A code that *you* happen to know? And I just, what? Cross my fingers you aren't the newly inspired town killer?"

Noah cocked his head to consider her. "Do I look like a killer?"

Slow and deliberate, she let her gaze wander over him before giving a noncommittal shrug. "Hard to say. Although, I think asking that is how they begin and end meetings of The Secret Psycho Killer Society."

A laugh, so warm and contagious it threatened to crack Ireland's aloof façade, bubbled up from Noah's broad chest. "Fair enough," he chuckled. "The control panel is in the basement. Type in the code, hit reset, then the code again. After that type in whatever numbers you want. You'll be the only one that has it. No one to distrust then, but *you*."

Flipping her bangs from her eyes, Ireland pressed the button to unlock her car. "Yeah? Sometimes I'm my worst enemy," she muttered through her teeth, before stepping off the stoop.

Her shoulder brushed his as she sauntered past. Keeping her expression pointedly neutral, she let the electric shudder that rocked through her be her secret to keep.

4

Ichabod

Ichabod shifted from one foot to the other, his stare locked on the lifeless hand peeking out from beneath the blood soaked sheet. His mind ticked back, trying to recall the first time he'd encountered a dead body. Undoubtedly, it had been during the war. Yet, for the life of him, he couldn't remember which death had been the first or the range of emotions it had stirred inside of him. Since then, each time he'd seen a life needlessly snuffed out, he felt that same endless void of sorrow for what might have been. Suddenly, he became painfully aware of the other townspeople gathered around. His chestnut eyes, made brighter by flecks of gold that swirled and crackled when he was anxious, flicked around the gaping crowd. Was he reacting properly? Their faces were tear streaked, pale, and aghast at the horror of the crimes. What deficiency lay within him that he actually had to contemplate if he should be frowning more?

He opened and closed his right hand, attempting to ease the tremors coursing down his arm, then filled his lungs to capacity and exhaled slowly. Moments like this made him thankful for a friend like Irv, who was blathering away beside him. Unbeknownst to Irv, he became Ichabod's beacon. Ichabod focused on his words, letting them draw him out of his head and back to the here and now.

"I searched the county records and there has not been an 'attack' from their alleged Horseman in decades." Irv's eyes flashed with an excitement he normally only got when discussing the intricacies of legal matters he often bored Ichabod and Rip with. "Up until now, many of the residents have played along with the warnings and rules the local officials have whispered in their ears to keep this 'legendary' hessian at bay, merely out of their own superstitious fears. Do not you see, Ichabod?" he gushed in an urgent whisper. "They were using a ghost story to keep the townspeople in line! Nonetheless, now they have had to resurrect their 'ghost.' I do not know what atrocity Madame Van Tassel and her hand maiden committed, or what knowledge they uncovered, yet I bid you mark my words, there are treacheries afoot here in Sleepy Hollow. Did you notice the nature to which their heads had been lobbed off?"

Bile rose in Ichabod's throat, and stung as he gulped it back, from his friend's straight forward description.

If Irving noticed Ichabod's sudden greenish hue, he failed to acknowledge it. "The Van Tassel woman suffered only one blow, a single slice from a powerful adversary. However, notice the wounds 'round her maid's throat. The flesh has been gouged and mutilated from repeated strikes. Someone hacked away at that poor woman. Which can only mean there were two attackers, not one lone!"

"Try to contain your enthusiasm, friend." Ichabod forced his nervous gaze up to scan the crowd. No eyes looked their way ... yet. "Others may misconstrue your zest for justice as a proclamation of guilt."

Their banter was interrupted by an anguished wail that visibly jolted the gawkers. "*Where is she? Where is my wife?*" Stares shifted to the ground as onlookers parted, allowing access to Baltus Van Tassel. He rounded the side of the building to the back garden of the inn. His robe blew behind him in his frantic strides, revealing the night clothes he still wore beneath. Receding grey hair, which flipped and puffed well past his ears in complete disarray, had gone unattended in his rush. As soon as his eyes fell on the lump, which was covered by a sheet, and the dainty sapphire slippers poking out from beneath, his legs gave out. He crumbled to the ground, crawling the remaining distance to her side.

"Selena! Selena, my love!" he sobbed, gathering the headless body in his arms.

Women, Mama Rosa included, shielded their eyes as the sheet fell away to reveal the full revulsion of their grisly embrace.

"Baltus, you must leave her be. This is a crime scene now," the town magistrate declared, and attempted to pry his friend's arms from the mutilated form of the woman he loved.

"This is no crime." Baltus's chin trembled; tears and snot dripped from his face while he eased his wife's body to the ground. "We became too lax and angered the Horseman somehow. This is our punishment. My dear Selena paid the ultimate price for our failure."

"This is ridiculous," Irv muttered, pushing his glasses up the bridge of his nose with his index finger. "They are not even considering the possibility of foul play."

The magistrate's white powdered wig slipped slightly askew as he heaved his grieving friend up on trembling legs. "Her death will not be in vain. We will double our efforts this evening. That dark spirit will be appeased and will leave us in peace once more. For now, you must let us record aspects of the scene for our records. It is our job to warn future generations of the Horseman's threat, to save them of this same fate." The magistrate glanced over his shoulder and nodded to the Van Tassel's young house maid. He was forced to snap his fingers to tear her red-rimmed eyes from the covered form of the fallen servant. "Elizabeth, help him home please. Tend to him and Katrina well during this difficult time, won't you, dear?"

"Of course, monsieur." The young maiden wiped at her eyes with the back of her hand, gave a quick curtsy, and rushed to collect her employer.

"Wait!"

Ichabod tried to catch Irv's shirt sleeve before he could do something rash, yet only caught the edge of his cuff, which easily slipped from his grasp.

It was too late.

His exuberant friend was bounding forward, his mission set. "Sirs, we must not let superstitious claims cloud us from an even darker possible truth! I will not deny you the folklore of the town, even so there is the possibility that these murders could be at the hand of someone that *knew* if they made it look like a horseman attack, no one in these parts would question it."

Baltus turned slowly, peering at Irv through eyes that fought to focus. "What are you suggesting, lad?"

"I practiced law downstate before the war. I have friends there that are trained to investigate crimes. I could reach out to them, ask them to come." Irv laid a reassuring hand on Baltus's forearm, seemingly oblivious to the still damp blood that stained the arms and front of the widower's robe. "We could find the truth."

Baltus stared down at Irving's hand as if wondering how it found its way there. "And what would you ask of me in return?" he asked in a tone ominously vacant of emotion.

"I would just need you to fund their voyage here and provide them quarters," Irv offered, his eager eyes pleading his request.

Rip inched forward from the outskirts where he'd lingered. "Shall I retrieve him before we're chased from town by a mob?"

Ichabod shook his head. "I think it's a bit late for that."

"I've heard of you, Ichabod Crane." Baltus yanked his arm from Irving's contaminating touch. The gaze he fixed on him filled with pure hate.

Ichabod's eyebrows shot up at the mention of his name.

"Actually, sir," Irv corrected, "my name is—"

"I'm done listening to anything you have to say. You have shown the kind of man you are. Attempting to exploit my sorrow before my wife's body is even cold?" Fresh tears gushed from Baltus's eyes, his voice trembling and breaking. "That is the very *worst* kind of charlatan. There's a special place in Hell for you, Ichabod Crane. And someday, Hell *will* claim you."

Without another word, Baltus stormed off, his maid scurrying to keep up.

"It seems Irv has tasked himself with making you new friends here in the Hollow." Rip grimaced and slapped a comforting hand on Ichabod's shoulder.

Ichabod saw his copy of *Grimm's Fairy Tales* slipping from his desk, yet couldn't catch it in time. The hardcover book flipped once in midair before hitting the floor with a loud *crack*. His students reacted to the noise as he imagined they would to cannon fire ripping a hole in the side of the school house. The pig-tailed Steinbeck twins burst into tears and huddled in each other's arms. The eldest children in class—Theodore, Mary Ellen, and Victor—immediately reached out for the youngest, fully prepared to shield them if need be. Bright blue eyes, framed by impossibly thick lashes, belonging to young Korine Lancaster peeked out from behind her older sister, Cecilia. Every last one of them was utterly, and justifiably, terrified. Their parents should have tried harder to shield them from yesterday's gruesome event, however in a small town such as this, Ichabod doubted it would be possible to keep such news quiet, even to small ears.

Ichabod tapped his fingers against his desk, mulling over how best to address this issue. "Children, quickly now," he commanded, zestfully bounding to his feet with growing enthusiasm for his idea. "I would like you to push all the desks to the outside of the room. Come now! Up and moving!"

With a fair share of unease, the children rose and met their teacher's barked order. Desks squealed and scuffed across the wood plank floor as they dragged them to their new resting place. The children then gathered in the center of the room, awkwardly awaiting further instruction.

Ichabod rounded his desk and eased himself to the ground, legs crossed in front of him. "Join me! All in a circle, knees together."

His order was met with much confusion. Theodore was the first to lead by example. One by one, the others slowly followed.

Ichabod held his tongue and refused to speak until the very last child took a seat. "Very good," he encouraged with a tight smile. "Do any of you know what a resource is?"

Mary Ellen tentatively raised her hand.

Ichabod nodded for her to answer.

"It is something that holds great value because it helps to benefit the community."

"Very good. And do you know what the greatest resource of Sleepy Hollow is?" He gazed around the room as the students looked to each other for the answer.

"*You* are," Ichabod answered for them. "Each and every one of you are the future of Sleepy Hollow. You are all so very valuable that every adult within this community would fight to keep you safe. The lot of our Hollow would eagerly draw their swords if it meant keeping you—

" his upper body swiveled as he pointed to each of them, "—and you, and you, and of course you ..."

"And me?" Korine asked, her voice the sweet tinkling of Christmas bells.

"Most definitely you, and they would not forget you, or even you Thomas—despite the fact that you are wiping your nose on your sleeve— or you, young sir. The entire town would do the very same for every last one of you." Looking into their faces, Ichabod could see the thick noose of their unease begin to loosen. "So, you see, you have nothing to fear. Your jobs—that must *not* be taken lightly—are to spend your days learning, playing, and tending to your chores while we adults handle any other pressing matters. Tonight you shall nestle into your beds and think lovely thoughts of candied treats whilst leaving unpleasant matters to the adults. Are we understood?"

Cautious smiles began to brighten young faces, their head bobbing in silently agreement.

"I'm sorry, but this matter is of dire importance and requires an audible agreement," Ichabod stated in an adopted façade of superior indignation.

A chorused holler of "Yes!" followed by a highly contagious case of giggles, echoed off the walls.

"Very good!" Ichabod clapped a hand to the floor, then pushed himself up to stand. "Now, I do believe it is time for you to head outside for your afternoon game of Kick the Can. Watch out for Thomas," he called after the children who were already scampering out the door. "He kicks like a mule!"

As the door banged shut, leaving empty silence in its wake, Ichabod dipped down to pick up the book that had caused the ruckus.

"You calmed the children with such ease. I wonder if you could work that same magic on the entire town," a soft voice said from the doorway.

Ichabod spun with a start, his hand immediately beginning to shake. His breath caught. He'd captured a few glimpses of the vision before him as she made her way across town, but never so near. The angels themselves would've envied her beauty. The color cascading down her back in thick waves, reminded Ichabod of freshly bloomed daffodils glistening in the sun. Lips, as succulent as ripe strawberries dipped in cream, parted to grace him with a smile bright enough to light the rest of his days.

Worried he was staring, Ichabod busied himself tidying his already neat desk. "I am afraid my methods are less effective on those jaded by age and life lessons."

She crossed the room without hesitating, or waiting for invitation. "I think you doubt yourself, sir. A kind heart is a treasure, or to use your own words, a resource. Its value cannot be measured."

Ichabod clasped his hands behind his back before she could see his flaring tremor. "I thank you for your kindness. Was there something that brought you to our school house? Can I help you in some way?"

He immediately regretted his choice of words, fearing she would misconstrue them as him finding her presence bothersome. Yet, before he had a chance to clarify his meaning, she pulled forward the basket that hung from her arm.

"When the nerves hit me, I bake. After the nightmare of yesterday, I found myself in the kitchen surrounded by three dozen apple fritters." She pulled back a corner of their cloth cover, allowing the wonderful aroma of cinnamon-apple to waft out. "I worried the children might be having difficulties as well, and thought perhaps bellies full of treats might distract them, at least for a short while."

Beauty and kindness was a potent siren song that made this vixen even more enchanting. "I will surely pass them along. And on behalf of my students, I thank you for your kindness, Miss …" Ichabod trailed off in hopes that she would fill a name he could fix to this mesmerizing vision.

"Where are my manners?" Her hand fluttered to her mouth, a rosy blush filling her cheeks. "I'm Katrina," she bowed her head and dipped in a slight curtsy, "Katrina Van Tassel."

Icy prickles replaced the blood pumping through Ichabod's veins. Here he was making small talk with this woman who had lost a family member mere hours ago. This was the moment he needed to extend his condolences, yet he couldn't seem to force them past his suddenly constricted throat. She was the daughter of Baltus *Van Tassell,* the same man that had publicly proclaimed him the lowest form of scoundrel. He wanted to ask her how she was fairing, explain there was a misunderstanding, utter some words that would allow her to leave here not thinking him a complete charlatan. Unfortunately, no such magical phrasing jumped to mind.

"And you, sir, what is your name?" Sweet words, spoken by an angel, who would surely cast him to Hell as soon as he responded. "Or shall I just call you Schoolmaster?"

Ichabod's arm gave a violent jerk as he pried his mouth open to answer with all the enthusiasm of a death march.

Before one syllable could leave his parted lips, the door flew open, allowing Mary Ellen to barrel inside. "Mr. Crane! Cecilia fell from the swing! She's bleeding terribly! Come quick!"

Katrina yanked the cloth from the fritters and handed it to Ichabod as he quickly rounded his desk. "Here, use this to stop the bleeding. Oh, wait!" she called a second before he stepped foot outside. "You are Ichabod Crane?"

He paused only a moment, to glance back and watch the disdain he was sure would spread across her lovely face, casting him down to a slithering reptile coiled under a rock. "I am."

"It is a pleasure to meet you, Ichabod." The warmth of her smile made his heart flutter, filling him with the comfort of … home.

5

Ireland

"I brought you a fern!"

Ireland glanced up from the file folders that covered her desk and smiled at the new arrival beaming from the doorway. "That's a lesser known form of greeting, however, in this particular office, completely acceptable."

"Sorry, I probably should've started with 'I'm Amber, your administrative assistant'." Amber crinkled her pert nose in a no-handed attempt to fix her silver-framed glasses. Her fluffy brown curls were barely contained by the hair-tie at the nape of her neck.

Ireland's leather chair squeaked as she rose to her feet and extended her hands to accept her gift. "Standard salutations are overused. You get points for originality." Directing an apologetic cringe at the fern, she added, "A living thing in my office? That's quite the commitment. I'm going to have to demand joint custody and supervised visitation to keep this thing alive."

"Oh, I can totally help with that! I read this fascinating article about the benefits of talking to plants, and since I'm usually talking anyway, I might as well direct it at our fern-baby." As Amber crossed the room, Ireland noticed slightly askew glasses weren't the only thing working against her. Her white blouse, with yellow polka-dots, was only tucked in on one side, and she appeared to be wearing two different shoes. "Sorry if it seems an odd gift, but I left the house in a rush. My mother always taught me that a little token of welcome can create deep roots of friendships, and that is exactly what I wanted to do! So, I stopped at the florist … and panicked. It was either this or an orchid and they are *insanely* temperamental!"

"You did your mother proud. Question, did she ever mention casting the occasional glance downward?" Ireland set the fern down on the corner of her desk, brushing the potting soil from her hands before subtly pointing at Amber's mismatched footwear.

Confusion furrowed Amber's brow as she followed Ireland's gaze. "Huh. Well that's an unfortunate first impression to make with your new boss."

"Okay, first, please don't call me your boss. We're the same age, and this is my first real 'grown-up' job. You use words like boss and I'm bound to freak out and rush off to have something pierced. Second, I saw nothing but a pretty fern. Any claims of odd footwear are simply speculation." With a playful wink, Ireland settled back into her chair. "In other, non-foliage related matters, Principal

Edwards mentioned a few of our seniors needed recommendation letters written for scholarship programs. Do you happen to know where those files are?"

"Absolutely," Amber bubbled, and began flipping through the mess of papers scattered on the desk between them. Her fingers flicked over the files with a speed that bordered on manic until she settled on a stack, which she pulled out and presented to Ireland. "Here they are! Organized with color tabs by the specific requirements needed for each, that way you can just go down the list and knock them out quick and easy. The key to the color tab is right here on top."

Ireland sucked air through her teeth, both impressed and terrified by her assistant's efficiency. "Fantastic. Could you please pull each students' file so I know who—"

"—they are and what their academic record looks like?" Amber finished for her. "On the filing cabinet behind you."

A knock rattled the office door before Ireland could accuse Amber of being some sort of voodoo mind-reader or an android— but she was convinced the girl was one or the other.

"Your first office visit!" Amber's shoulders raised with her high-pitched squeal of delight.

Ireland stared for a beat, her glance flicking around the narrow office as she tried to figure how she would maneuver to the door around Amber, who seemed to be firmly planted. Unless she learned to crawl across the ceiling Spidey-style in the next five seconds, it wasn't going to happen. With no other choice, she leaned in toward Amber to whisper, "One of us should get the door."

"Oh! Allow me!" Amber gushed. Turning on the heel of her brown shoe, she led with the black one to take the stride and a half to the door.

Opening it a crack, she peeked out, then glanced back over her shoulder to whisper in a soft but urgent tone, "It's Principal Edwards and a student."

"You can let them in," Ireland whispered back.

The door squeaked on its hinges as Amber pulled it open and took a meek step into the background.

"Miss Crane, do you have a second?" Principal Edwards asked with a painfully forced smile.

"Absolutely." Ireland wet her lips anxiously as her gaze darted from the principal to the student and back again.

Amber snuck out, and quietly shut the door behind her. Principal Naomi Edwards folded her hands in front of her, her voluptuous figure putting strain on the buttons of her eggplant-colored blazer. Beside her stood a cute, golden-haired teen whose arrogant swagger and cocky leer made him look like a stand-in on a *CW* show.

"Miss Crane, this is Mason Van Brunt. It seems he couldn't get through the first day of school without being sent down to see me." The principal's full lips pursed while she cast a disapproving glance at the disinterested teen. "Which makes a consecutive four for four of his high school career. This time he sexually harassed our fifty-year-old PE teacher, who also happens to be a Tai Kwon Do instructor." Out of the corner of her mouth, she muttered, "You're lucky she didn't kick your teeth out the back of your head."

Snorting his amusement, Mason tipped his head to peer up at her from under one hitched brow. "What can I say, I appreciate a well-maintained G.I.L.F."

Principal Edward's forehead puckered in confusion. "A gilf?"

"Grandma I'd like to—"

"And that's enough out of Mason!" Ireland rocketed out of her chair, cutting off the teen's off-color comment.

"*Anyway,*" the principal continued, shooting Ireland an exasperated eye roll, "Mr. Van Brunt's parents have been notified, and they are on their way to collect him." She handed his file off to Ireland, then stabbed one French manicured finger at the chair, gesturing for him to sit. "Until they arrive, I thought you two could get acquainted, maybe even figure out what demons lurk in him that make him act a fool at any given moment."

39

Mason didn't argue, but flopped down in the chair. Principal Edwards gave Ireland a quick nod and mouthed the words "good luck" before pulling the office door shut behind her.

Ireland suppressed a nervous gulp. Sure, she'd taken the necessary classes, had done all the specialized training, and on paper was more than qualified for this job. However, this wasn't a case study she would be graded on. This was the real deal. Stalling for time, Ireland leaned back in her chair and cracked open Mason's file. She didn't have to read long to get to the disturbing parts. "Ya know, it's hard to pick which offense in here is the most disturbing, but ... I think I'm going to go with sexually assaulting the statue of the school mascot. That one has to be my favorite."

"What can I say ..." He shrugged with what he probably thought was a flirty grin. Truth be known, it landed closer to stroke victim. "My charms are an acquired taste."

"Yeah, the 'charms' of guys like you are normally remedied with topical creams." The words were out before Ireland could even attempt to filter them. She kept the file up high so he couldn't see her aghast shock at her own statement.

Leaning forward, he tried to force a smolder. "What was that, sweetness?"

Ireland pressed her lips together in a firm line and calmly laid his file on her desk. The flaring of her nostrils was the only indication of the storm that raged within. One simple little pet name, that was all it took to make her pulse pound through her veins, feeding into the white hot rage that made her want to grab him by the hair and smash his face into the corner of her desk. Rational thought tried to weigh in, whispering that this innocent youth had no way to know that her asshat ex used to call her that. Ireland held firm to that reminder as she took a cleansing breath and leaned forward with her elbows on her desk. "I get this little act of yours, believe me I do. Before your voice changed, and your balls dropped, the girls didn't really notice you. Did they, Mason?"

His brown eyes widened in shock, a rosy glow filling his cheeks. "I ... I don't know what you're—"

Ireland held up one finger to stop him. "Oh, I'm not done. I'm guessing you were probably picked on, too. Bullied, and downright made to feel like a nothing. Am I right?"

"What's the matter with you, lady?" He slumped back in his chair and folded his arms over his chest. Mr. Swagger seemed to have run out of leers.

"Then," Ireland knew she was toeing the line of effective guidance counselor, but couldn't seem to stop her rolling rant, "puberty hit and you went and got yourself a makeover. Worked out, started tanning, discovered some random sport you actually have a knack for. Heck, maybe you even had one of those fun music montages like in the movies. End result? A whole new Mason. You could've had your meathead happily ever after ... but no. You're so afraid of fading into the background again that you have to go out of your way to stay in the spotlight and make sure no one *ever* forgets you again. I'd ask if I'm right, but those white lines around your clenched lips tell me all I need to know."

"You bitch," Mason growled through his teeth.

"I have been called much, much worse. So, here's what we're going to do. You and I will meet here a couple times a week. We're going to start planning for your life after high school, make goals for when you're no longer surrounded by kids that know about the time you got a stiffy in P.E.—"

"*How do you know about that?*" Mason raged, his face blooming a deep tomato red.

Ireland held up both hands in surrender as she bit down hard on the inside of her cheek. "I didn't, I swear. It's just a random thing I threw out there because it happens to a lot of guys your age."

Mason exhaled, fading back to dull pink.

"We just need to work together, to get you looking at the bigger picture of your future and passed the BS of high school. Along the way if we can get you to graduation, and maybe have a few days thrown in there where you can get by without being a total d-bag, that'll just be an added bonus!" Feeling pretty damned good about herself, Ireland offered him a warm smile as a proverbial olive branch. She had gotten her point across in a way, which she felt, spoke his language. Maybe she could be that cool school counselor that all the kids come to love.

Mason let his chin fall to his chest, and rubbed one hand over the back of his neck. "Wow, you just have it all figured out, don't you?"

Ireland noticed a hint of amusement in his tone. For reasons she couldn't yet explain, it reminded her of a ticking time bomb.

"See, you're new here and really don't *get* how things work just yet. So, let me enlighten you." The smug golden boy leaned in, glaring daggers across the desk. "Why don't you go out back and take a look at the sign by the brand, spanking new football field. The fancy little plaque you'll find has four little words on it," he counted them off on his fingers, "Donated ... by ... Charles ... Van Brunt. Then, maybe sashay your fine ass down the hall and take a gander at the new auditorium with its state of the art light and sound systems. And, wouldn't you know it, you'll find a matching plaque there. My dad practically *owns* Sleepy Hollow. You wanna know why I've gotten away with everything I have *without* getting expelled? It's because no one *dares* cross my father. In simple terms: You. Can't. Touch. Me." Leaning back in his chair, he laced his fingers behind his head. "But if you still want to have regular meetings where we sit here, braiding each other's hair, and writing in our dream journals, that's fine by me. Just do me a favor and wear a low-cut top, at least make it worth my while."

Ireland's mouth opened and shut, however the only words flashing through her mind were of the four letter variety. It was taking every ounce of willpower she had not to let those fly out.

"So," Mason said with a victorious smile, "what should we talk about for the rest of our time?"

The awkward silence was broken by the buzz of the intercom. "Miss Crane, Mason's step-mother is here."

"Send her in," Ireland requested with a telling amount of insistence.

Ireland rose to her feet, expecting *Versace* and *Jimmy Choo's* to come flouncing through her door. Instead, she was met by a fresh-faced blonde rocking jeans, a hoodie, and a warm smile.

"Hope you don't think this means I'm buying you lunch, kid." His step-mother smiled and attempted to ruffle Mason's hair.

The surly teen pulled away, a look of disgust souring his face.

If she noticed, she feigned oblivious as she extended her hand to Ireland. "Hi, I'm Ana Van Brunt, Mason's step-mom."

"You aren't my step *anything*!" Mason snapped, springing from his chair with enough force that it rocked back on two legs. "You have a *piece of paper*! That doesn't make you a Van Brunt. It makes you another toy my dad *owns*!"

Mason forced past her, his shoulder slamming into hers, as he stomped from the room.

Awkward silence filled the air as Ireland and Ana watched his stormy exit.

"They're so sweet at that age," Ireland mused with syrupy sweetness.

Ana indulged herself in a giggle at her step-son's expense. "He's had a tough time coping with his parent's divorce, and his dad and I getting married."

"That can be tough on a kid." Ireland nodded. "How long has it been?"

"Since he was five."

"Oh, so it's still a fresh change, then." Ireland chuckled.

Ana nodded, her ponytail bobbing against the back of her neck. "We're still in the adjustment period. Any day now it's going to get better. Anyway, I'm sorry about his behavior. I'll encourage his father to have a talk with him. If you want me to have him call you, I can give him the message."

"Yeah, that would be great."

"Well, I better get out there before he keys 'whore' onto the side of my car ... again." Even while Ana's smile held firm, Ireland could sense the sadness in her; a deep melancholy that longed for repair.

"Ana?" she called after her.

Sunlight shone through the lone office window as Ana glanced back, revealing a light dusting of freckles that peppered the tops of her cheeks. She paused with one hand on the door frame, her eyebrows raised in expectation.

"I'll help with Mason any way I can," Ireland promised. "I give you my word."

Ana didn't offer an agreement of any sort, but let her gaze fall to the floor. When she glanced back up, her eyes glimmered with unshed tears. "Welcome to Sleepy Hollow, Miss Crane," she muttered through a tight smile, then strode off without another glance back.

6

Ichabod

"Wait until you see the spectacle going on in town!" Leaning against the side of the school, Rip launched off of his perch as soon as Ichabod stepped outside. The unexpected surprise nearly caused the skittish teacher to drop the stack of books and papers he was taking home to complete the class marks.

"How long have you been lingering out here?" Ichabod skittered side to side, struggling to adjust the weight of the books before they went tumbling to the ground.

With an exasperated roll of his eyes, Rip caught and steadied the pile. "Perhaps an hour or so? Your school days are *frightfully* long."

"Give up on seeking gainful employment altogether, did you?" While Irv had found employment as a file clerk at the courthouse—a position he was grossly over-qualified for—Rip seemed content to live off the good nature of his friends. However, the generosity of both men was quickly running thin.

"Ichabod," Rip seized his friend by his narrow shoulder and leaned in as if to impart his own special brand of wisdom. "Do you have any idea how many ladies in this town are currently in need of comfort? It would be a disservice to them all, and downright cruel, for me to seek other vocations during such a volatile time!"

Shaking his head, Ichabod shrugged out from under Rip's touch and clomped down the school house stairs with his cargo in tow. "You truly are a hero to the people."

Rip either missed Ichabod's blatant sarcasm or purposely chose to ignore it. "And it is right time the people realized it!" He beamed as he matched strides with Ichabod. "Now, I suggest you brace yourself, sir. The Hollow is attempting to ward off ghouls with a display, the likes of which, I guarantee you have never seen!"

Heavy clouds hung low in the sky, smothering any of the sun's hopeful rays before they could attempt to penetrate this ominous world of grey. As they strode further into town, Ichabod and Rip were assaulted by the powerful aroma of rosemary and sandalwood.

"The entire village smells of a funeral procession," Ichabod said, covering his nose and mouth with the cuff of his sleeve.

"That would be the good Reverend." Rip nodded to a modest cottage situated next to the fork in the road, which split the drives leading to the ostentatious Van Brunt and Van Tassel estates. Dressed in robes normally reserved for his Sunday sermons, the Reverend waved a smoking roll of potent herbs in front of the doors and windows. "He plans to do every home in the Hollow, to prevent the Hessian from entering."

Shutters were already drawn for the night. Any window not fortunate enough to have them was covered by sheets. "As if a simple piece of cloth could hide them from their fabled monster," Ichabod muttered under his breath.

On either side of the cobblestone road, men drove waist-high stakes into the ground with sledge hammers. The sorrowful hush of the skittish town was shattered by each strike that resonated with a haunting echo. The door to the Hollow Inn opened. Five of the local women filed out, led by Mama Rosa with her arms full of as many carved jack-o'-lanterns as she could carry. The three ladies behind her held the same cargo. Madame Lancaster trailed them, heaving a large basket overflowing with long, thick candles. The likes of which were normally used to ward off night's smothering embrace.

Rip gasped and recoiled. Ichabod followed his gaze and gave a shudder all his own. Rosa's mother, Eleanora as they'd come to know her, rounded the corner from the back of the inn. The word 'witch' was often tossed around in reference to her, yet fear prevented *any* from ever uttering such a claim in her presence. Cradled in her bony embrace, she held a large drum mixing pot with a ladle hooked along the side.

"What do you suppose?" Rip's chestnut brow furrowed as the women busied themselves setting a jack-o'-lantern in front of each stake.

Madame Lancaster plucked the stem top from one, and stood back to allow Eleanora access. The old woman hauled the pot forward with remarkable agility for someone that appeared to have missed their own wake. Eleanora set the pot down and gave the contents a quick stir, a bit of frothy crimson sloshing over the edge.

"Is that ... goat's blood?" Ichabod gulped. What little color he had in his alabaster complexion drained chalk white.

"I sincerely hope so." Rip grimaced. "Perhaps they figure its properties are multi-useful? Can ward off plagues and a murderous ghost?"

Eleanora dipped the ladle in and scooped up a spoonful. Leaning in, she sniffed the brew and expelled an appreciative moan.

"I fear I must warn you, if that ladle finds its way to her lips, we will be revisited by my lunch," Ichabod stated without the slightest hint of a jest.

"And mine will provide it company," Rip seconded.

Instead of tasting the bloody cocktail, Eleanora slopped it inside the waiting jack-o'-lantern. A few drips splashed against the rind and streaked down like bloody tears. She took careful attention, catching them with her thumb then wiping them off on her apron. Her wide, toothless smile resembled that of the jack-o'-lantern whose stem she replaced before rising to her feet with the pumpkin in tow. Holding it out before her, face to gruesome carved face, she cradled it between her palms like a cherished lover.

"Line the streets with ghoulish treats," Eleanora began in a sing-song rasp that sent shivers prickling down Ichabod's spine, "else the horseman ye shall meet."

Slowly, she raised the pumpkin high above her head, offering it to the not yet present moon, before plunging it straight down onto a waiting stake. Blood spurt from its carved eyes and mouth, coating the post that impaled it with splatter and pumpkin matter. Madame

Lancaster plucked the core out once more to drop a candle into the holed core and light it with a long wooden match. Grisly shadows danced across the gore splashed ground with each flicker of the flame.

Ichabod wanted to avert his eyes from this garishly barbaric demonstration, yet before he could tear his gaze from the pooling blood, Eleanora stepped through his line of sight. Her sunken stare caught his and held firm.

"Offer blood to thine who rides." The usual ominous melody left Eleanora's cadence. Moving on to the next stake, she spoke the eerie message as pointed instruction meant specifically for him. "Or the next to die may be *your* bride."

"Good thing you aren't married, aye, chap?" Rip said with a nervous laugh that snapped Ichabod from his trance.

Ichabod forced a tight smile despite the knot of fear that settled into his gut, spreading its venom through his veins. "Yes, good thing indeed."

Despite only having met her once, his thoughts immediately turned to Katrina. He was well aware of his station in life and knew she would never be his. Even so, he vowed to himself, as long as a threat remained in the Hollow, he *would* keep her safe. He had to.

The pair found themselves so engrossed in Eleanora's show that they failed to notice Abraham "Brom" Van Brunt crossing the street and stomping their way. With the heel of his hand, the formidable Brom shoved Ichabod's shoulder, sending him stumbling back to keep his feet under him.

"Pardon, sir!" Rip snapped. His tone one of accusation, not apology, as he grasped Ichabod's arm to steady him.

Ichabod tipped his head back, then back some more, to take in all of the barge-sized man before him.

"The hens that cluck with gossip and rumors claim you were graced by the company of Katrina Van Tassel this day," Brom growled through his clenched, square jaw. "You are aware that we are to be wed, are you not?"

Ichabod had encountered many men like Brom, especially in the military. Giant, bruiser types that used their size to intimidate and purposely targeted those they dubbed as weak. Men such as these used to make Ichabod's knees knock … until he fought alongside those so-called roughens in the war. They had trembled, suffered, and wept just like all the others. Therefore, breaking the spell their intimidation once cast. Still, this being a new town and fresh start, Ichabod figured it best to keep the peace.

The schoolmaster pulled himself up to full height. Unfortunately, that still didn't make a dent in the size difference between them. "Rest assured, Mr. Van Brunt, Miss Van Tassel was there to comfort the children after yesterday's ordeal. Nothing more."

Brom's copper-weaved coat, inlayed with elaborate gold-threaded embroidery, pulled taut across his barrel chest as he folded his hands behind his back. "Then you have seen that the beauty of her heart rivals that of her pleasing exterior?"

Ichabod chose his words carefully, keeping his tone calm and steady. "That may be true, sir. But rest assured, if that same heart belongs to you, it is quite safe. I mean your courtship no threat."

"As if you could." One corner of Brom's thick lips tugged back in a haughty sneer. "Her *heart* is of little consequence to me. Her father and I are in talks to join our families. Our union is imminent. The joining of the Van Tassel and Van Brunt houses will be beneficial for all involved. The birth of an empire."

Rip stepped forward, positioning himself between his friend and the glowering Brom. "And how does the lady feel being used as a bargaining chip?"

Brom ground his teeth together, glaring down at Rip as if he were a bug that needed to be squashed under foot. "I would not ask a woman for her opinion any more than I would ask which of my steer would like to be this weekend's roast."

"Clearly, his new age thinking is what drew Katrina to him," Rip muttered out of the corner of his mouth.

"Our union is a smart match." Brom raised one eyebrow in a show of superiority. Ichabod doubted Brom had heard Rip's barb. He wasn't the type of man that would disregard such a blatant show of disrespect. "She will come around when her father explains it to her as such."

Ichabod gently pushed Rip out of the way to offer Brom his hand and a smile. "Then, let me be the first to congratulate you. I am sure the bride's longing for romance will be quenched by your keen business savvy and negotiating skills."

Confusion flickered across Brom's face, yet the respectful nature of Ichabod's physical gesture allowed him to shake off the thoughts of possible insult and accept the offered hand. "Yes ... well, thank you."

Ichabod responded with a brief nod and retracted his hand from Brom's sweaty mit.

"You men should seek shelter. Leave these matters to those of us prepared to deal with them." Brom made those his parting words before turning on his boot heel and striding off to rejoin the work crew.

As Ichabod watched Brom's broad back shrink into the distance, moisture sprinkled down on his shoe and pant leg. His face folded into a cringe at the red dots that stained the fabric from the pumpkin Eleanora drove down onto a spike not three feet from him. The decrepit old woman giggled mischievously at the mess she'd caused. Her cracked and blistered lips pulled back in a wicked grin. The wink she granted him caused shivers to quake in the very marrow of his bones.

7

Ireland

Ireland sniffled and wiped her nose on the back of her hand. There was a killer on the loose—dire matters at hand—yet here she was, standing in a cemetery openly weeping. No, not weeping; that sounds calm and reserved. What she was doing was a hiccupping mess of snot and tears.

"Because this is how normal people respond to a work of art." Ireland punctuated her self-chastising with an exaggerated eye roll.

It had started simple enough, a walk through town to enjoy the beautiful colors of the autumn trees that were hard to find in the concrete jungle of Manhattan. She'd followed a trail, enjoying the crunch of leaves under her feet. The path weaved through town, allowing her to bask in its peace as it led across the back grounds of the Old Dutch Church cemetery.

Then she saw her. The Lady in White—according to the plaque at her feet—was another Sleepy Hollow legend. This one being of a woman who died tragically the night before her wedding. After frequent postmortem sightings of the forever grieving bride-to-be, she was then memorialized in statue form. The stone work was a thing of disturbingly tragic beauty. The long, flowing gown she never got the chance to wear had been carved in stone as her permanent garb. A chapel length veil was draped over her head, its blusher parted in the middle to reveal only the center of her face. The remainder of her seemed to be concealed by a shroud of despair.

Tentatively, Ireland stretched out her arm and let the tips of her fingers trace over the cold, rough stone of the woman's face. There was something so familiar about the peaks and plateaus of her features. Although it didn't make a lick of sense, Ireland half expected the nameless girl's given name to roll from her tongue.

"Maybe she reminds you of *another* stone person that you formed an unnatural attachment to." Ireland laughed through her tears, causing an incredibly unattractive snort she was thankful she was alone for.

Physically shaking herself out of this onslaught of lameness, Ireland shoved her hands into her pockets and crossed the grounds back toward the sidewalk at a steady gait. "Don't look back, Ire. You might see a cherub angel tombstone and lose your shit … again."

Mother Nature waved her hand, adding a touch of dusk's violet haze to the sleepy town. Already the residents of Tarrytown were settling in for the night. The low hum of traffic and the occasional chirp of early rising crickets provided a serene soundtrack for her stroll home. Why, then, was this peaceful hush causing Ireland's heart to pound in her chest like a caged animal desperate to escape?

Suddenly, Ireland jerked ramrod straight, her head snapping one way then the other, scouring the landscape for ... something. Her brow creased, sweat dampening her palms. Was that her heart beat? Had it escalated to the point of audible? No. That incessant thump, drumming its way closer by the second, was coming from ... everywhere.

"Holy hell, those are hoof beats," she murmured to herself.

They echoed all around her, bouncing off each tombstone to tease and taunt her. Ireland considered herself a skeptical person. If she didn't see it with her own eyes, she had a hard time believing it. Yet, phantom hoof beats in the wake of the discovery of a headless corpse was enough to make a believer out of her. She jogged the remaining distance to the exit, feeling the burning need to be *anywhere* but the cemetery immediately, if not sooner. As the ornate cast-iron gate squealed open under her grasp, Ireland crouched behind it and peeked around the side.

"Jinkies, Daphne, there doesn't seem to be anything there," Ireland joked at her own expense, then exhaled a shaky breath and forced herself to step out onto the sidewalk.

From behind her came the sharp crack of hooves finding pavement. Bothersome bangs fell into her eyes as Ireland whipped around, a gasp frozen on her lips. Around the bend came a snow white horse pulling a carriage. The couple in the back were lost in each other's arms, while a rather uncomfortable looking driver pretended he couldn't hear the noisy smacks and slurps of their kisses. The horse peered Ireland's way as it trotted past, its ears perking with interest.

Ireland let out a breath she hadn't realized she'd been holding; her glib commentary effectively silenced. Turning on shaky legs, she started her trek home, forcing herself to maintain a slow, calm pace despite her deep desire to sprint home like a dog with its tail on fire. With each calm, measured step she whispered to herself that everything was okay.

It was just the carriage ... just the carriage.

She was doing a good job convincing herself, too. Her heart rate slowed out of the red zone and she had been able to resume regular respiratory function. A small voice in the back of her mind picked that moment to inject a bothersome piece of trivia she'd purposely chose to overlook.

The carriage horse rounded the corner in a steady flat-foot walk. What you heard was a thundering gallop.

"You know you're being nutso, yet you continue to walk." Ireland indulged herself in a douse of self-belittling as she stomped down the rickety basement stairs. She had every right to be annoyed. She'd been home for two hours and had spent that time nervously pacing from the endorphin remnants of her adrenaline rush.

The key pad was down there somewhere and her latest crazed notion—the pot of chamomile tea had been a complete bust—was to chase away her lingering chills with a little peace of mind. Maybe by resetting the code, clicking the deadbolt into place, and possibly hiding under her bed, she could finally get some sleep and *not* go to work tomorrow looking like a zombie.

The old basement had that standard damp and musty odor. Ireland yanked the cord over her head, causing the bare lightbulb to swing and cast long shadows through the darkness. Her gaze scoured the floorboards overhead for another light, but didn't spot one. Thankfully, she'd had the forethought to bring a flashlight. Clicking it on, she shined a blue-tinted circle on to the dank walls as she turned in a slow circle at the base of the stairs. No need to venture any farther into creep-dom than absolutely mandatory. To her left, next to the water heater and an old set of shelves holding dusty paint cans, she spotted the control panel.

"One, two, one, five. One, two, one, five," Ireland chanted the reminder as she scurried over on tiptoes. She mimicked Noah's deep tremor while acting on his instructions. "Code, reset, code again, then zero, four, two, two and ..."

"System armed," a robotic female voice assured her.

"Thank you, Security-bot. When the rise of the machines comes, you will be the last I termin—" Ireland's sentence trailed off. A soft, glowing diamond of light appearing on the floor by her foot. She turned, following the flickering beam to the crevice in the wall it appeared to be cast from. Without thinking, or hesitating in the slightest, Ireland squatted down to investigate. Maybe it was coming from outside? A crack in the foundation allowing light from an outside street lamp to seep in? That theory quickly disproved itself when she peeked inside. It was a separate room with stone walls just like those around her. It couldn't be a utility room, the furnace sat behind her, humming and occasionally clanging like a flatulent old man.

Ireland rose to her feet, brushing off the grime from the walls on her hands, and peered down the length of the wall. She expected to find a door to a fruit cellar she'd overlooked. There was nothing to see except stone and dirt. Her slim shoulders rose and fell in a casual shrug, her interest in this mystery quickly fading. As one final gesture of defeat, she raised her foot to block out the light with her toe before giving up and retreating upstairs. That light touch was all it took to set off a chain reaction. The point of impact deteriorated, causing a few rocks around it to do the same. Ireland jumped back, covering her nose and mouth with the crook of her arm as a small cloud of dust and debris mushroomed out from the wall. The mess settled quickly, pulling back its thick curtain of unbreathable air to unveil a gaping hole about a two foot by two foot diameter.

Ireland pursed her lips and cast a longing gaze up the stairs. Oh, how she wanted to run up there, call Noah the Handy Man, and make this *his* problem. Unfortunately, she already knew she wouldn't. Stupid, blind inquisitiveness would insist she investigate.

"You know what this same type of curiosity did to the cat," she grumbled to herself as she squatted and shone her flashlight into the room, no bigger than the fruit cellar she thought it to be. "It got it trapped forever in a dank, dark room never to be heard from again."

Ireland paused, contemplating her own warning, then curled into a ball and shimmied through the cramped opening. "I seriously need to work on my decision making skills."

A fit of coughs hit the moment she sucked in her first breath of stale, stagnate air. The strong fruity odor gave weight to her theory of what this space had been used for. Gradually she turned, illuminating each wall with her flashlight until …

All the air was forced from her lungs, leaving her gasping. On a ledge notched out of the wall, a candle burned, its wax just beginning to melt and streak down the sides. Someone had very recently lit that, which meant … *she wasn't alone.*

Fear rooted her where she stood. One turn, or glance in the wrong direction, and she ran the risk of see something move behind her that would make her bladder fail and every horror movie she'd ever watched come to life.

"Hello?" Ireland called out in a breathless squeak. If anyone actually answered, there was a high likelihood her heart would leap from her chest, give her a quick nod, and scurry off to save itself.

To her great relief, silence was her only answer.

She forced her lead feet forward, closer to the flickering candle. Melted wax puddled at the top of it then trickled down the sides, cutting through dust nearly an inch thick. Mason jars lined the shelf beside it; some empty, some holding canned fruits and jams. A few were even labeled moonshine. Regardless, all of them were covered with a dense layer of grime. Whoever had been here hadn't stayed long enough to disturb anything. Slightly more reassured, Ireland exhaled and allowed herself to poke around and investigate.

Her lip curled as she stepped over the ugliest garden statue she'd ever seen in her life. "Because who doesn't want to highlight their landscaping with a concrete, sleeping hobo? There's a reason they hid your ugly ass in the basement, dude."

Shaking her head, she moved on to an old trunk in the corner. It creaked beneath her hands as she forced the lid open. Inside were the kind of old clothes museums would pant over: long, flowing dresses with intricate bodices, hooded capes fastened with buttons formed into family crests, thick wool dress uniforms that Ireland guessed dated back to the Revolutionary War. All antiques, all in pristine condition. Yet, they filled her with the same sorrow that the statue had—only minus the unexplainable rush of water works. Feeling as though she was scavenging graves, she shut the lid and laid a hand against it in silent apology.

Brushing her hands off on the legs of her yoga pants, Ireland rose to her feet and cast the flashlight beam out for one last sweep of the small space. Her gaze locked on the last remaining mystery—the candle. If it weren't for that she would have no problem closing this room back up, like the time capsule it had become, but ... someone had been in here. If she ever wanted to be able to close her eyes or shower in this house, without feeling like the walls were watching her, she was going to have to call Noah over for a quick inspection. Instantly, that thought filled her with a new kind of dread.

"Dammit, why can't he be an old, fat guy? It would make life so much easier," she grumbled under her breath as she crossed the cramped space with determined steps.

Her false sense of security blinded her from the heavy, grey eyelids that snapped open behind her. Just as her lips pursed to blow out the candle, a cold, bony hand closed around her calf.

8

Ireland

"Wha—what happened?"

"You grabbed my leg and I whacked you with my flashlight." Ireland let the flashlight handle rise and fall, smacking it against her palm in an open threat. "You picked the wrong house to break into, pal. You don't mess with New Yorkers, we mess back. Now, you need to tell me who the hell you are, and you better *pray* I like the answer."

Internally, Ireland winced, shocked by the hostility in her tone. Then again, it wasn't everyday she found a creepy little troll living in her basement.

"The sleeping spell! It's broken! That must mean ..." Dull grey eyes, encircled by a yellowish-hue, gaped up at Ireland like a meteor was about to strike directly behind her. "*Was there a beheading? Has the Horseman returned?*"

Ireland's flashlight wielding arm pulled back defensively. "Whoa! How did you know about that? Did you have something to do with that man who was killed?"

"So, it's true then," the scraggly, bearded man mumbled to himself. "If he's risen, that must mean," his panicked stare locked with hers, "you're a Crane?"

"Yeah, I'm a Crane," Ireland hissed through clenched teeth. "*Who the hell are you?*"

"I am ... did you tie my hands and feet?"

"Damn skippy, I did."

He tried to sit up, which proved challenging with his hands tied behind him. "May I ask why?"

"Maybe I had a surplus of zip ties after securing a bookshelf to the roof of my car when I moved." She let one shoulder rise and fall in a shrug that would've appeared casual had in not been for the murderous gleam in her eyes. "Or *maybe*—and go with me on this one—it's because you *attacked me in my friggin' basement!*"

His bushy, unkempt eyebrows pulled together in confusion. "To the roof of your what? What year is this?"

Ireland's lips twisted to the side as she folded her arms over her chest. "Seriously? You're gonna play that angle? Dude, if this is some sort of drug thing and you're coming down from a bender, you should *really* look into clean living."

"No toxins can be blamed for my state, miss," the filthy stranger clarified, tugging against his restraints. "A sleeping spell was cast, meant to preserve my body so I could carry out an important task."

Her eyebrows disappeared into her hairline as Ireland stared down at the scrawny, smelly man hogged tied on her couch. "You might wanna look into getting your money back for the preservation part."

"My name," he pushed on as if Ireland hadn't spoke, squaring his shoulders to the best of his ability despite his awkward position, "is Rip Van Winkle. If I'm awake, it can only mean that the Horseman has returned to Sleepy Hollow, and we are all in very real danger."

"Wow. That's impressive in a delusional, bat-shit, crazy kind of way," she deadpanned. "Exactly how many books did you weave this fairytale from?"

"You must listen!" The plea in his eyes trumped that of his tone.

Ireland's forced brave front was getting harder to maintain by the moment. This man seemed truly sick, the kind of illness that required a straitjacket and padded room. There was no telling what he was capable of. This idea, of dragging him upstairs and playing vigilantly while she questioned him, had turned into colossally bad judgment on her part. She should've called the cops immediately while he was unconscious. Now, all she could do was pray those ties held. "The only thing I *must* do is steam clean that couch to get your funky smell off of it."

"You keep up that cavalier attitude and you'll be dead!" Rip yelled with enough force to make the tendons of his wrinkled neck bulge.

Ireland didn't recall grabbing the box cutter off the coffee table. Yet there it was, clasped in her white knuckled grasp as she lunged for him, the blade stopping millimeters from his throat. "Don't even think about threatening—"

Her ultimatum was cut off by Rip's eyes rolling back and his body slumping against the couch. The only sound left in the room was his rhythmic snores that could rival a hibernating grizzly.

"Huh." Ireland's hand relaxed as she retracted the blade. Her first slap, which landed against his bristly bearded cheek, was a tentative one. The second packed a bit more of a wallop. "Hey. Hey! Wake up!"

Rip came to with a start, bucking hard enough beneath her to send the box cutter flying and Ireland reeling back. "Wha—what happened?"

"Do you say that every time you wake up? You're kind of like that little blue fish in the Disney movie." Ireland bent to retrieve the box cutter, her voice calm and steady.

"I didn't understand half of the words you just spoke. Please, just tell me, did I fall asleep again?"

"You did, actually." Ireland turned the box cutter over in her hand, admiring the sharp angle of the blade. "Rip, would you mind if I performed a little experiment real quick?"

"What kind of—*oh! Please, no*—zzzzzzzzzzz."

In retrospect, leaping at him with the knife poised probably wasn't the most ethical course of action, fortunately it *had* led Ireland to the answer she was looking for. Her smelly little friend seemed to suffer from stress induced narcolepsy. That greatly diminished any level of threat he *may* have been. It did make the issue of what to do with him of greater concern. Much as she wanted to, and she *really* did, she couldn't bring herself to call the cops on him. She'd watched enough movies to know the horrendous things that could happen to an old guy in prison that was never conscious to defend himself. Her chest swelled before she released a begrudging sigh. Not too long ago, before her life got turned upside down, she had wanted to adopt a stray from the pound. Suddenly, that idea was seeming far less appealing.

Crouched beside the couch, Ireland sliced Rip free from his restraints.

When the old man came to yet again, she anticipated his first words before he opened his mouth to croak, "Wha—what happened?"

"Alien attack. Don't worry, I stopped them shortly after they probed you." She glanced up … and her attempted smile faltered on her lips.

The color drained from Rip's face, and the whites of his eyes bulged from their sockets. His gaze locked on Ireland's exposed forearm.

"*Where did you get that*?" he asked in a hollow, ghostly whisper.

Ireland glanced down at her arm, searching for what she was missing in this troubling equation. "My tattoo? An artist in Manhattan did it for me."

Rip shifted to the side to dig a medallion, threaded on a silver chain, from the pocket of his grungy slacks. "*This* is the talisman of the Headless Horseman, an object created and prayed over by the most powerful holy men and shaman in the world. It is the *only* thing that can control the Hessian. The very existence of this artifact has been carefully and intricately concealed for centuries. I have been in possession of it for … a *very* long time. It has been *my* will that kept the beast at bay, confined to his purgatory prison." His gaze traveled to her face, where he searched for answers to questions he had yet to voice. "And you, my dear girl, have somehow found yourself branded with this *exact* same symbol."

Rip's dry, calloused hand encircled Ireland's wrist as he deposited the silver-dollar sized medallion onto her open palm. Ireland ran her thumb over it, not trusting her eyes or even the ridges beneath her touch. It had to be a coincidence ... after all, pirate swag and sugar skulls were all the rage. That had to be it—just a blind stroke of luck—that explained how the skull design she held so perfectly matched her own. While her tattoo contained a bit more detail, there was no denying that the core image—a skull set against a crossed sword and axe—was exactly the same.

Nothing more than a coincidence, Ireland reiterated to the sudden pounding of her pulse.

"I was meant to teach you the techniques and methods to control the Horseman and stop the carnage." Rip's voice rose in intensity with each word. "But to find this? *His* talisman branded in your skin?" His head fell back, as he pleaded to the plaster ceiling, "Heaven, help us all! I ... I don't know what this means! I don't what to—"

The desperate plea cut off as he slumped back against the couch, instantly drooling.

After about twenty minutes of watching Rip snore and twitch, and numerous less than kind attempts to wake him, Ireland figured out that the degree of the scare must play some part in how deep and long his naps would be. Whatever it was he believed about her tattoo had rattled him straight into hibernation. Which then left her with the annoying dilemma of what to do with him. He sure as heck wasn't staying in the house, or continuing to squat in her basement. Those weren't even options. A little creative thinking became mandatory. The shed in the backyard was by no means the Ritz Carlton. However, after adding a flashlight, sleeping bag, a couple of old pillows, and a picnic basket full of snack foods, Ireland felt she was doing a good deed by giving this vagabond a comfortable-ish place to rest and eat before she booted him out of her life forever.

Her hands encircled his scrawny ankles. "Ugh, buddy, you smell like week old Tai food and sour milk." She dry heaved, trying to cover her nose with her shoulder as she forcefully yanked him off the couch; her hope being that his cranium bouncing off the floor might jar him awake. The thump shook the floor beneath her feet and rattled the glass of the front bay window. Unfortunately, Rip had no problem at all sleeping through mild head trauma.

"You're not going to work with me even a little bit, are you?" she groaned at her splayed guest who had long since out stayed his welcome.

Hating life in a major way, and inventing new expletives to demonstrate that, Ireland hooked her arms under Rip's pits … there by getting more closely acquainted with the pungent flavor of his stench than she cared to. Years of hard living had reduced him to little more than bone. Yet, dragging what she guessed to be around a five-ten, limp frame from the living room to the dining room, and around the table to the sliding glass door, proved to be no easy task.

Ireland slid the door open, letting the rush of cool air that swept in refresh her sweat-dampened skin, and peeked out into the night. Her nervous gaze flicked one way then the other, to ensure her neighbors were nowhere in sight. Briefly, she paused to commit a giant no-no and scratch her fresh tattoo, which was irritated by the rough polyester of Rip's shirt. Ireland then adjusted her grip to get a firm hold, and made a mad dash outside. His thick-soled boots scuffed across the deck boards, thumped down the stairs, and rustled through the grass, providing a soundtrack of realism to Ireland's act of insanity.

"One week in a new town and I'm hiding a body in my shed," she mused, curling her slipping fingers around the fabric of his shirt for better traction. "Nothing unusual about that."

With sweat trickling down her spine, Ireland flung the shed door open. Shuffling penguin-style, she maneuvered her drooling cargo over the sleeping bag and eased him to the ground. She even took the good measure to shove the pillow—she fully intended to burn after he used— under his head and kick his legs onto the sleeping bag with the toe of her shoe.

"It's been real, Rip," she said, flipping the open side of the sleeping bag over him. "Rest up, then go peddle your crazy somewhere else."

A sleep-fart acted as his only response.

"Good talk." Ireland took a step back, out of the shed, and pulled the door shut behind her.

For a moment she paused, pressing her palm flat to the rough wood siding of the shed door. This was ridiculous, impractical, and downright dangerous. She didn't know this man or what he was truly capable of. Common sense screamed at her to display even the slightest iota of self-preservation by calling the cops and turning the obviously troubled man over to them.

A wry scoff huffed past her lips, blowing back her long side-bangs that had fallen in her eyes during her body-toting workout. Despite the warning siren blaring in her mind, she couldn't do it. Something deep within her told her this was a man that needed a little kindness; for someone to protect him, even if that meant from himself. The certainty of that realization hushed the worrisome chatter within and provided her the only sense of peace she'd found in ... well, a long enough time to make it seem a pretty damned crucial message.

Ireland's moment of reflection was interrupted by a low rumble directly behind her. Hot breath puffed against the back of her neck, sending electric chills of danger coursing through her. A frightened yip escaped from her constricted throat as she spun on her would be attacker ... only to find herself completely alone. She and the few crickets that chirped their sweet serenade to the night were the only occupants in her 'four mower swipes' sized yard. Fear, like bubbles churning in acid, boiled through her, popping and oozing their own toxic thoughts of what could be lurking in the darkness straight into her bloodstream.

Rubbing her arms to ward off her sudden rash of goose bumps, Ireland forced herself to maintain a steady stride back to the house. "Great job picking your fresh start town, Ire," she mused.

The sliding door slid shut behind her before she heard the darkness omit a guttural neigh in response.

71

9

Ichabod

Ichabod's slender fingers tickled across the piano keys, the haunting melody of *Canon in D* filling the inn's gathering room. Long shadows, cast by the flickering candles, danced across the walls like merry little nymphs oblivious to the chaos outside. Suddenly, a sour note broke the melodic spell. Ichabod sat up straight and stretched out his back, only then noticing that his arm was quaking with a fresh onslaught of tremors. He flexed and straightened his digits, hoping it would relax them enough for him to quench his longing for the melodic keys, the memory of which still warmed and tingled his fingertips. Exasperation at the relentless spasming brought his gaze up, a groan of annoyance sneaking past his lips. There, reflected in the glass of the sea side painting hanging over the piano, he saw a ghostly female form reaching for him as she floated up behind him.

Ichabod gasped, spinning with a jerk.

Katrina emitted a small squeak of surprise and clutched her heart at his abrupt reaction. "I am so sorry if I gave you a fright! I saw your hand trembling and wondered if I could be of aid?"

"No, I am fine," Ichabod nervously chuckled. "Or, I will be once my heart remembers how to beat in rhythm."

Concern creased her otherwise flawless face. "Again, I must apologize. Elsewise, are you all right? Was your hand cramping from playing?"

"I wish that were the case." Ichabod peered down at the hand that frequently betrayed him. The tremors had dulled, but not enough for him to resume playing. "During the war I took a bayonet to the shoulder. The nerves were damaged. By the grace of God, it was not severe enough to render the limb useless. Unfortunately, during moments of strain or stress, it tends to shake." He glanced up at the lovely Katrina, suddenly uncomfortable with the level of weakness he'd displayed. "*Ahem*, I do not speak of this often."

Candle light warmed her face with the sweet, ethereal glow of an angel. She stepped closer, her head cocked with interest. "What eases it when it flares?"

Ichabod found no judgment or pity on her face, only genuine concern. It was that which kept him talking on this tender matter. "Relaxation, primarily. Once I can soothe the strain that is plaguing me, it tends to correct itself."

"Perhaps a bit of companionship could soothe you?" Blonde waves brushed Katrina's lovely face with the tender caress of the calm sea lapping against a white sand shore as she nodded to the settee in the corner. "I would happily sit a spell."

A hot blush rushed to Ichabod's cheeks and ears, forcing him to shift his gaze to the loose string on his cuff button. "Your presence evokes many emotions, miss. The effects of which are far from soothing." Instantly, Ichabod's head snapped up, stunned by the forward nature of his own words. "A thousand apologies, Katrina. I have no excuse for such banter. It's even more disgraceful considering you're on the verge of marriage."

Katrina's cornflower blue eyes widened in surprise. "I am? May I inquire as to whom I am betrothed to?"

"Brom Van Brunt, of course."

"Ah." Katrina gathered her billowing skirt and made the two strides necessary for her to situate herself on the settee. "Brom has tried on multiple occasions to convince my father to bestow my hand to him. Yet there is one factor that boorish Van Brunt has failed to consider."

Unable to keep his eyes off her, Ichabod swiveled on the bench as she moved. "And what, may I ask, is that?"

Katrina's tight smile did nothing to hide the sadness that seeped into her eyes like slow moving snow clouds, heavy with their weighty burden. "That my father knew real love with my mother, and would never allow his only daughter to settle for anything less."

"You must think me a heel." Ichabod shook his head, aghast with his own insensitivity. "I have failed to offer you my condolences for your loss even once. I am so very sorry, I cannot even begin to imagine the devastation you must be dealing with."

74

Katrina smoothed her skirt with her palms, then folded them in her lap. "Thank you, that is very kind. However, the woman that died yesterday was not my mother but my stepmother. The second Mrs. Van Tassel, a title that is quickly becoming a cursed one. It has been five years since my mother was claimed by the fevers. Selena married my father three months ago. The loss was primarily his as I never got much of a chance to know her."

"If your father experienced love in its truest form, how could he bring himself to remarry at all?" For the second time that night, Ichabod desperately wished he could retract his words. They seemed to slip past his lips without filter. He blamed it on her beguiling beauty and the overwhelming desire to know absolutely everything about her. Thankfully, she didn't appear off put by his forwardness ... yet.

"There are five Dutch families that have been in Sleepy Hollow since the area was first settled; the Van Tassels, the Van Brunts, the Landcasters, the DeMarrs, and the Lovenstiens. While all have prospered at varying levels, they have remained a close knit group. As long as I can remember, they have had frequent meetings behind closed doors, making decisions that will affect the entire town. Officials that will be nominated for election, widows in need of aid, how crops are faring, anything and everything involving the wellbeing of the town is discussed. It was they who suggested Father make his home whole once more by taking a wife." Katrina huffed a humorless laugh as she leaned to the side of the settee and curled her legs under her. "Those same men are also the reason I had to turn to Mama Rosa once again for a place to rest my head."

A protective fire flamed in Ichabod's chest. *"They forced you from your own home when a deranged madman is on the loose?"*

"Not *forced*," Katrina corrected. "Merely suggested strongly after they showed up with barrels of ale and the intentions of helping my father drown his sorrows. Father doesn't like to be viewed as weak by anyone, least of all his own daughter. Whenever he feels the need to partake in spirits, which is quite seldom, he asks that I stay away so that my vision of my heroic papa is never soiled. "

Ichabod's mouth opened ... but he immediately snapped it shut. While his own parents had died years ago, the memories of the loving, nurturing upbringing they'd bestowed on him still lived on. He couldn't imagine being in a family where weakness couldn't be displayed. Wasn't the whole purpose of a family to support one another?

Before Ichabod could decide on a proper response, the front door of the inn flew open. Irv stomped inside, slamming the door behind him hard enough to shake the wall. He stood in the foyer, framed by the gathering room doorjamb. Globs of stringy orange sludge mixed with tear-shaped seeds hung from his shoulders, dripped from his hair, and swung from the frames of his glasses.

Katrina gasped and clamped a hand over her mouth.

Ichabod tried with little success to suppress his grin. "What, pray-tell, happened to you?"

Irv pivoted their way, his posture ramrod straight and nostrils flaring. "I *may* have suggested that putting up a lookout post, and manning it with glorified vigilantes, may not be the preferable option to the current situation facing the town. And that our resources *may* be better utilized employing more bodies to patrol the streets as legally hired, paid law enforcement."

"I take it the message was not well received?" Ichabod said, biting the insides of his cheeks to stifle a laugh.

A wad of pumpkin innards fell from Irving's hair, slapped against the tip of his nose, and landed on the polished wood floor with a wet *squish*. "Not as well as one would hope. I am going to retire for the night to scrape and bathe this off. Good night."

"Night!" Ichabod and Katrina chorused, letting their amusement spring forth in a chorus of giggles.

As Irving began his march down the hall, Rip and a lovely young brunette with a narrow waist and full hips emerged from that same direction. The brunette's face instantly flushed, her gaze averting to anywhere but at those who bore witness to her shameful retreat.

"You smell of pie," Rip pointed out to the steaming Irving.

"I am aware," Irving snapped and strode on, leaving a trail of seeds and sludge behind.

"Thank you, Ichabod Crane, for taking the time to show me your wonderful collection of books and discussing the literary merit of each with me," the brunette declared loud enough for all to hear as she fluffed the flattened back of her hair. "And now, I bid you good night."

Without so much as a glance back, she made her retreat. Ichabod and Katrina exchanged confused glances before turning to the rumpled, yet contently happy, Rip for clarification.

"Did she just call you Ichabod?" Katrina inquired.

Rip ran his fingers through his mahogany locks, allowing the motion to continue straight up into a wide-arm stretch over his head. "She did. I figured Ichabod's name has already been villainized in town, no point in sullying my own name as well! Feel free to go by Rip if you'd like." After shooting a saucy wink to Katrina, Rip ducked back down the hall to his room.

"Your friends are ... delightful." Katrina pressed her lips together, her cheeks rosy with laughter.

"They are more my brothers than friends. We fought beside each other in the war. I don't know much in life, but I *do* know that those two men will stand beside me no matter the situation."

"You are very—" Katrina hid a yawn behind the back of her hand, "—fortunate to have them both. Goodness, I am terribly sorry. I didn't sleep well after yesterday's events, and it seems to be catching up with me."

"Don't feel you have to stay up on my account. By all means, feel free to retire." Ichabod waved his hand in the direction of the rooms.

Katrina's narrow shoulders sagged. "I would if I were able. However, the room Rosa gave me is right beside her late husband's barn where she is allowing the men to construct the lookout post. I'm a light sleeper and won't be able to rest until they do."

"Then, let me offer another option." Ichabod rose to his feet and offered Katrina his hand. Her skin, like the soft whispered touch of satin, brushed his as she accepted his offering. With a gentle hand, he helped her to her feet. "I am fortunate enough to be able to sleep through most anything. Perhaps we could switch quarters for the night so you may enjoy the solitude of my room at the far end of the inn? It's a good distance from the working men. You shouldn't be bothered by them at all there."

"That's so very kind, Ichabod, however I would hate to be such a bother."

"It's no bother at all. I will help you collect your things and then it's off to bed with you." Ichabod hooked Katrina's hand around his arm, grabbed the burning lantern from the back of the piano, and escorted her down the hall.

"I'm not sure it's proper, sir, for you—a single man—to enter the quarters of a woman rumored to be betrothed, no matter how adamantly opposed to said union that woman may be." Katrina held her head high, adopting a mock haughty air.

Ichabod pulled free from her grasp. Turning to face her, he dipped into a formal bow. "My lady, I shall wait in the hall only to help carry your belongings. Therefore ensuring public opinion of your virtue is *never* called to question."

"How very noble of you." Katrina giggled, gracing him with a small curtsy. "These are my quarters."

Ichabod held up the lantern as Katrina retrieved her room key from the velvet coin purse sewn at the waist hem of her dress. The lock clicked and the door swung in. Katrina turned to Ichabod to borrow the lantern. Instead, she witnessed his face falling slack with horror.

"Ichabod? What is it?"

"Katrina, don't turn around!" Ichabod yelled, a moment too late.

He tried to grab her and pull her to him, yet instinct spun her head toward the darkness. She sucked in a shocked gasp, followed by a blood curdling scream. Thundering footsteps from various parts of the inn hammered toward them. Katrina buried her head in Ichabod's shoulder, allowing him to gather her in his arms as she shielded her eyes. The lantern rocked back and forth in Ichabod's trembling hand, illuminating fresh bits of the gory scene with each swing and sway.

Blood.

Splattered across the furniture.

Smeared into the carpet.

Streaked on the walls.

Laying on the bed, in a pool of crimson life, rested a headless corpse dressed in noble attire reserved for men of regal station. In its hands, the body clasped one single black rose, positioned over its chest like an offering. Scrawled above the bed, in wet letters that glistened in the lantern's flames, was one lone word—*Katrina.*

10

Ireland

Ireland woke with a start, immediately bolting upright and smacking her head on the underside of her nightstand. "Ow, shit!" Her exclamation turned panicked as the impact knocked her alarm clock down on top of her. If those glowing numbers were right, her alarm had failed to do its *one* job and she had exactly twenty minutes to get to work. "Dammit! Stupid alarm!"

She scrambled off the floor, not bothering with the question of how she'd ended up there. No time for that now. Sprinting to the bathroom, she raised her arm to take a quick whiff and determine the degree of shower necessity. Instantly, her face crumbled in a cringe. Showering was a must. She yanked her clothes off in the hall to save time, stumbling over her pajama pants when they tangled around her ankles.

Without pausing to adjust the temperature, Ireland cranked the shower on and jumped in. The prickles of ice water could be her punishment for oversleeping. She was mid-shampoo rinse when soapy bubbles streaked down her arm and set it on fire with burning pain. A bit of citrus-passion fruit scented soap stung her eyes as she peered down to investigate. About four inches beneath the crook of her elbow she had a slice straight across the width of her arm. The shallow wound was angry red and puffed up beneath the thick coat of dried blood that covered it. Holding it beneath the streaming water, Ireland ignored the bite of pain as she rinsed it clean, all the while trying to form some idea of where it had come from. She didn't remember scratching herself when she moved Rip, but that seemed as likely a prospect as any. Glancing over each shoulder and down her front, she checked for any other marks. There were none. Just the one, lone slice … that almost looked deliberate. Realizing today's long sleeves would serve the multi-functional purposes of concealing her tattoo *and* preventing speculation she was a cutter, Ireland shrugged off the mystery and returned to her frenzied rush.

The school campus was already buzzing with activity as Ireland threw her MINI Cooper in park, and bolted from the car in hopes of beating the first bell. She made it two strides before it rang, thereby altering her goal to the *second* bell.

She gave a brief nod to the custodial crew gathered at an exterior wall of the gymnasium, scrubbing away with brushes and rags. Some kid must've decided to try their hand at graffiti art. If they'd been caught, she'd most likely be seeing them soon. Probably right after the principal played a little "bad cop" and doled out the punishment.

A chorus of squeaking shoes, slamming lockers, and incessant chatter greeted her as she yanked open the door and strode in, her low heels clicking against the faded linoleum. Turning right at the first T in the hall, she made her way to her office through a sea of offered smiles and shouts of hello from the students she passed. Inhaling a deep, cleansing breath, she forced herself to be a grown up and hold her smile steady as Mason Van Brunt slammed his locker shut and spun her way, an arrogant smirk curling across his lips.

His eyes narrowed in a vindictive glare as he fell into step behind her, close enough for his liberal use of cologne to singe her nostrils. "Want to continue our talk about the importance of a name in this town, *Crane*?" He spit her last name as if it were a vile curse that soured on his lips.

"Buying into the hype of your own town, Mason?" Ireland frowned.

Unfortunately—or fortunately, considering the kid was kind of a tool—Mason was already gone, having ducked into his classroom. Rounding the corner into the guidance office, Ireland shook off his half-assed attempt at intimidation and held up her coffee to Amber in place of a wave. "Morning!"

Amber raised one finger, muttering a short, "Uh-huh," to whoever was on the other end of the receiver cradled to her ear.

Without breaking stride, Ireland whispered a quick, "Sorry." She could at least set her stuff down before getting the rundown of the daily happenings.

Apparently, the "happenings" were a pow-wow in her office. Principal Edwards leaned against Ireland's desk, her arms folded over her chest. Two uniformed police officers killed time by browsing her wall of educational pamphlets. All three turned her way, wearing shockingly similar stern expressions, the moment she stepped into the room.

"People here to see you!" Amber called out as soon as she replaced the receiver.

"Thanks, I got that," Ireland muttered and pulled the door shut behind her.

"Nice of you to join us." Principal Edwards shot a pointed glance to the wall clock.

"Sorry, a student stopped me in the hall." That wasn't *completely* a lie. "What can I do for all of you this morning?"

The nearest officer, attractive in a fit, silver fox kind of way, pivoted to face her. His thumbs were looped through the front of his holster. "We need to know where you were last night, Miss Crane."

A nervous giggle bubbled up Ireland's throat, but she quickly choked down. "At home ..."

Discovering a squatter in the basement and interrogating him while he was tied up on my couch.

"... unpacking."

"Can anyone attest to your whereabouts?" the other officer, who the years had not been as kind to, asked.

The homeless guy, before I knocked him out—thrice.

"No, sorry, I was all alone. What's this about?"

While the officers exchanged questioning looks, Principal Edwards pushed off the desk and rose to her feet. "It seems that last night *someone*," she drilled that last word in hard and deep, "thought it would be fun to graffiti the side of the gymnasium with one single word. Do you have any idea what that word might be?"

A slew of smartass answers ran through Ireland's mind. Having the good sense to know they would not be well-received, Ireland opted for the demure approach. "No, ma'am, I don't."

"It was Katrina," Principal Edwards linked her fingers in front of her, her eyebrows raising in expectation. "Do you have any idea what a message like that could mean?"

Ireland felt a hot flush of guilt rush to her cheeks, even though the feeling was completely unwarranted. "I ... no, why would I? I don't even know anyone by that name. It was probably a student broadcasting their crush of the week."

"That's what we thought at first, too," the silver-haired officer stated, rocking from the balls of his feet to his heels and back again. "Until we discovered that the name was written in blood. Blood, which we tested and found a direct match to from a health screening done at NYU. Would you like to take a guess who it belonged to?"

"Me?" Ireland's pulse drummed in her temples. That couldn't be right, there was just no way.

The slice in her arm tingled with sudden, startling awareness. Was it possible someone had entered her house while she was sleeping, cut her arm to collect her blood, and did God only knows what else? One name flashed in her mind above all others. One that had opportunity.

One that had already shown signs of instability. One that might just use her act of kindness against her. *Rip.* He had been in the basement before. He had to know another way in that made her locked door irrelevant. Had he drugged her? Stolen from her? Had his filthy hands been on her?

Principal Edward's sneered words snapped her from her unnerving reverie, "If this was some kind of joke, it is an incredibly disturbing, gruesome thing to do in a facility full of children."

"I have no idea how this is possible, but I promise you I had nothing to do with it." Even Ireland heard the shocked, hollow ring of her words. "Why? Why would *anyone* do that?"

"You must understand how far fetched a notion it is for us to believe you had *nothing* to do with it." The principal made no attempts to hide the judgment that dripped from each word.

"I understand that." Ireland squared her shoulders and stared directly into her employer's round face. "But with all due respect, Principal Edwards, your doubts don't change the fact that I had absolutely *nothing* to do with this. I have no idea how my blood ended up on that wall. I'd like the answer to that as much, if not more, than you do."

"Miss Crane, if that *is* the case then you need to be very careful. An act like this could be viewed as an open threat. Someone in Sleepy Hollow is trying to send you a message, and it isn't a friendly one." The heavier of the two officers pulled a card from his pocket, pinched between two fingers, and handed it to her. "If you run across any problems at all, call us immediately."

"Thanks. I'll add this to the one Officers Potter and Granger gave me," Ireland stated with a forced smile of gratitude as she dropped the card into her briefcase.

"Who?"

"Keep in mind," Officer Silver-hair interjected, cutting off further conversation with his gruff tone, "that if you *were* behind this, these type of occurrences are *not* tolerated here in Tarrytown. I sincerely hope this is the one and *only* time we have to talk to you about something like this." He acknowledged Principal Edwards with a brief jerk of his chin. "Naomi, if you have any other issues don't hesitate to call."

"Without a second thought or moment's pause," she assured him, her stare never wavering from Ireland.

With barely a nod in her direction, both officers left. Leaving Ireland alone with the principal who may as well have had cartoon steam lines rising off her head.

"Why don't you take the rest of the day off, Miss Crane?" Principal Edwards worded that as a question, however the implied meaning was anything but. "To give some serious thought to how we can ensure nothing like this *ever* happens again."

"Yes, ma'am." Ireland readjusted the strap of her briefcase on her shoulder, spun on her heel, and marched from the school with one lone thought driving her forward.

Rip.

The shed door flung open hard enough to bounce on the hinges. Ireland stood framed by the doorway, her chest rising and falling with each ragged breath. Rip paused, mid-chew. His wide eyes stared up at her as the hand lifting another cracker to his mouth froze.

Ireland let the box cutter slip from her fingers. It landed on the sleeping bag beside him with a dull thump.

"Pick it up," she hissed through her teeth.

"Wh—why?" Rip stuttered, his face clouded with fear and confusion.

"Do it!" she barked, knowing full well that her handle on her emotions was slipping. She forced herself to inhale a deep, shaky breath and steady the harsh rise and falls of her tone. "Now."

Reluctantly, Rip did as she said. "Now what?"

Ireland squatted beside him, shoving her sleeve further up her arm to reveal the slice beneath. "You were a coward to attack me in my sleep," she growled in a hushed whisper. "Now I'm awake and expecting it. Go ahead … try it."

Her tough and fearless act was due, in large part, to the courage bolster of a can of pepper spray shoved in her back pocket. If he actually lunged he was going to get a face full of nastiness followed by a ride in the back of a police car.

"Someone … did that to you?" Rip maintained eye contact as he eased his hand to the ground and let the cutter slip from his grasp.

"Not someone, *you*."

"Miss, I just awoke," Rip said, his face a mask of sincerity that Ireland almost bought … *almost*. "I haven't even had time to bite into that sandwich you were thoughtful enough to make for me. I rose, heeded nature's call, and then came back here and ate *a* wafer. That's it."

"*Don't lie to me!* You waited long enough for me to go to sleep, broke into the house—the same way you did before—sliced my arm, and raced over to the high school to write the name 'Katrina' on the wall in *my blood.*" Even as she voiced her accusation, doubt began to seep in.

In the short time she'd known him, Ireland found Rip to be a lot of things—odd, off putting, no friend to those with noses—but he never struck her as stealthy or quick; two traits that would be mandatory for whoever broke in. Still, she was puffed up with her own frustration and couldn't back down. Staring murderous daggers, she waited for his reaction.

Rip's stare flicked frantically from side to side as he mentally put together pieces. "If someone broke into your home and performed such a ritual ..." He trailed off, his trembling hand rising to stroke the length of his beard. "The Horseman is calculating, but only in regards to acts of extreme violence. An undertaking such as this would require finesse. Something completely out of character for the beast. That can only mean," his eyes widened into large Os, searching Ireland's face for answers she couldn't give, "he's no longer working alone. Someone else has learned to control the Hessian!"

Those were his parting words. His body followed his rolling eyes straight back, where he banged against the side of the shed and slumped there, a string of drool leaking over his slack lip.

Ireland shook her head with a wry huff of laughter. "You're a weird little troll. You know that?"

Sadly, no answers could be found in Rip's snores. She'd have to wait for him to come to—again. Ireland rose to her feet, turning at the waist to stretch out her back. There was plenty she could do to pass the time: unpacking, settling in, calling her boss every five minutes to beg her not to fire her over this … The problem with any of those things was that she would need to going *inside* the house—her sanctuary that had been violated.

Ireland's bangs blew into her eyes as she glanced over her shoulder at the yellow cottage-style house with its white gingerbread trim. From the first time she saw pictures of it online she'd fallen in love. It was so quaint and homey, with its wood floors and decorative moldings, that she could picture the life she would have here. That picture did *not* include a bum sleeping in her shed or visits from nighttime arm slashers. Even so, this house—this tiny, little *home* that vibrated each time the furnace kicked on—was *hers*.

Her fresh start.

Her first solo go at this grown-up thing.

Her very own space.

No way was she going to let some jerkoff with a knife ruin that for her. That decided, she would give herself today. One day to be freaked out and indulge her fears … then get over it. Tonight, she would change the code, sleep with the pepper spray on her nightstand, and claim her space once more.

Her plan made, Ireland shut the shed door and strode off to immerse herself in a healthy dose of avoidance.

11

Ireland

"Mom? *Mom?* No, this isn't something that needs to be discussed at tonight's bonfire …. I'm fine, really. It was just a question … No, you don't need to get Dad … Hi, Dad … Like I was telling Mom … No, praying to the moon goddess isn't necessary … Yes, I'm sure. I was just looking for legal advice, you know from back when you were still sane?" Ireland cringed, wishing she could reel the words back in the very second they left her mouth. Sure enough, her dad launched into his well-practiced rant about how he and her mother had freed themselves from the constricting ties of corporate America by starting a new life on the road, living in what was essentially a shed mounted to a flatbed trailer.

Leaves crunched under Ireland's tennis shoes as she strolled alongside North Broadway, a main street through Tarrytown, giving the occasional "uh-huh" and "you're so right" to her father. The sun warmed her skin, while her hoodie warded off the slight chill in the air. In retrospect, she would've rethought her chosen route if she'd realized just how big the Old Dutch Cemetery was. She'd been walking alongside it for so long that she was having a hard time remembering a time in her life she *wasn't* staring at tombstones. Being surrounded by death was *not* conducive to her goal of setting her mind at ease.

"Yes, Daddy," she said, tuning back in as her father turned the conversation back around on her. "I'm sure you're right. This absolutely must be the universe trying to teach me a lesson … What lesson? Uh…" a wrong answer meant a second wave of the incessant rambling typhoon, "… well, clearly, that I … *um* … put too much importance on materials things?" Her fingers crossed in hopes that her answer would suffice.

Some people wouldn't consider a topic veer to the upsides of hemp underwear a win, but those same people probably didn't know Theodore Crane. Ireland's puffed cheeks exhaled a relieved sigh as she continued to interject the appropriate off-handed comments to keep up the guise that she was listening.

The crescendo boom of a gong on her father's end of the line a few moments later cut their conversation—thankfully—short. Immediately, her father rushed to get off the phone. Past experience had taught Ireland better than to ask what the signal was for. Previous answers had ranged from meal time to tantric fun.

"Okay, Dad … Thanks again for the help … Love you, too … Hug Mom for me." Only after clicking her phone off did Ireland realize where her mindless meandering had landed her—right at the feet of the weeping bride statue.

"You, again." Ireland's lips screwed to the side in distaste. "What? Did you think just because you're sitting there all mopey, I was going to get misty-eyed every time I saw you?"

She hadn't been expecting an answer. The menacing snort behind her *really* made her wish she hadn't gotten one. Slowly, on the balls of her feet, Ireland turned. Three tombstones away a smoke grey stallion anxiously pawed at the ground. Seated on his back—like a silent beacon of death—was a black cloaked figure, his head concealed by fabric and shadows.

"Nice costume, cowboy," Ireland swallowed hard to fight off the tremble in her voice, "but don't expect the locals to be fans of that look."

She took a step forward on the off chance that he would let her scurry back to the exit undisturbed. The hiss of his sword sliding from the sheath at his hip squashed that hope in a harsh and definite fashion.

Ireland stumbled back, gaining a little distance as she raised her hands defensively. "Great job with the intimidation tactic, really. But it's the middle of the afternoon. You try anything and you're gonna have an audience before that horse of yours can get three strides in."

Slowly and deliberately, the rider shook his cloaked head, calling her bluff. And he was right. Sleepy Hollow was a ghost town—no pun intended. Ireland had seen *maybe* two cars since she'd left her house. Everyone was at school or work. With her heart thudding in her chest hard enough to resonate through her ribs, Ireland inched her way back.

The horse matched her step without being cued.

This was *not* the fabled Headless Horseman of Sleepy Hollow. Of that Ireland was sure. For one thing, his crudely tossed together costume consisted of black jeans, the cape, and bright white tennis shoes. However, he *had* been twisted enough to don the ensemble and strap on a sword, and *that* made him a very real threat. Ireland edged further back, little by little, until she could round the side of the statue and position it between them. With the stone woman as her buffer, she spun, her feet pounding into the grass as she pumped her arms and sprinted down the knoll.

Behind her came the sharp clang of metal and the thundering hoof beats of her stalkers galloping in pursuit. Ireland desperately wanted to chance a look over her shoulder, to see how fast the gap between them was shrinking. However, every scary movie she'd ever watched warned of what a bad idea that would be. Instead, she forced herself to ignore the growing pinch in her side and pump her legs harder still.

The moment her steps pounded over the planks of the Sleepy Hollow Bridge, she counted to determine her lead time.

One Mississippi …

Two Mississippi …

Bang, ba-bang, bang!

No lead at all. She wouldn't make it off this bridge.

A flannel clad arm shot out from between the sidewall beams of the covered bridge. "Ireland! Take my hand!"

She didn't hesitate, but launched herself at the offer of help. Turning her hips to allow Noah to yank her through the narrow opening, splinters snagged and ripped at her clothes as he pulled her through to safety. The momentum of her jump knocked them both back, rolling them down the stony embankment until they skidded to a stop on the bank of the river beneath. Instantly, Noah bolted upright, his finger pressed to his lips as he listened for signs of her pursuer following.

The heavy silence was broken by a hyena-like laugh, youthful and sharp. Ireland pulled herself up, on to skinned and bloody elbows, and craned her neck around the underside of the bridge.

By the rail, still astride his panting horse, Mason Van Brunt pulled back his hood. A victorious grin split his face. "Miss Crane, did I forget to mention that my father *also* supplies the horses used for the equestrian team? And we just so happen to have bits of a Horseman costume laying around for parades since he *is* our school mascot."

"What the hell, Mas?" Noah groaned. "Shouldn't you be in school?"

"Easy, Van Tassel. I was working Brimstone for the team competition Saturday when I saw your girlfriend walking alone like an open invitation." One shoulder rose and fell in a casual shrug, a rosy flush of self-amusement brightening his cheeks. "I just couldn't resist." Still laughing, he yanked the horse's head around and nudged him forward.

Only then did Ireland find her voice ... or at least she thought it was her voice. The breathless rasp with its distinct pitch of boiling rage made it practically unrecognizable. "Good luck getting a college referral letter now, *you sociopathic little prick!*"

Noah bit the inside of his cheek hard to stifle a laugh he dare not free. "So, those classes you had to take on the proper way to deal with kids? You apparently aced those?"

"That's not a kid." Ireland pulled herself off the ground and brushed the rubble from her rump. "*That* is the devil incarnate."

"Ah, he's a good kid. Just going through an asshole phase. Happens to the best of us." Noah eased himself off the ground, picking off the grass and sticks that clung to the thick flannel of his shirt.

"Some people just make the mistake of getting stuck there." Ireland glared after Mason as his shadow faded into the distance.

"The La Brea Tar Pits of asshole-ism." Noah pressed his lips into a thin line and gave a mock sympathetic nod. "They claim many each year."

Ireland snorted a laugh, thankful to have a reason to after … *Mason.* "Not that I'm not grateful, but what were you doing under here?"

"Fishing." Noah nodded at his pole and tackle box open and waiting under the bridge. "I'm about done. Nothing's really biting. Can I walk you home?"

"You live right next door, *Mr. Van Tassel.*" Ireland added extra emphasis to his name as she folded her arms in front of her and hitched one inquisitive brow. "How could I say no to such a *prominent* member of the community?"

Noah sucked air through his teeth and rubbed one hand across the nape of his neck. "Yeah … about that. I didn't lie, per say. I *am* the handyman for all of our family's properties. I just withheld the part where I'm also a partial owner."

"Why not just say that?" Ireland raised one hand, palm up.

"Around here people think the names Van Tassel and Van Brunt equal dollar signs," he explained as he gathered his fishing paraphernalia. "Can you really blame me for wanting to distance myself from that? It gets every lady and open-minded dude in this town panty-throwing anxious. Speaking of, did you want me to hold your coat so you could ..."

"Ya know, I think I'm good." Ireland chuckled as she led the way up the steep banking incline toward the path that would lead them both home. "So, is that why you stuck up for Mason? You used to be him?"

"Nah, my parents made sure we always stayed humble. They made us daily chore lists, insisted we get jobs to pay our own expenses, and lived in the same modest house they brought my sisters and me home form the hospital to. Little things like that made all the difference. Vic, the one who passed, was my second cousin. Our sides of the family were never close because *his* family used their name for power. We were the black sheep for not doing the same. You could say Vic was actually the Mason of our family. Not that he even remotely deserved what he got in the end."

"That sucks about your cousin. I'm really sorry for your loss. However, it sounds like your parents did it right. Mason's aren't doing him, or society in general, any favors by allowing him to be a tool." As she walked, Ireland clamped her hand over the mysterious slice on her arm. It had cracked open with a fresh rash of radiating pain when Noah yanked her over the bridge. Through the thick fabric of her hoodie sleeve she could feel blood seeping through, sticking to the fibers.

"You okay?" Noah halted and caught her arm, intending to push her sleeve up and investigate the wound. The touch of his rough, calloused hands were gentle, yet insistent. "Did I scrape you on the way through?"

"No!" Ireland snapped more harshly than she intended as she snatched her arm away and tugged her sleeve back down. Her ears burning red hot at his shocked reaction, she cleared her throat and tried again with a bit more couth. "I cut myself unpacking. There's a reason they call them box cutters and not box ticklers."

Ireland clamped her mouth shut—before something even more moronic than 'box ticklers' could tumble out—and ducked around Noah. She let each stride toward the cemetery gate punctuate her point that she didn't want him to press the matter further.

"Okay, then," Noah stammered in confusion as he retrieved the fishing supplies he had cast aside and rushed to catch up.

Long legs and a wide stride allowed him to get to the gate before her. With a gentlemanly flourish, he held it open and waved her through. "I know you're new in town and don't know too many people. Maybe we could do dinner—"

"Oh. Oh, *no!*" It had been long enough since she'd been propositioned for a date that it took Ireland a minute to figure out that's what this was. She took the realization like a bucket of ice down the pants. "I just meant ... I don't do ... *that.*"

"You don't eat?" Noah's eyebrows had practically leapt off his head at her display of crazy.

"I don't date," Ireland clarified. "*Ever.*"

Noah didn't break stride, but leaned to the side to consider her. "Freshly cut and colored hair. Probably a drastic cut, too, judging by the way you keep playing with where it falls at the back of your neck."

Ireland quickly dropped her hand to her side.

"Add to that a tattoo on your arm new enough to still be peeling. I have three sisters and know the female break-up signs all too well when I see them. I'm gonna guess it was a pretty nasty one?"

Ireland stared down at her shadow, appreciating its simplicity and complete lack of complications or judgment. "The worst—like, ever—in the world. I gave up everything for him and let myself become the person *he* wanted me to be just to make him happy. He thanked me by banging the neighbor's dog walker on the coffee table I had just refinished."

"Did they smudge the finish?" Noah asked with a look of genuine concern.

In spite of herself, Ireland erupted into a sharp bark of laughter. "I didn't stop to check. I was too busy trying to maneuver the refrigerator into the hallway."

"I'm sorry," Noah chuckled in confusion, "I'm going to need you to elaborate on that."

"I bought the fridge." Ireland flicked her long, side bangs from her eyes, already shaking her head at her own idiocy. "In that moment it seemed of *dire* importance that I take it with me. He could ruin my life, but he couldn't take my fridge." At Noah's perplexed stare, Ireland rolled her eyes. "I know. It made sense at the time. Scooting it back and forth, inch by inch to the door. I even had to ask for a wrench to unhook the water line. Then, when I couldn't figure it out on my own, Brantley—the dreaded ex—volunteered to help. After that I got it as far as the door before I remembered it took a team of four movers to get it up the six flights of stairs, because it wouldn't fit into the elevator."

Noah's face turned from pink to red as he stifled his laugh behind his dirt-smudged hand. "So what'd you do with it?"

"His little chicky had thrown some pants on and was holding the door open for me. I gave up and told her to keep him *and* the fridge. Then, tagged on the word 'whore' to make myself feel better."

That did it. Noah threw his head back in a loud guffaw. "If they made a movie of that," he swiped at his tearing eyes in between chuckles, "I would watch it every year on my birthday."

"Yeah, well, now you see why I don't date. I can't afford to lose any more major appliances," Ireland said as they rounded the corner, her canary yellow house coming into view.

"Ah, the guy was a tool. You just haven't found the right one yet." Noah bumped her playfully with his shoulder.

Ireland hiked one brow, casting a sideways glance his way. "Are you saying you're different?"

"Me?" Noah jabbed a thumb at his chest. "No, not at all. I'm a complete scoundrel. An ass of epic proportions. Maybe over dinner, *as friends*, I can tell you how to avoid guys like me."

Ireland stopped at the walkway to her door and craned her neck, checking for signs of movement inside the large bay window. "Dinner, as *friends*. Where I don't expect you to pay or hold doors and you don't expect make-up or sex."

"I'll be rude, and you'll be purposely homely. It'll be magical," Noah laughed, and jabbed a thumb over his shoulder toward his house. "I'm going to go, before I say something stupid that'll change your mind.

Night, Ireland. And, for what it's worth, I'm glad you weren't killed horribly by a fictional Horseman tonight."

"Thanks, me too!" Ireland called after him. Only *she* noticed the slight tremor of nerves in her voice and knew all too well the cause.

It was fear of what she would find awaiting her inside that prompted her to pause, letting Noah disappear behind his own closed door before she slid her key in the slot and pushed open the door. A cold knot of fear twisted in her gut the moment she stepped inside. Ireland crept through the house on tiptoe, her muscles set on a hairpin trigger to flee at the slightest provocation. Mentally, she cursed her extreme lack of athleticism. Right then would've been the ideal moment to have golf clubs or baseball bats laying around as impromptu weapons. Instead, she walked with her head on swivel, scouring every inch of the house for traces someone else had been there. Behind curtains, in closets, under her bed, she checked every possible hiding spot. Each time uttering a silent prayer she wouldn't come face to face with *anyone,* before holding her breath and taking a peek. Thankfully, this unorthodox method seemed to work. Just as her confidence that the house was secure was beginning to build, and that knot of unease began to loosen, she reached the door that led to the basement stairs.

Ireland's hand closed around the knob and yanked it open. A shaky breath escaped through pursed lips at the hungry maw of darkness that lay before her, eager to swallow her whole.

"It's probably good," she gulped, before shutting the door and locking it. For good measure, she dragged a dining room chair over to wedge it, propped up on two legs, underneath the doorknob.

Comfort in her surroundings slowly returning, Ireland tugged her hoodie over her head. The fabric of it stuck in the dried blood on her arm. She cringed at the painful pull of it and broke it free as quick as she could. Tossing the soiled garment onto the washing machine, she eyed the wound, finding it in desperate need of a good washing and a little antibiotic ointment. On her way to the kitchen sink to do just that, she noticed the scrap of paper stuffed into the seal of the slider. The door shushed across its track as she cracked it open, allowing the slip of paper to blow inside and flutter to the ground at her feet. Ireland bent to retrieve it, turning it over to read the spotty inked message written with a pen that obviously had given Rip fits.

> *The talisman may still be of use. I have ventured into town to do some investigating. My return shall be swift.*
>
> *-Rip*

Ireland's tongue flicked across her top teeth as she chuckled. "Yeah, that should go *swimmingly*."

Still shaking her head, she relocked the door then strode to the kitchen sink to clean her arm. She let the water run a minute, checking the temperature with the tips of her fingers before sticking the top of her forearm under the faucet. The sting of it prompted a cringe she couldn't stifle. Holding it still, she allowed the water to completely flush the wound. Thankfully, the pain lessened after a moment. Water was pouring over the cut, working its cleansing magic, when Ireland caught a faint movement out the kitchen window. A prickly warning skittered down her spine, snapping her head up. Her apprehensive gaze flicked across the yard, finding nothing ... *at first*. No tiny critter scampered through the grass that desperately needed mowing. No slightly crazed homeless man returned to the quarters he had somehow claimed in the shed. Yet, she could've *sworn* there was something there.

Ireland shut off the water and leaned forward. The late day sun had hidden its face behind thick grey clouds, making it necessary for her to squint into the ill-timed obscuring gloom. In the center of the yard the grass was depressed, a crescent shaped divot dotting the center of it. From behind her, a soft knock rattled the front door. Ireland pulled back from the counter, about to turn away, when the divot vanished. The grass within it sprung back up to a slightly crushed version of its original state. A small gasp eeked past Ireland's lips before she could slap a hand over her mouth to contain it. She watched—through bulging eyes—as the shape reappeared, closer this time. As if something had taken a wide step forward. Then another. The steps of an unseen entity moving across the yard at a steady pace.

"Miss Crane?" a muffled male voice called out, followed by a second knock.

Ireland wanted to respond, longed for another set of eyes to confirm what she was seeing. Unfortunately, her tongue seemed to be frozen to the roof of her mouth. Ghostly steps that couldn't possibly be real had robbed her of the art of basic articulation.

"Miss Crane? Tarrytown police, can you open up please?"

The steps came to a sudden stop at the edge of the deck, any trace of them instantly vanishing. With her heart thudding in her chest, Ireland shoved herself away from the counter. She rounded the edge of the breakfast nook, catching a bar stool in the process and sending it crashing to the floor. Refusing to let it slow her, she hopped over it with an awkward half-twist to maneuver herself to the slider. Cupping her hands around her eyes, she waited ... and watched.

"Miss Crane? Is everything okay?"

A barely audible hiss from the other side of the door caused Ireland to lean in further, her forehead touching the cool pane.

"We know you're in there, ma'am, and need you to open up!"

Hot breath fogged the opposite side of the glass—right where Ireland's face was.

"*Son of a ...*" Ireland threw herself away from the door. Mid-backpedal, she stumbled over a dining room chair and crashed to the floor in a pile of limbs and furniture.

"*Miss Crane?* Kick it in!"

Wood splintered as boot met door. The door cracked open with enough force to bang off the wall behind it. In the amount of time it took for the two officers to run to her aid, guns drawn, the fogged breath had already dissipated, leaving behind no trace it had ever been.

"Are you okay, miss?" the heavier officer—who she'd met earlier in her office, and whose badge read Sheppard—asked in a breathless pant as he grasped her elbow and helped her to her feet.

Ireland reluctantly tore her gaze from the now vacant glass. "I *uh* ... slipped on my way to the door. Sorry, didn't mean to scare anyone."

"No harm no foul," his silver-haired colleague stated, his chest puffed as he admired the battered door. "Gonna need your landlord to have a look at that, though."

"We're sorry if we gave you a start." Sheppard slid off his hat and wiped the sweat from his brow with his forearm. "We just came to help your uncle home."

Ireland's eyebrows rose to meet her hairline. "My who?"

A bushy face, creased with deep lines and wrinkles, ducked around the open door frame. "There's my favorite niece." Rip smiled through brown-stained teeth.

"My *uncle*." Ireland nodded her comprehension.

"We found him in the middle of the street unconscious." Silver-hair pivoted enough for her to read Burke on his badge, as he drummed his fingers against his holstered gun. His expression did nothing to hide his distaste for the man currently slinking into the house like a scolded puppy. "Blew clean on the Breathalyzer. How? I have no idea."

"Your carriages move at ridiculous speeds," Rip offered in way of explanation. "I found it alarming, hence the loss of consciousness in the street."

"He does that." Ireland clarified to the disbelieving officers, her face a mask of apology. "Super fun at parties."

"Keep an eye on him. Something like that happens again and we could have a much worse problem on our hands." Officer Burke gave a curt nod, which acted as his only good-bye, before he strode from the house.

"Glad everything here was okay." Officer Sheppard stared after his partner for a moment, before offering Ireland an uncomfortable smile. "Sorry again about your door."

Ireland followed him to the door. It wouldn't latch, but could be dead bolted in place. As soon as the lock clicked, she spun on an unsuspecting Rip. Her quaking hands gestured wildly from her rising panic, barely kept in check. "First, some nut job breaks into my house to steal my blood. Now," she stared out the window, as if an explanation for what had happened could be found floating there, "I think an invisible horse just tried to trample me in the yard. And, yes, I know that sounds insane, don't give me that look! I sound like a friggin' lunatic, just like you have every second since we met! However, I'm beginning to think you're the only one that knows what the hell is going on. So, fine! You win! You say you know all about this boogity-boogity crap? Well, have a seat, Rip, because you and I are going to have a nice long talk!"

He didn't utter a peep, but fell straight back, thumping to the floor in a heap.

"Yeah, no, by all means take a friggin' nap first," Ireland grumbled and blew her bothersome side bangs from her eyes.

Sweet smelling steam wafted from the tea pot as Ireland poured a cup of freshly brewed ginger tea into a cup for herself and one for Rip. Her gaze flicked from the flowing russet liquid to the old man rousing on the floor. He rolled to his side, off the throw pillow she'd stuffed under his head, rising up on legs that wobbled under his slight weight. Rip didn't make eye contact or utter a sound when he accepted the offered mug, but turned and shuffled into the front room. Ireland brought the mug to her lips and slammed it back—much to the displeasure of her then scorched gullet—before she deposited it in the sink and followed him. Mentally, she tried to prepare herself for the gush of lunacy she knew was coming. Unfortunately, a little voice in the back of her mind warned that even if her head could flip back like a garbage can lid she *still* wouldn't be open-minded enough for what she was about to take in.

The man, now seated on her couch, was no longer the bumbling wacko she'd come to know Rip as. His entire demeanor had changed, grown noticeably somber; the severe and forlorn look in his eye giving away that this was a man who had seen more than he cared to admit. His slack posture stiffened, the firm set of his jaw causing his bushy beard to bulge off his face like steel wool.

"Ichabod Crane was a real man," he began, "not just a character in a fable. I knew him well enough to say, with absolute certainty, that he never deserved the fate that befell him—of being known as a victim of the Headless Horseman and nothing more. He was as good a man as any person could ever hope to meet."

Ireland eased herself to the floor across from him, crossing her legs at the ankle in front of her. "No offense, but I read the book—many times, actually. Ichabod Crane was a money-hungry hound dog that set his sights on Katrina Van Tassel because her daddy had money. He only gave up on that because a fabricated myth ran him from town like the coward he was."

"No!" Fiery passion ignited in Rip, sharpening his grey eyes to pure steel. "That was ... a misunderstanding. Irving *had* to write it that way."

"Irving? As in Washington Irving?" Ireland tried, unsuccessfully, to hide the amusement in her tone. "You mean the author you stole your name from?"

"One and the same. However, I didn't steal my name from him. I *am* Rip Van Winkle."

Ireland nodded slowly, allowing herself time to choose her words careful. "At the end of that book, Rip Van Winkle gets so mad he rips himself in two. In that same situation you would take a nap."

Nose hairs waved in the breeze as Rip snorted a humorless laugh. "Aye, we came up with that after *way* too much ale. It seemed more … *menacing* than the reality." He stared down at his dirty trousers, a fresh wave of sadness furrowing his brow. "Irv and I fought alongside Ichabod during the Revolutionary War."

Something in his desolate tone clamped down the claim of shenanigans that danced on the tip of Ireland's tongue. If this was his delusion, one he believed in quite adamantly, who was she to rob him of it?

"That's where I saw the true heroism of that man for the first time." Rip stared out the window into the setting sun, as if his memories were playing across the sky in a private viewing just for him. "He saved not just my life, or Irving's, but our entire battalion. Just under a dozen of us that had been sent to march north in search of shelter and aid for more of our men. Winter was at her harshest, and we lacked the resources to combat her fury. So, we walked. Through the wind, through the snow, through the pain, leaning on each other to draw strength when our own was tapped. When we saw the glow of the farm house, with its home fires burning, it beckoned to us like the most alluring of mirages. Thankfully, the old couple inside welcomed us. The old man made his living as a large animal vet, his wife his constant aid. They used what training and experience they had to care for each of us; tending to our wounds, warming our chilled bones and filling our starved bellies. We were so close to death, we didn't even think about our footprints in the snow. They led the enemy right to us. They surrounded the house, threatening to kill us all. The couple informed us of another way out—a storm cellar under the house. It was a ten pace sprint to the outhouse, then fifteen more to the tree line and safety. Together, we reached the decision that it was too dangerous to all go at once. It would draw far too much attention. Ichabod volunteered to stay behind, shouting taunts at the enemy and generally making a ruckus in the house to create a diversion. It was he who timed it out, releasing us one by one. Irv and I hung back to help until Ichabod practically forced us out. It was me that tripped, making everything that followed *my* fault. My foot found an exposed tree root and I went down, loud enough to draw attention from the nearest enemy soldiers. Ichabod had no choice but to run if he stood any chance at escape. A soldier gave chase and stabbed Ichabod in the shoulder with his bayonet. Ichabod gained control of the weapon, pulling it from his hemorrhaging wound and turning it on his attacker. Irv and I came back for him and dragged him to safety from the rain of musket fire." Rip craned his neck to catch Ireland's gaze, a rush of tears filling his eyes. "He was the bravest, most kind-hearted man I have ever known. If you truly do share his blood, you should consider yourself blessed."

"It's a pretty common name," Ireland said as she awkwardly picked a fuzzy off the yoga pants she'd changed into. "I have to ask, if he was such a stand-up guy, why the smear campaign after he died?"

"The truth had to be protected, and sometimes there's no better place to hide things than in plain sight. We offered people a legend, laced with fabrications, so the truth would be concealed from those that may use it for harm if they ever discovered the truth."

"And what truth would that be?" Ireland asked, her patience audibly wearing thin. "That ghosts are real? That the thing going bump in the night might be there to claim your head?"

Rip's arthritic finger traced along the rim of his coffee mug. "Far worse. That the Horseman is a constant. He may find a worthy head, allowing his spirit to be sated and move on, but then his victim shall rise up in his place. Worse yet, the Hessian can be controlled. If that talisman were to fall into the wrong hands, he could be turned into a weapon that could be wielded in the most bloody and horrifying ways imaginable. I was told a Crane would come, and when you did I was meant to teach you how to control him—to take my place. Then, you showed up with that mark." His gaze flicked to her tattoo, before shaking his head with a pang of distress washing over his face. "You may think it was your own free will that inspired you to add what you thought was a frivolous piece of art to your body, but someone, somewhere had sinister motives and knew all too well the ramifications of branding you with that. Best I can figure now, the two talismans are canceling each other out. Our new goal must be to figure out how to get at least *one* of them working, or many lives will be lost … possibly even your own."

110

"So, you're saying that thing in my yard was ... what? The Headless Horseman come to claim me?"

"I didn't see it to say." Rip shrugged, pressing his chapped lips together in a thin line. "It's a possibility. The police officers presence could've thwarted his advance. If that *is* the case, we should salt the doors and windows to prevent his spirit from entering. Especially since it was most likely *he* that slashed your arm, meaning he's walked these halls before."

Ireland expelled a breath she hadn't realized she'd been holding, and let her head thump against the wall behind her. "I hate this friggin' town."

12

Ichabod

Ichabod crept into the hall, quietly pulling the door to Katrina's bedroom within the Van Tassel manor shut behind him. "She sleeps now. The poppy seed tea calmed her," he explained to her anxious looking father.

"Thank you for bringing her home," Baltus gushed, his hands nervously wringing his handkerchief. "What did you say your name was, young man?"

Ichabod's mouth opened, fully intending give the truthful answer, when an image of him being thrown from the premises flashed before his eyes. "Washington Irving, sir," he lied. "You can call me Irv, as most do."

Baltus clapped a grateful hand on Ichabod's shoulder. "You are an upstanding lad. Although why you choose to associate yourself with the likes of that scoundrel, Ichabod Crane, I shall never know."

"He is not all bad," Ichabod muttered through a tight, forced smile. "I can attest to that."

"*Humph*," Baltus snorted, and straightened his ruffled collar with a haughty air. "And what of the body? Were they able to identify it? Peter Van Brunt was beside himself with fear that he may have lost his only son, Brom."

Ichabod's gaze fell to the plank wood floor. The grisly scene replaying, for what seemed to be the millionth time, behind his eyes. "The body belonged to Daniel, the Van Brunt's stable hand. Why he was targeted or displayed in such a gruesome matter has yet to be uncovered."

"Such a tragedy." The candelabra strung overhead cast a glimmering glow that reflected off of the top of Baltus's head where the hair had long since receded. "For so long we thought, not that we had bested the ghostly beast, but that we had somehow stumbled on to some sort of accord. It appears we were very much mistaken."

"You had an agreement with the man known as the Headless Horseman?"

Baltus shook his head, the corners of his mouth sinking into a sorrowful frown. "As much as anyone can negotiate with a creature from Hell with nothing to lose."

Common sense whispered to Ichabod to keep his mouth closed. Yet, it was his fear for Katrina's safety that spurred him on, forcing the words passed his lips. "Sir, have you ever considered that this is not a spirit, but a madman with an agenda all his own?"

Baltus rubbed the back of his head, his gaze forced away by visible guilt. "For reasons you cannot begin to understand, I will simply say no. I know that not to be the case."

Before Ichabod could protest further, a hammering at the front door cut him off.

"That must be the house boy," Baltus explained, his steps already inching him down the hall. "I asked him to fetch more fire wood. Excuse me, please."

After a brief nod of dismissal from his guest, Baltus disappeared down the hall in the direction of the foyer. With him gone, Ichabod let desire get the best of him. Easing Katrina's door open, he stole a peek at the sleeping angel. Her blonde hair fanned across her pillow; her chest rising and falling in a soothing rhythm. Ichabod knew his place. He didn't belong here; in this home, or this town for that matter. Even so, as he stared at that vision of loveliness, he knew he would not step foot out of Sleepy Hollow until she was safe and her own words bid him leave.

"No! *No!* I beg of you! Show the mercy I *know* you capable of!" Ichabod's head snapped up to see Baltus edging away from the door, his face ashen with panic.

Ichabod took a brazen step forward. His rush to intervene coming to an abrupt halt when the blade of a sword winged through the air. Blood sprayed from Baltus's neck, hitting the floor in thick splatted successions, like a rock skipping over the water. A crimson slash broke through the skin of his neck. Slowly, it grew. Opening. Gaping. Dribbling gore, as his head rolled off the stump of his neck.

Ichabod didn't wait for it to thump to ground. Spinning on the ball of his foot, he dove into Katrina's room and latched the door behind him. He crossed the room with determined strides, gathering her in his arms before sinking to the floor to hide them both between the wall and her bed.

Katrina roused with a groan, which Ichabod stifled by clamping a firm hand over her mouth. As she squirmed and fought against him, he urgently hissed against her ear, "Katrina, I can assure you there has never been a better time to panic. Yet, you *must* be still. The killer is in the house."

Katrina twisted her head. Frightened eyes, bright with unshed tears, sought confirmation on Ichabod's face. He nodded, pleading with his eyes for her to be still. A thud in the hall snapped both of their stares toward the sliver of light shining in from under Katrina's door. Heavy footfalls echoed down the hall, drawing near with an ominous *thump, sss, thump, sss.*

Ichabod squeezed his eyes shut, uttering a silent prayer. Not one of fear, but one of mercy. If one of them were to meet their end, and that likelihood was increasing with each nearing boot clomp, Ichabod prayed it be him. If the trembling woman in his arms—who smelled of a sweet blend jasmine oil and honey—could be spared, he would gladly sacrifice his life.

The footfalls halted … right outside of Katrina's door.

Katrina whimpered behind Ichabod's hand, burying her head against his chest, as the shadow of two large boots blocked the sliver of light. Once more, that menacing hiss sounded. Bile stung the back of

Ichabod's throat. He weaved his hand into Katrina's hair to hold her still and spare her the horrific sight of her father's unseeing eye staring beneath the door crack—his head impaled on the end of a long blade.

Ichabod's ferociously beating heart threatened to tear from his chest as the doorknob jiggled beneath the stranger's grip. With frantic need, his gaze scoured the room in search of a weapon, an exit, *anything* that could help them. Tragically, he came up empty handed. Tightening his grip around Katrina, he dotted a kiss into her hair and tried to reassure himself it wouldn't be the last.

Suddenly, in the most astounding of miracles, the boot shadows pivoted away in a hurried rush that caused their heels to click together. The figure strode back down the hall at a near run. Katrina's head rose to peer at Ichabod, unspoken questions swirling in her beautiful eyes. Were they safe? Was he gone? All Ichabod could manage was a slight shake of his head. It was too early to tell, and far too big a risk to climb from their hiding place and check. Instead, Ichabod rolled to his back, letting his head fall to the floor, as Katrina's muffled sobs soaked the front of his shirt.

13

Ireland

The plush terry cloth robe slipped from Ireland's shoulders with a whispering caress before pooling in a heap around her ankles. Marble tiles chilled her bare feet as she stepped into the walk-in shower. The tips of her fingers slid across stainless steel. With a flick of her wrist, the trio of showerheads flowed to life. Welcoming heat came at her from all angles, pulsating over her curves with a rhythmic seduction. Ireland turned, a groan escaping her as the streams massaged all the right places. Steam rose, fogging the handle and creating a cloud of humidity that hugged her frame. Tipping her head back, she let the droplets rain down on her face and across her closed lids. Her lips parted, welcoming the rush of warmth that flooded between them. Until it assaulted her tongue with a rush of coppery warmth that clamped her throat shut with a wretched heave. Her hands cupped to catch the droplets, her eyes widening as thick crimson pooled in her palms, seeping between her ivory fingers. Formerly white tiles were now smattered and smeared with blackish-red gore that sprayed from the nozzles. Ireland threw herself from the shower, her feet *slipping beneath her. She reached out to steady herself, but found nothing to hold on to. Nothing there to pull her back from the brink, except her own need for self-preservation ... and a shadowed silhouette in the corner. Instinctively, she covered herself with her arms. Squinting, she craned her neck to see the figure that was slowly turning to face her.*

"Mason?" Her voice echoed around her before she could even speak it.

He stared straight ahead with fixed, unseeing eyes. Blood trailed down his face from various points of origin, soaking the front of his shirt. "Cloak of night, brings Horseman's plight. His pricy toll, will be a soul."

"Mason? Are you okay?"

A hard blink and his eyes found focus on her. A desperate panic flared his nostrils, forcing his breath to come fast and ragged. "Help me, you have to help me," he pleaded, his teeth pink with the blood that streamed past his lips.

Her trembling hand reached for him, then recoiled at her own inept state of confusion. "H-how? What do I do?"

"You have to save us," Mason's words became more garbled by the fresh rush of gore that bubbled up the back of his throat. His once handsome face contorted in rage. Leaning forward he balled his fists and screamed with a force that bulged the tendons of his neck, "Save us!"

Ireland bolted upright, sputtering. Her pulse was pounding through her veins. The details hung with her—the bitter taste of copper exploding in her mouth, her feet slipping in the blood, Mason's desperation—making her stomach roll in revulsion. Her shoulders curled in, lurching with a potent dry heave. Swinging her legs off the bed, she barely had time to sprint to the bathroom before the contents of her stomach wretched from her trembling form.

On shaky legs, she eased herself to the counter to rinse her mouth under the faucet. Cupping her hands under the cold water made a particular part of the dream all *too* real. Ireland blinked hard, forcing the memory back down to the farthest reaches of her mind. Steadying herself with one hand clamped on the edge of the counter, she concentrated on her breathing. What started as choked, ragged breaths forced through constricted lungs, eased to a passable pattern of normalcy. Only then did her gaze wander up to the frantic looking woman staring back at her in the mirror. She searched her pallid face, made shiny by the nausea sweats, for answers. Unfortunately, she found nothing there except a haggard looking chick in need of a good solid REM cycle.

Back in her bedroom, her cell phone buzzed on the night stand. Ireland ran a shaky hand over her face as she rushed to answer it, all the while trying to remember how one goes about sounding normal. "Hello?"

"Ireland, it's Principal Edwards." An uncharacteristic tremble of emotion cracked in the principal's greeting. "School has been canceled today, but we—we're going to need you to come in as soon as you can. Mason Brunt was found early this morning," her voice broke with a hiccupped sob, "*dead.* We need you to come in to offer grief counseling to any students that may need it."

Ireland's mouth fell open. A garbled, barely audible response tumbled past her lips, as the phone slipped from her hand and clattered to the floor. Her hands curled around the sheets, grasping the cotton fabric in a white knuckled hold, the world whipping around her with a deafening roar.

14

Ireland

"Mas was a dick, but I'm an even bigger dick. I *totally* know that about me. How do I know I'm not next?"

"I have enough credits to graduate *and* a scholarship to NYU. Do you think I could apply for early graduation in case I, ya know, don't make it out of this town alive?"

"I made out with Mason after cheerleading practice. That's only a few hours before he died. How do I get past that? No one is going to want to go to prom with me. I'm, like, the Black Widow!"

Ireland shook two aspirin into her waiting palm, the pills rattling from the bottle. Despite her impending migraine from a slew of the inane, the teens she'd counseled had kept her distracted from the frightening questions playing at the back of her mind on a constant loop—mostly. It was only in the lull between students that those dark ponderings broke through, refusing to be ignored. A long shadow, cast by the tall frame in her doorway, fell over her cluttered desk just as she choked the pills down with a swig of water.

"Today has been absolute shit." Noah leaned against the doorjamb, his hands stuffed in the pockets of his faded, army green coat. Sandy blond hair fell across his forehead in a deliciously messy disarray. "A kid being killed so ... brutally. This is a nice town, despite the legends. Things like this don't happen here."

Her chair squeaked beneath her as Ireland leaned back, nodding in downhearted agreement while allowing him to purge the thoughts eating at him.

"Beerfest is in town. They have a warming tent that serves brats and precarious amounts of alcohol. I won't buy. You won't slap on any lipstick. We'll just go slam back a few, until we take the edge off or fall off our chairs. Whatever comes first." He cocked his head, considering her from under his lowered brow. "What do you say?"

Ireland snatched a pen off her desk just to give her fidgety hands something to occupy them. Mason had appeared to her, begging her to help him, right around the time someone was chasing him down outside his father's stable. The details of which she'd learned after watching the televised police press statement in the teacher's lounge. That *couldn't* be a coincidence. All day she'd been counting the seconds until she could scurry home and spill the details of her nightmare to Rip, in hopes that he could make sense of it. Now, her day was winding down and her eagerness had replaced itself with absolute *terror* over what he might say.

Before better judgment could talk her out of it, she slapped her pen down against the desk top. "I say, hell yeah."

Noah's eyebrows rose in shock. "With no further persuasion needed? I had a whole speech prepared."

Her chair rolled back as Ireland pushed herself to her feet. She shouldered her briefcase and draped her coat over her arm. "Tell me over our second pitcher, and maybe add voices to make it fun."

"No way!" Ireland laughed so hard her cheeks ached, but couldn't seem to stop. "You don't get to swoop in here with your woes of dating some top-heavy, pharmaceutical rep and try to take the crown I *earned* for the worst break-up story! Did you miss the refrigerator thing? Do I need to tell it again or maybe pantomime it? Because I think that would really sell it."

"Not only did I hear the fridge story, but I've decided to play it in my mind every night so I can fall asleep with a smile." His third beer had raised the decibel of Noah's voice enough that there would be no secrets at their table this evening. "I will give you that it's funny as all hell, but it still doesn't win the prize. I'm telling you, I can top it."

Ireland's eyebrows raised in challenge. "You think so, huh?"

"I know so."

With a wave of her hand, she prompted him to continue. "Then by all means, convince me."

"My ex ..."

"Brittany? Bambi? Candy?"

"Tandy."

"That was it! I knew it was a stripper name. Go on."

Noah paused to shoot her an exasperated eyeroll before continuing on, "After we moved in together she insisted on bringing her stupid pet snake into our apartment. I hated that damned thing. Went out of my way to pretend it wasn't there. The day I broke up with her, she left all of her possessions behind, said she'd have a friend come get them. But she *did* take one thing with her ... the snake's terrarium. Dumped her little friend in the middle of the living room floor and walked out with the tank. Hand to God, that thing slithered into my couch to hide! *Who does that?*"

"Holy monkey-balls! What kind of snake was it?"

"*Does it matter?* A slithering, legless bastard moved into my couch! I had to call animal control to come get it out. Even then I couldn't sit down to watch a game without feeling like it was crawling on me. So, I moved. Grabbed my toothbrush and let the ghost of that little creepy-crawly have the place to himself. See? Reptile infestation. I totally win the bad break-up story." He punctuated his sentence with a tip of his red Solo cup.

Ireland shook her head and matched his swig, the humor vanishing from her face. "Brantley wasn't my type, *at all*. He was total upper crust. Champagne wishes and caviar dreams. Not that any of that appealed to me. I liked him more for his ... hell, I don't even know anymore. Maybe he offered a stability I hadn't had since my parents went all whack-job, children of the moon. Whatever it was, I fell *hard*. We met senior year of college, about a month before I was supposed to leave for a pretty friggin' prestigious internship for Child Psychology at Mercy

Hospital. Brantley talked me into staying—the first of many bad decisions he would talk me into. He enjoyed living off of Daddy's money—who was some big wig on Wall Street and basically owns a few blocks of Manhattan. Anyway, he convinced me we didn't need to study or basically be productive members of society at all when we had 'love'," she air-quoted the word, acknowledging it as the lie that it was, "and a limitless bank account. I let him persuade me to put all my goals and ambitions on hold to spend my days jet setting with him in between tennis lessons and fashion week. I'm not going to say it wasn't fun at first, because that's a bold face lie, but by the end I was miserable. I lost myself and everything I believed in. Then, one day I put my key in the door and walked in to see my fiancé's bare-ass pumping away with a twenty year old that could make a rock look intellectual. To this day, I believe he purposely did it to get caught because he was too much of a coward to admit he was just as unhappy as I was." Ireland took another, longer, swig then wiped the foam from her lips on the back of her hand. "I would've happily taken a snake on the loose over that."

Noah jabbed his cup in her direction. A bit of the foamy brew sloshed over the cup rim. "Technically speaking, there was a snake on the loose in your scenario, too."

Ireland gulped down a laugh induced spit-take.

"You know what you need?" Noah leaned in, his flannel clad elbow brushing hers. "A good vice."

Ireland traced her finger over the rim of the cup. "I don't really think—"

"Hear me out," he playfully argued. "Instead of shutting out men altogether, just supplement a crutch to lean on. Not booze, smokes, or anything that could hurt you long term. But maybe a boy toy you can vent those physical aggressions on. FYI, I would happily offer my services to you in that regard." He didn't leer, because that would've made it skeevy, but raised his eyebrows in the innocent expression of someone genuinely trying to help.

She knew he was kidding, yet still had to wet her lips and take a minute at the hot flush that filled her cheeks and burned its way across her earlobes. Maybe it was the beer goggles, or her libido clearing its throat in a less than subtle reminder that "the pulsate setting on the shower nozzle" doesn't count as a relationship status. Whatever the cause, Ireland found herself fighting the impulse to close the gap between them and find out for herself if the soft curve of his lips tasted as good as they looked.

In a fluttering mess of confusion, and a slight case of the alcohol spins, Ireland bolted from her wooden folding chair. The abrupt move caused it to wobble on two legs, threatening to tumble over backwards. "I'm sorry. I—I have to go."

"Whoa, wait." Noah's hand encircled her wrist with a gentle touch that set her skin on fire. "That was a joke. You got that, right?"

It took every ounce of willpower she had to shrug away from his touch and side-step to position a chair between them. "Yeah, absolutely. I just *really* … need to get home."

"You sure?" Noah nodded toward the four-piece band doing sound checks in the corner. "The band is getting set up. They do great covers of some kick-ass classic rock."

Ireland let her gaze wander the length of his arms. He'd never held her, yet somehow she could feel the sensation of his hands on her, like they'd been there a thousand times before. Knowing all the right places to—

"Yep, I'm sure," she managed to squeak. "Another night, maybe? Wanna walk me home?"

Please say no. Please say no. Please say no, her voice of better judgment mentally chanted.

"Absolutely." He grinned, his gaze brightening with a mischievous gleam.

Oh, crap. Better judgment grabbed its coat and retired for the night.

15

Ireland

"So, I have to ask, you said your parents went all 'children of the moon'. Does that involve howling, or was it some kind of metaphor I didn't get?"

Ireland hid a belch behind her hand and cringed at the bitter after-taste of it. It may have been a chilly night, but she couldn't tell; the wonders of beer had made her impervious to it. "They used to be corporate lawyers. Both of them. I spent a lot of time with nannies while they went out and fought for Big Business. Then, marijuana was legalized—"

"Let me guess, Ozzie and Harriett went on the protest?"

"I wish," Ireland sighed. "They quit their jobs and went on the road touring with the Renaissance Festival as card carrying suppliers."

Noah paused for a beat, mid-stride. "I ... did not see that coming."

"Yeah, neither did I. Now, every conversation with them involves the Earth Goddess and how backed up my chi is—whatever the hell that means. They only visit if the tour is nearby. Those are the moments when it *really* sinks in that Mom traded *Chanel No.5* for patchouli oil and Dad went from wine connoisseur to hydroponics expert."

"No wonder you sought some stability with the douche-bag ex," Noah muttered, kicking a stick off the sidewalk in front of him.

"Nah, it wasn't all Brantley's fault," Ireland mused, feeling a bit more forgiving in her haze. "I let love change me. I just have to learn from it so that it doesn't ever happen again."

Noah bumped her with his elbow, the glow of the street lights casting deep shadows over the hollows of his face. "We all change for love. It's just a matter of what you let it change you into."

Ireland stopped walking and turned to face him, her almond-shaped eyes narrowing. "That's pretty deep for a handyman."

Noah took a slow step forward, one brow hitched in a Cary Grant-style leer. "I *am* deep. I got that from a fortune cookie."

The laugh that played across Ireland's lips faded as she stared up into Noah's face. Darkness sharpened his features, adding an allure of sultry mystery. "I don't wanna walk in on you with another girl." Her still bleeding heart let that proclamation slip out before her foggy brain could filter it.

"Then always knock first," Noah answered with a teasing smirk.

Daring herself to take the plunge, Ireland eased in a little closer. "You're kind of an ass, aren't you?"

The rough skin of his knuckle brushed her jawline, sending waves of white hot desire coursing through her. "Just enough to make me lovable."

"Ireland?" a familiar voice interrupted.

Ireland hadn't realized they'd stopped in front of her house, or that they were on their street for that matter. Be that as it may, even in her inebriated state she knew *that* voice. Well enough for the hair on the back of her neck to spring up and every muscle in her body to clench tight. *"Son of a bitch."*

Noah read the instant change in mood and stepped back. Squinting into the darkness, he attempted to make out the shape of their mood killing guest. "Who is that?"

"We've had some fun tonight." Ireland ignored his question to hiss one of her own through clenched teeth, "You've gotten to know me well enough to say that I'm not a *complete* head case, right?"

"I guess so. Why?"

"Good. Then please disregard what you're about to see." With no further explanation, Ireland turned on her heel. Her goal? Blood or payback. Either would suffice.

It was easy to toy with the idea of forgiving Brantley when she was a couple drinks in and he was a few hundred miles away. However, having him show up on her doorstep unannounced and uninvited tore the Band-Aid off the wound of their break-up and ground a handful of salt into it.

"What the hell are you doing here?" Ireland stomped across the yard, her chest rising and falling in angry snorts like a charging buffalo.

Noah matched her stride, most likely out of concern he was going to have to pull his date for the evening off a well-dressed fella wearing a hurt-bunny expression.

"I thought I told you I never wanted to see you again!" Ireland raged. "I believe the phrase 'crawl up your own ass and die' was used. Or was that in some way unclear?"

Noah stepped in front of her to position himself between the two of them. "I'm going go out on a limb and guess you're Brantley?"

Brantley sneered at Noah's offered hand in open disgust. Choosing then to ignore him altogether, he craned his neck to speak directly to his seething ex, "I came here to talk some sense into you and bring you home. However, now I see you've had your own little indiscretions."

"Indiscretions!" Ireland lunged at Brantley, her hands curled into claws. Noah swung one arm out behind him, catching and gripping the sleeve of her hoodie tight to hold her back. "There *is* no indiscretion here! I am a *very* single woman. If I decide to let this guy do things to me that make my legs bend backwards that's no one's business but *mine*!"

"Oh, you're bringing me into this? Awesome," Noah said with a humorless chuckle. "It's only awkward if we let it be, kids."

At one time Ireland had found Brantley irresistible, with his tailored suits and JFK, Jr. good looks. Now, as his lips curled into that knowing smile that used to make her melt, she felt nothing but the uncontrollable desire to slap that look clean off his face. "Babe, come on. Do you really want to throw everything we had away over one little slip? It's time to get over the diva act and come home."

Noah cringed and rubbed his free hand over the nape of his neck. "Wow, dude, that was *exactly* the wrong thing to say."

"There was no *slip*," Ireland stated as calmly as she could with her pulse thudding in her temples. "And this is not me having an unjustifiable tizzy. This is me telling you, in no uncertain terms, to take all of your lies and BS, and *get out of my life*."

Brantley squared his shoulders and adjusted his tie. His glare sized Noah up, as if noticing him for the first time and finding him tragically lacking. "It seems you have your heart set on slumming it."

Ireland threw herself against Noah's steadfast arm, struggling to get past him. He pivoted to catch her shoulders and hold her back. "Okay, let's hit the pause button right there. Nothing good is going to come of this, so let's make a clean break, let time and clearer heads work their magic. Brantley, as the owner of this property I'm going to have to ask you to leave. I don't want to call the cops, but I will if I have to. The only other option here is me turning this little lady loose and letting her kick your ass Amazonian style. Fortunately for you, I care enough to be her voice of reason that you aren't worth it."

"Now I get it." Brantley shoved his hands into the pockets of his jacket and rocked back on his heels, a smug smile slowly spreading across his face. "She got herself a new sugar daddy. He's no different than me, Ire. Don't kid yourself about that. Sooner or later he'll get tired of your crap and go looking for a little touch elsewhere, just—like—*me*."

"All right, that's enough." Noah's hands dropped from Ireland's sides, his right hand balling into a tight fist.

Ireland caught his arm just as Noah pulled back to swing.

"No." Her low whisper rang hollow, detached of all traces of emotion. Everything seemed to be zapped out of her the moment her present intermingled with her inescapable past. "Let it go. He's—no, *I'm* not worth it. Just … go home, Noah."

Ireland ducked passed Noah, stepping close enough to her ex to catch a tangy whiff of his liberally applied aftershave. "Brantley, you can stay out here as long as you need. Pitch a tent if you want. I don't care. But know that it won't change anything. I'm done," she looked from Noah to Brantley and back again, "with *all* of this."

Without another word, she strode inside.

Ireland didn't pause or break stride before storming straight through the house and out the slider. Her heavy steps banged across the deck and down the stairs into the yard. Throwing the shed door open, she caught Rip mid-Oreo, the flashlight in his hand illuminating a collection of the best works of Edgar Allen Poe.

"Last night a kid from my school appeared to me in a dream and begged me to help him. This morning I learned that someone killed him. Sliced off his head right outside his Dad's horse barn." Rip's face blanched. Still, he didn't interrupt Ireland's agitated rant. "You're pretty much nuts, but you're also the only one that seems to have any idea what's going on."

"You'd be surprised how often those two traits coincide," Rip held up one finger to interject.

"Either way, the couch is more comfortable than the shed. And, truth be told, I'm scared of falling asleep alone. I ... don't know what'll happen next or what freaky thing I'll wake up to."

Rip rose to his feet, genuine compassion puckering his brow. "It would be my honor to look out for you, miss."

Ireland said nothing, but stepped back to allow him passage, waving her arm in open invitation to the door.

16

Ichabod

"We just need a moment of her time." Ichabod attempted to push past Mama Rosa to gain entry to the section of the inn reserved solely for her and her mother. "She is the only person that seems to have any insight into the Horseman. She may be able to help our cause!"

"She is a sick woman," Mama Rosa argued, standing firm to deny him passage. "In addition to her Horseman ramblings, she also strokes her shoe like a cat, and calls it Madame Persephone. Do you think that will be of help as well?"

"What of Katrina?" Irv clamped a hand on Ichabod's visibly trembling shoulder and interceded on his near manic friend's behalf. "After all she's been through, she needs a final rest to this chaos. Use your better judgment, please. Not just for her sake, but for the entire town."

Katrina's grip on Ichabod's hand tightened. "I can speak for myself, sir." Her chin thrust out in an attempt at indignation that fell short. It would have been far more convincing if her face wasn't still puffy from the reoccurring sobs that shattered her time and time again since the moment she'd learned of her father's death. "That madman killed my father," Katrina's voice broke with emotion, yet she forced herself to press on, "if your mother knows anything at all, the simple act of sharing it could save lives."

Mama Rosa's gaze searched Katrina's face. Something she found there coaxed a sigh of surrender from her lips. Turning on her heel, she marched down the narrow hall, jerking her head for them to follow. The hallway came to a T with closed doors in either direction.

Rosa gave a short rap on the door to their right. "If she grows agitated," she warned, "I *will* demand you leave. Which you will do without question. Are we clear?"

"Ma'am, we've met your mother," Rip claimed, from his well-chosen spot at the rear of the pack. "If she becomes agitated there's a good chance we will all run screaming from the room."

"Well and true," Rosa admitted and pushed open the bedroom door.

With the leery steps of those forced to descend the gates of Hell, the group crept into the room led by Irv, who held the lantern. Instantly, they were assaulted by the pungent mix of dried flowers and mothballs. Four heads swiveled, openly gaping at the room around them. Every inch of wall space was covered with crucifixes. Sparse furnishings decorated the small space. A lone chest of drawers leaned against one wall. A narrow bed was situated in the center of the room. Eleanora lay on the bed, still as the dead, with her hands folded over her chest.

"Quite honestly, I was expecting less organized religion and more chicken feet." Rip swiped the dust off the top of a nearby cross with his fore finger, then brushed the digit clean with his thumb.

Rosa threw a sharp elbow into his ribs.

"Apologies," he huffed, struggling to regain his breath.

Ichabod crept across the creaking floorboards on tiptoe, Katrina tucking herself in tight behind him. "Eleanora?" he whispered quietly to her sleeping form, equal parts urging her to wake and terrified she actually would.

The slight woman failed to stir.

"Eleanora?" He tried a second time, with a bit more volume.

Still nothing.

Irv's face popped into Ichabod's peripheral vision. Tipping his head back, he crinkled his nose to force the frames of his glasses higher. "Is she breathing? Can you tell?"

"Mother?" Mama Rosa rounded the bed, her tone reflecting an edge of concern.

Ichabod leaned closer, tilting his head to the side to see if her chest was rising and falling. He heard what he thought was a slight rattle, yet detected no movement. Swallowing the lump of fear that rose in his throat, he pressed his ear lightly to her gaunt chest.

From that position, he didn't see her eyes snap open. His first indication of her rousing came in the form of clawed hands that clamped down on his head—one pressing into his face, the other the back of his head.

"*Shhfferrrnut!*" The flailing hands of the schoolmaster slapped against the mattress. Desperate as he was for freedom, he feared hurting his skeletal captor.

"Mama! Mama, everything is okay," Rosa soothed, scrambling to unclench Eleanora's fingers, which dug crescent shapes into Ichabod's cheeks and forehead. "These people have some questions for you ... about the Horseman."

The decrepit woman's vise grip relaxed, and her freakishly strong hands sunk into the mattress to push herself up to sitting. Ichabod wasted no time righting himself, the red flush in his face slowly fading.

Eleanora's dull grey gaze scanned over the faces eagerly peering back at her. With a brief nod, she began, "To learn the secrets ye must know,

you must first hear a tale of woe."

"Can we do this without the awful, cryptic rhymes?" Irv groaned, steadying himself with a hand on the post of her footboard.

Elenora's toothless mouth worked furiously, grinding lips over gums, as she glared Irv's way. "I do not like him," She muttered to Rosa out of the corner of her frown. "He is cheeky."

"Hear that?" Rip grinned, making no attempts hide his visible amusement at Irv's expense. "You are cheeky."

Rosa gave her mother a comforting pat of the shoulder before addressing the group, her face folded in apology. "Ever since she was struck ill, it has been easier for her to speak if she rhymes. You should hear us composing our list for market. Quite an entertaining event."

It was easy to joke for those that hadn't born witness to two grisly deaths in as many days. Irv and Rip would most likely nestle into their pillows that very night without having horrifying images splashed behind their closed lids. Unfortunately, that was not the case for Ichabod or Katrina. They had both stared death in the face this very night. It having stalked them from the shadows, revealing momentary glimpses of the meaning of true horror.

Katrina fell to her knees beside Eleanora's bed, clasping the old woman's hand in both of hers. "Others mock when you speak of the Horseman and declare you mad. Yet I believe with all of my heart it was that blood thirsty ghoul that claimed the life of my father. Please, if you know of anything that can help us banish him to Hell where he belongs, I beg you to speak!"

Eleanora's eyes widened. One hand—ravaged by swollen, arthritic knuckles—rose to cover her mouth. "If Baltus did fall, means trouble for all." Eleanora shook her head, her coarse hair fanning out from her head. "Before the Hessian rose,

with ghostly woes,

he lived as a man o' arms

enduring war's troubles and harms.

His British leader spoke the command

to burn this town and pillage the land.

'Leave no persons standing' the captain did order,

condemning each soul to hell's very border.

Obeying the command and doing his duty,

one soldier ravaged homes and claimed their booty.

His mission halted and his conscious arose

when he found a babe in swaddling clothes.

Beneath his coat, he hid the babe's head.

Finding him shelter behind an old shed.

His conscious sated, he returned to his task

'til he stumbled upon the mother, wearing panic's mask.

While her fists beat against his chest,

the soldier dragged her to where the infant did rest.

Family reunited, he returned to his battalion.

Only to meet the boom of a canon.

His body should have been burned, like so many others,

'cept for the demands of one grateful mother.

Without those cleansing flames to silence his soul,

The Hessian rose from his earthly hole.

A hero's head he seeks to claim,

to those who fall short he shall kill or maim.

The town under siege, our safety deluded,

many were killed," her eyes brimmed with tears as she turned to

Rosa, "your father included.

T'was the babe grown to boy that discovered their bond.

Humanity of spirit connected, and a new day dawned.

Baltus was that lad that banished the ghoul.

Then, taught us the methods to ward off his rule.

If the Horseman turned on the boy he once saved,

all bets are off, our precautions waived.

Is only one thing could break humanities role,

one with sinister motives has taken control.

Fill with dread, not mourning, at the death of the waif.

Yet heed this warning ...” Her wide, frightened stare flicked to each of their faces, *“no one* is safe.”

17

Ireland

Ireland couldn't remember how or when Noah returned, nor did she really care. All she knew was she was reveling in every minute of his attention. Her hands traced over his back and further down, rising with the soft curve beneath. He moaned against her neck, his mouth nipping and kissing its way back to hers. Her lips parted, allowing an appreciative sigh to escape. Noah's lower lip teased across her mouth, tempting her to be the first to dive into the deep pool of need brewing between them. Her back arched beneath him. The skin-on-skin contact only fueled their building urgency. Both unwilling and unable to wait a moment longer, Noah shifted himself on top of her. His unspoken offer would deliver what she longed for the most—a journey to that blissful brink. It took both hands and every ounce of willpower Ireland had to push him away, thereby denying herself the gush of release she yearned to lose herself in. Nonetheless, this wasn't right. Not yet. For him, she would demand perfection and accept nothing less. With a gentle finger pressed to his lips, *she shushed him. The heat radiating from her stare confirming to them both that this interlude was most definitely to be continued ...*

Ireland woke with a groan, sexually frustrated but sporting a naughty little smile from her dream romp. Only then did she remember her house guest. She giggled and bit down on her lower lip, sincerely hoping she hadn't weirded Rip out by making her dream tryst audible. Rolling onto her back, she threw one arm over her head—and found Rip sitting at the foot of her bed, wide-eyed and shaking like a nervous Chihuahua.

"*What the shit, Rip?*" Ireland bolted upright, clutching the edge of the comforter to shield herself.

"Had to stay awake, had to tell you," he chanted, slowly rocking back and forth. No sooner did the words leave his mouth then his stare went blank and his body toppled straight back like an axed tree. He only fell a few inches before jerking himself awake and resuming the off-putting sway. "Had to stay awake, had to tell you."

"Just when I think you can't get any creeper, you astounded me by reaching a whole new plateau. What did you do to yourself? You're twitching like a meth head."

"Went into the kitchen. Consumed any products that claimed to boost energy. Ate a bowl of those disgusting brown rinds."

"Rinds? That's coffee, dumbass. You're supposed to brew it."

Rip rambled on as if she hadn't spoken, which—judging by his herky-jerky gestures—he might not have been aware she had. "Then I drank your last three of those products involving some sort of red bovine, followed by half a dozen vials that claim to bestow energy for an allotted period of time. Every part of me tingles. Quite honestly, I think I could fly if the moment required it."

"Let's not test that theory," Ireland replied, wiping the sleep from her eyes. "I don't know what ingesting all of that at once will do to a person, but it's safe to say you're a walking, talking science experiment now."

"It doesn't matter!" Rip's voice rose to near hysteria that he quickly tried to rein in with a few calming breathes. "I had to tell you. You must know."

Ireland recoiled, her hands rising to steady him, or fend him off—she wasn't sure which. "Easy, I'm right here. Whatever it is, just go ahead and tell me."

Rip's mouth creaked open. His gaze fixed, pupils dilated. Straight back he went, crashing to the floor with enough force to shake the house.

Ireland ignored the lack of modesty offered by her tank top and shorts as she leapt to her feet and ran to his side. "Rip? Come on, buddy!" Each word was punctuated by a slap or shake. "After a warning like that I'm gonna need a little more info. Plus, I *really* don't want to explain a catatonic homeless guy in my bedroom to the paramedics."

Rip woke with a start, sucking in a deep gulp of air like a man free from submersion. His hand locked around her wrist in a vise grip; his breathless voice wavering as he rasped, "It's … you. You *are* the Headless Horseman."

"Oh, well that's just ridiculous." Ireland's hand slipped from behind Rip's head.

His melon bounced off the wood floor just as sleep claimed him.

Ireland sat at the breakfast nook and sipped her tea, albeit a bit begrudgingly since Rip had polished off the last of her coffee. Her fingernails drummed against the countertop as she waited for him to wake up. No sooner did he rise up on shaky legs that threatened to buckle beneath him, then she launched into the speech she'd mentally rehearsed during the hour he'd been out. "I packed a bag full of food, water, and even threw in a little cash. The temperatures are going to be dropping soon, so if you want to carry on with this squatter lifestyle you're so keen on, I'd suggest you head south to avoid the dropping temperatures. There should be enough money there to get a bus ticket."

"Miss, I implore you—"

She silenced him with one hitched brow and a glare. "I'm not mad. Actually, I blame myself. Life has sucked balls lately. Maybe I thought a little … *strange* would shake things up. Whatever it was that caused my bout of crazy is officially over. It's time for you to go."

"I know this is hard to believe, but you must listen!" Rip stomped his foot, his face reddening. "Last night, you rose from your bed. I saw it with my own eyes. I watched as you ventured down into the basement and came back wearing clothes from the trunk. A black cape concealed your head. A sword hung from one hip, an axe on the other. Where you got those, I haven't the slightest. You vanished into the night, Miss Crane. And when you came back," he glanced down at his hands, obviously seeing something there she couldn't, "blood covered your gloved hands.

Shoo me off if you must, it will not make whatever this is go away. Sooner or later, you *will* have to come to terms with what is *fact*."

"Can you hear *you*? I mean the ridiculousness of that claim isn't lost on you, is it? The *Headless* Horseman. By title alone I am instantly disqualified because of one, very noticeable, trait." Ireland circled her head with her hand. "If that were true, and we're talking pigs flying out of my ass probability here, where would my head factor into this equation? Does it come off? Hang in a satchel at my waist? Oh! Maybe it bursts into flames like in that Nicholas Cage movie!"

"I understood shockingly little of that." Rip's mouth pinched in a tight scowl. "However, as words are often hard to believe, I prepared a back-up plan."

With a wide, determined gait he strode through the kitchen, rounded the utility area, and disappeared down the basement stairs. He returned a brief moment later, toting an axe.

Ireland sprang to her feet, her hands raising defensively while she inched toward the door. "Okay, maybe I was being unreasonable. Why don't you put the axe down and I'll make an extra effort to put on my listening ears?"

"The time for words has passed." Rip stalked toward her, the axe gripped tight in both his hands. "Now, you must see."

Ireland shrank back, her eyes squinting shut just as Rip whipped the axe … and presented it to her handle first.

"There's a partial handprint left on the handle, in blood. Look at the small, narrow shape of it. It's undeniably female."

Cautiously, Ireland accepted the axe—mostly because she wanted it out of Rip's hands. The crusted, red print was of the side of a hand: the pinky, ring finger, and part of the palm. Matching her hand to the print, she found it a close fit. Fortunately, not close *enough* to add merit to Rip's claim. Weighing the weapon in her grasp, she *did* feel an unexplainable stir of familiarity. Instinctively, her other hand rose, curling around the wooden hand in a standard two-handed hold. The flashes hit hard and fast behind her eyes. Memories, which she shouldn't have, sent her stumbling back with their blind force.

Charles Van Tassel cowering against the side of his freshly polished car, his arms raised to shield himself.

Mason Van Brunt casting a terrified glance over his shoulder as he sprinted toward his house ... and its promise of safety.

A slumped figure she'd hit from behind tumbling to the ground at her feet.

And the blood—pools, sprays, and geysers of it. Her sweet reward for a job well done.

The axe slipped from Ireland's grasp and clanged to the floor. Her legs folded beneath, her breath coming in choked gasps. "Oh ... dear God, I remember. I ... *how could I*? How could I do that? Mason was just a *kid*. He had his whole life in front of him and I—"

Rip crouched beside her, cocooning her in wiry arms that no longer smelled like the back end of a water buffalo thanks to the shower Ireland had allowed him to take. "It wasn't you," he soothed. "Not really."

"It was me!" Ireland argued, her hands clenching around his shirt sleeve in white knuckled fists. "I remember ... enough to know that. How

147

could this happen?" Her voice cracked and faded to a barely audible whisper. "I had no control. I never would have ... any of it ... *ever*."

"Actually, I gave that quite a lot of thought after you returned, while I waited for you to wake. I think it has to do with your talisman mark. Whoever gave that to you knew *exactly* what the consequences would be. Its lone purpose *wasn't* to cancel out the other talisman. On the contrary, that inked symbol acted as a formal invitation allowing the Horseman's spirit to enter you. It's quite fascinating really. Almost a shame Irv isn't here, this would've been a prize discovery to him."

Finding his cavalier approach too much to bear, Ireland shoved his arms away and scrambled to her feet. "I have to go. I have to turn myself in. People lost their loved ones and need to know what happened to them."

Snagging her purse and keys off the counter, she stomped toward the door, seemingly oblivious to the fact that she lacked crucial things like shoes and pants. Rip darted in front of her, slamming his back against the front door before she could turn the knob. "I really have to object to that. Perhaps we could wait a beat? Let cooler heads prevail?"

Ireland pivoted on her heel and strode straight for the slider. "I appreciate you trying to protect me, but I'm a monster. I fully deserve whatever they do to me."

"Noble as that would be, I'm not trying to protect *you*," Rip shouted after her, a mix of desperation and panic raising the octave of his voice. "The Horseman takes hold during your times of rest. Think of what will happen to those locked in a cell with you when that transformation takes hold. *Do you want more blood on your hands?*"

Ireland stopped. Her shoulders slumped in defeat. "Then what do I do?" Her desperate plea cracked as a hiccupped sob forced its way through. "Kill myself? I'll do that before I let myself hurt anyone else."

"The Hessian is already dead and he lives in you. Take your own life and you will rise again, without a shred of humanity to hold you back." Rip inched his way closer, a cautious hand raised as if he were nearing a wild mustang. "Unless you can think of some way to rid yourself of that rather permanent brand, we will just have to find a way to overpower and control it."

Her selective hearing pinpointed only one part of Rip's suggestion, *rid yourself of that*. That was the answer. It had to be. If the mark was gone, she would be free. Her purse thumped to the floor at her feet. Ireland stumbled forward, through her emotional fog, purposely detaching herself from her body and what she planned to do to it.

It's a vessel, nothing more, she reassured herself as she opened the cabinet in the hall, allowing the drop down ironing board to fall into place. *Any pain you feel is fleeting compared to what you've done.*

Ireland plugged in the appliance that ticked with life as it warmed. Ninety seconds, that's how long it took to reach full heat. The convenience of that was why she bought it in the first place. For some reason that seemed ironic now.

"Ireland, I worry you're not quite thinking clearly here," Rip stated from behind her in the overly cautious tone usually reserved for talking jumpers off of ledges.

Forty-six, forty-seven, forty-eight …

She stared straight ahead, her silence and the clicks of the iron's heating element acting as his only answer.

"We can figure this out together. We know the Horseman can be controlled. That gives us an instant advantage."

Sixty-one, sixty-two, sixty-three ...

"Whatever your plan here is, I assure you that you do *not* have to do it." Rip crept closer, moving to unplug the iron.

Ireland pivoted her upper body and threw her arm out, denying him passage in the narrow space.

Seventy-eight, seventy-nine, eighty ...

A slow hiss of steam eeked from the silver plate.

"Oh, no." Rip's face blanched. "Ireland, what are you *doing*?"

Eighty-seven, eighty-eight, eighty-nine ...

Her trembling hand closed around the grip. "What has to be done."

Her arm turned skyward as she laid the iron on it flat. Pain seared like a thousand needles. A wash of tears flooded her eyes. Even so, Ireland denied herself the right to yell out, viewing that as a privilege she'd given up the moment she took the life of a child.

Biting the inside of her cheek hard enough to taste blood, she held the iron steady. The smell of burning flesh filling the cramped hall. Behind her, Rip wavered and crashed to the floor, his head barely clearing the edge of the kitchen counter.

Only then did she pull the iron away, peeling off chunks of her skin with it. A choked gasp caught in her throat and prevented even a whisper of a breath from passing. A perfect iron shaped mark marred her flesh. Red, cracked, and oozing blisters had already formed. Except for on the tattoo. That remained perfectly intact, not a blemish to be seen.

18

Ireland

"These are nasty wounds," the dark-haired intern, who Ireland guessed to be maybe a year or two older than her, stated weaving in another tight stitch. "How did you say you got them?"

Well, random health care professional, Ireland mentally mused from the midst of her pain-killer induced fog. *It seems that tattoo you're staring at has somehow turned me into a serial killer. I thought self-mutilation may be a cure for that. Judging by the blood-soaked towel I came in with, and the fact that I've blacked out twice since I've been here, it's safe to say that is not the case.*

"I wanted to mow my lawn one last time for the season. Hit a big rock that jammed between the mower blades." Despite the fact that her tongue felt like it had swollen to three times the normal size, her lies flowed with a remarkable ease. Ireland thanked whatever this nice woman had injected into her arm for that. "I called my boyfriend and asked him to help, but you know how guys are."

"Boy, do I." The doctor flipped her hair over her shoulder and scoffed in disgust. "Let me guess, he said he'd be there and never showed."

"You guessed it." Even she could detect the slight slur of her words and did her best to enunciate. "I got ticked and tried to do it myself. Not a smart move. Burned myself on the exhaust and sliced the hell out of myself on the blade. Next time I'll know to turn it off first. Worst part, other than feeling like a complete moron, is that I still didn't get it fixed."

"Don't beat yourself up too bad." With a gentle hand, the doctor slathered ointment over the burns and fresh stitches, before positioning gauze over them and taping them into place. "I think the lawn mower did that enough for you. You got lucky, actually. That top slash was nearly to the bone. It's a miracle it didn't severe your hand completely. I've seen it happen. Plus, a big silver lining here is that gorgeous tattoo still looks perfect. Did you have that done somewhere here in Tarrytown? The color and shading is amazing."

"No, in Manhattan," Ireland mumbled, staring down at the corner of the loathsome mark peeking out from beneath the taped on gauze.

After the *second* attempt at burning it off failed, Ireland had gone for the knife. Dragging it across her skin and splitting her arm with a crimson gash. She could—and *did*—cut around it. However, something about that enigmatic mark wouldn't let her break the surface of it, or saw beneath. Attempts to were thwarted with a resistance that seemed iron clad.

153

The pretty doctor sat up to stretch her back. "I think that should do it. Let me go get your discharge instructions for the care of the wounds, then you'll be free to go."

A forced smile and half-hearted nod were the closest to a reply Ireland could manage.

The doctor slid back the curtain. Draping her stethoscope around her neck, she paused to flip her gaze back to her patient. "Oh, and you might want to consider withholding sex from that boyfriend for a while. At least until he learns to be a better listener!"

Ireland kept her fake smile in place, knowing full well it didn't reach her eyes. She let the sorry attempt die as soon as the good doctor sauntered off to the nurses' station to prepare the paperwork.

Relieved to be alone, Ireland flopped back against the pillows; her good arm draped over her eyes as her head swam from the combination of blood loss and a potent medicinal cocktail. Only then did she realize how truly lucky she was that she made it to the hospital without blacking out behind the wheel. Then again, how good can one's decision making skills be after finding out they go all *Darkly Dreaming Dexter* in their sleep?

"I'm not crazy! I know what I saw!" a male voice shouted loud enough to resonate through the entire ER.

"Sir, we need you to calm down. You are disturbing the other patients. If we have to sedate you, we will."

"Don't you threaten me! Do you know who I am?" the enraged patient spat. "I could buy and sell this entire town three times over! You *will* treat me with respect!"

Ireland would know that self-absorbed, whiny tone anywhere.

Brantley, her inner-self groaned, a split-second before bolting her upright with a fresh rush of panic. Had he still been outside her house after she charged off as the Horseman? There would be no explaining that away if he'd been witness to it all. *Had he told the cops*? Funny how just a few hours ago she had been so determined to turn herself in, and now that same lingering possibility had her instantly petrified. Not "funny ha-ha" but more, "huh, I don't *actually* want to fry in the electric chair."

Easing herself off the bed, Ireland tiptoed from the room. The smell of antiseptic burned her nostrils as she set off to find her raving ex. No fedora or whip was needed for this particular quest. She simply followed his increasingly agitated shouts to the bed at the end of the hall, which was surrounded by nurses, a couple doctors, and hospital security.

"Ireland!" Brantley snapped as she peeked around the curtain. "Nice choice of town! Some idiot dressed as the Headless Horseman attacked me last night!"

"I'm sorry, miss. You can't be in here." A grey-haired security guard held up one hand to halt her, the thick paunch around his middle straining against the buttons of his starched uniform shirt.

"Back off, rent-a-cop. She's my fiancée." Brantley's face, bright with a hot flush of red, was partially covered by the bandage wrapped around his forehead. Other than that, he seemed to be perfectly fine. Still a raging ass—but that was to be expected.

"*Ex*, oh, so very ex," she clarified to the small crowd.

A couple of the nurses hid their giggles behind their hands.

"Can I have a minute with him?" Ireland asked. "I think I can calm him down a bit."

"You always *did* have effective methods for tension release." Brantley leered, leaning back against his pillows with his arms folded behind his head.

Ireland clapped her hands in front of her, her eyebrows shooting into her hairline. "And *there* is a prime example of how he got that ex title!"

"At this point, I'm willing to try anything," the perturbed looking doctor admitted as he shooed away the rest of the crowd. "However, if you can't calm him down, I *will* have him sedated until his test results come back. Then, hopefully, we can boot him out of here." Shooting one last glare at Brantley, he followed the departing crowd out.

"Let me guess," Brantley smirked. "You heard I was here and had to come running. Deny it all you want, Ireland. You still have feelings for me."

Picking a fight wouldn't get her the answers she needed, even though it would feel *really* good. So—as much as she despised the idea—she had to choke down her loathing and play nice.

With a lift of her chin, she gestured toward his bandaged head. "Want to tell me exactly what happened?"

Brantley pulled his hands out from behind his head, gesturing wildly as he ranted. "What happened was I got attacked by a cloaked lunatic! This *person*," he spat the word as if it tasted rancid on his tongue, "on horseback charged right at me and hit me with the butt end of his sword! He knocked me out and left me on the side of the road. *Who does that? What is the matter with people?*"

"But, I mean, it wasn't *actually* the Headless Horseman, because the person had a head … right?" Her own dread at his answer spawned her voice to rise to a squeak.

"Of course it wasn't the *real* Headless Horseman." He cocked his head to gift her with his best sneer of annoyance. "You're a college educated woman, Ireland. Try using your head."

Ireland ruffled a hand through her short hair, chuckling a dry, humorless laugh to the floor. "Yeah, what was I thinking …"

"What it was, was a nutcase with a sword in one hand and a friggin' axe in the other! Probably the same freak that has killed two people in this town already. Speaking of which, thanks for cluing me in on *what* was going on!"

Her narrow shoulders rose and fell in an exasperated shrug. "In our lengthy, yet surprisingly *non-existent* phone calls?"

"I'm just saying." Brantley smoothed the front of his hospital gown in the same fashion he would one of his designer suits. "I may have thought twice before driving up here. I mean you're hot, Ire, but you're not *that* hot, if you know what I mean."

Ireland did her best to turn her gritted teeth into a painfully forced smile. "That's funny. I had that same thought when you proposed."

Brantley scoffed and rolled his eyes. How different life must be for someone who genuinely believed themselves to be God's gift.

More than anything, Ireland wanted to rip him to shreds. Not in a bloody Horseman fashion, but in the far more gratifying way of using just the power of her words. Unfortunately, she still had questions that he, as the only living survivor of an alleged Horseman attack, could answer. The best she could hope for was getting the information before she bit her tongue clean off. "You said your attacker was on horseback. Any idea where they got the horse?"

Or how a novice rider was able to stay on a charging steed?

Brantley threw his hands in the air, like her ignorance physically pained him. "How could I possibly know that? I didn't exactly have time to strike up a conversation before the guy *knocked me out!*" He simmered down for a brief moment, his narrow-eyed stare locking on the pastel curtain in front of him as if the glimmer of a memory played there just for him. "Although, now that I think about it, I think he *did* get off his horse for a minute. Right before I blacked out, I-I think he leaned over me and pressed one finger to my lips." With a shudder, he physically shook himself from the trance. "I probably imagined that. I was pretty looped out, hence the head wound."

Blood rushed to Ireland's face with enough force that she feared her ears were steaming. In her dream last night, she had pressed her finger to Noah's lips.

Oh, God! Was I having a sex dream while nearly killing my ex? There was wrong, an elevator that went six stories further up, and then this.

Ireland clamped her lips together in a thin white line and fought for even a semblance of composure. "This person, they had a cloak on,

right? Could you see their face at all? Enough to tell that they actually ...
you know …. had a head?" She tried to remember a time in her life she
sounded more like a raging lunatic. One didn't spring to mind.

"*What the hell, Ireland*? I was nearly killed last night! You seem
more concerned with some random dude on horseback than my
wellbeing." He jabbed an accusing finger in her direction. "That, right
there, is why we never would've worked out! You're insensitivity to my
needs."

That was it. The switch that turned off her nice. "No, you diddling
other women was more the deciding factor there. Ya know, it's really a
shame that the horseman didn't aim for your *other* head. But, hey,
there's always next time!"

"*We are so over!*" Brantley raged, his face morphing from red to
purple. "Get out of my room!"

"*Glad to see you finally agree with general consensus!*" As she
stormed from his life for a second time, Ireland deeply hoped *this* one
would stick.

19

Ichabod

"Tonight was meant to be the Harvest Ball," Katrina said as she slid between the folds of her crimson and taupe gown. "Now the town is meeting, trying to concoct a plan to stop a being that death itself couldn't tame."

Ichabod sat on the edge of the bed with his back, respectfully, to Katrina while she changed. His loaded musket lay across his lap. In the reflection of the window in front of him he could see the soft curve of her hips as they tapered into her narrow waist. He cleared his throat and shifted his gaze to the floor. His chin tipped to the side, ever so slightly, to ask, "Are you secure in our plan?"

"I am to attend the summit on the arm of Brom Van Brunt," she reaffirmed as she pulled her long, blonde locks out from the back of her gown and began tightening the laces of her bodice. "Then speak with as many people as I can, searching for anyone that may have motives leading to the Horseman."

Ichabod nodded. Mostly to himself, he muttered the remaining details they were depending upon, "Rip will be inside as well. That man can finesse a crowd with a skill that truly baffles. If there are secrets to be found, he will uncover them. Irv will be outside with me, primarily because the Horseman isn't the only one in this town that would like to see *his* head on a spike. We will be on horseback, patrolling the grounds with a few other men that have volunteered. You will have nothing to fear."

Her elegant gown in place, Katrina turned to Ichabod wearing an expression equal parts timidity and fear. "What of Brom?"

The bed squeaked as Ichabod shifted his weight to face her. "Boorish as his ways may be, he cares for you. If you adopt the guise that you have interest in him, he will do all he can to protect you inside the gathering, while I provide you the same service outside."

"And," her long lashes brushed the tops of her cheeks as she cast her gaze to the floor, "you aren't bothered by me being on his arm?"

In the midst of the plotting and planning, Ichabod had slipped into the role he knew well of military strategist. He had detached himself from the emotional aspects—until that very moment. The reality of his request sank in like a heavy stone. He had asked her to take another man's arm, asserting her place beside *him*. The implications of that dug into his gut like a dull blade, churning and twisting deep.

"The mere idea of that makes me ache," he stated, forcing the words through his suddenly parched throat. "Yet I would endure this hardship, and countless others, to keep you safe."

She moistened her lips with a flick of her tongue, seemingly wrestling with words that gave her pause. "Ichabod, when this is over … w-would you call yourself mine?"

Ichabod closed his eyes. The euphoria of that question washed over him, cleansing him of all his sins with the promise of tomorrow. Rising to his feet, he took her velvet soft hand in his. A love he hadn't known possible illuminated her striking face. "From the moment I saw you, my heart belonged to you alone. If by some miracle you were to give me your love in return, I would need nothing else to sustain me the rest of my days."

Katrina's palm tenderly brushed his cheek. "You have already claimed that."

Allowing no further hesitation, Ichabod gathered her in his arms. Katrina tipped her head back, the soft curves of her body molding to his. Full lips parted in an alluring invitation it would take a stronger man than him to resist.

With his lips still tingling from the memory of her kiss, Ichabod watched Katrina leave the inn with Brom. She had met him on the front stoop, forcing a desolate smile while Brom did his duty by offering his condolences. After which, the sizeable man pulled her to him in an embrace meant to comfort. Ichabod bristled, his shaky breath only easing when Katrina quickly extracted herself from Brom's smothering hold.

She wouldn't succumb to Brom's charms. After everything they'd been through, he felt confident in that. While the constable and his men cleared away the grisly scenes Katrina and he had happened upon, they couldn't erase the scars left on her tender heart. It had been Ichabod that calmed her after they discovered young Daniel's jarring corpse. It had been *his* arms that held her as she quaked with agonizing sobs after learning of her father's death. Brom claimed he wanted to marry Katrina, yet this was the first time he had reached out to her since her loss. Ichabod had to guess that his true motivation for escorting her that evening was just another part of his plan to assert them as a couple within the community. Brom's private agenda trumped matters of the heart once more. The ramifications of this ruse were settling in Ichabod's gut like having ingested rotted meat, causing acidic bile to churn and rise with a painful sting at the back of his throat.

"Have you noticed all the bearded men here in the Hollow?" Rip mused as he sauntered into the gathering room. "That look is really quite distinguished. I'm thinking of growing one."

Ichabod couldn't be bothered to respond as he watched Katrina hook arms with Brom and begin their stroll across town.

"What are we looking at?" Rip joined Ichabod at the window, then clamped a reassuring hand on his shoulder. "Ah, I see. Rest assured, I shall keep a close eye on her for you. I'll even intervene if I see the oaf's sweaty mits lingering."

Ichabod cast a cursory glance at his overly-candid friend and shook his head. "Not a penny to your name, yet somehow you have managed to acquire a dapper new wardrobe. Should I bother to ask how?"

Rip straightened his posture, adjusting the ruffled cuffs that poked from the ends of his burnished brown coat. "Feel free to ask, my prowess is a matter of pride for me."

"I fear that same 'prowess' may get us chased from town."

Rip's noncommittal shrug was all but canceled out by his 'cat that ate the canary' grin.

With a shake of his head and a huff of much needed laughter, Ichabod retrieved his musket from where it leaned against the wall. "Head to the church and stay alert. I'm off to find Irv and begin our patrol. Tonight, we end this Horseman's reign of terror."

20

Ireland

"Thank the heavens you've returned!" Rip seized Ireland in an awkward bear hug, made all the more unpleasant by his filthy clothes, which smelled like the underside of a rhino. She *had* to find him something else to wear. "There was blood all over the kitchen and you were gone! I was sure you were dead!"

"And that my reanimated corpse rose to wreak havoc through the town?" Ireland pried herself from his bony clutches. "This isn't a show on AMC."

Rip tipped his head, his expression blank. "I don't understand that reference."

"Let me summarize it by saying, I'm fine." Ireland ducked around him, strolling into the kitchen to drop her purse and keys on the counter. "And, after repeated, incredibly painful experiments, I can say with absolute certainty that the tattoo won't let me get rid of it. For reasons I can't fathom or explain that thing has self-preservation down pat."

"Tell me more about the person that applied that ink." Rip's fuzzy brows drew in tight as he stroked the length of his beard. "They had to have enchanted the mark somehow."

"He was a regular dude." Ireland shrugged, rubbing the tape around her bandages that had begun to itch. "Bald head, lots of ink, used cuss words as a form of punctuation. I really doubt he was behind this. If there's a type for that kind of thing, he isn't it. Whoever it was, the bigger question is why would they want to? What possible reason could they have for letting this ... *thing* ... loose?"

"To turn the Horseman—you, as it were—into a rogue killer that can't be controlled or stopped." Rip twisted the very end of his beard around his index finger. "Not that I have the foggiest idea why that would be anyone's goal."

"Because they're a dick?" Ireland offered.

"A what now?"

"Dick?" Not only was her comment significantly less funny when she had to explain it, but doing so crossed the line into downright uncomfortable. "A ... uh ...penile phallic symbol."

"Oh." The rises of Rip's cheeks, not covered by wiry beard, bloomed with color. "*Oh, my.*"

"It's a figure of speech ... that I won't be using again thanks to this moment of abject mortification." Ireland shoved her hair behind her ear just to have something to do with her hands. "Can we move past this and never speak of it again?"

"Yes, let's." Rip feverishly nodded.

Ireland took a deep breath and exhaled slowly, her gaze drifting out the back slider. She'd been at the hospital longer than she thought. Late afternoon shadows stretched across the yard. "We need to come up with a plan before that sun sets and I go for another ride. It's doubtful the next person will get off as easy as Brantley did."

Rip's upper body pivoted in her direction, his hands folded in a posture that hinted at his Old English roots. "What did you have in mind?"

Ireland flopped down on a bar stool and let her head thump against the countertop. "Not killing anyone tonight was pretty much the end of my plan."

Rip rocked from his toes to his heels and back again, his fingers steepled beneath his chin. "I have an idea, however it *will* require further research. Is there a library in town?"

Ireland didn't bother to raise her head. Laminate countertop muffled her voice. "Unless you're planning to stock pile them and whip 'em at me when I go all crazy dark side, I don't think books are the answer."

Lost in his own thoughts, Rip paced the length of the kitchen. "There was a woman from my time, if I could pinpoint her whereabouts or that of her living relatives—"

Ireland raised her head enough to rest her chin on her hands. "I don't know if you're aware of this, but your situation is actually somewhat rare. About ninety-nine, point nine-five percent of the people from your time have been reduced to *dust*."

"No, she wouldn't be living. Even so, the information is still there, within the tissue, it would just be a matter of extracting—"

"Stop!" Ireland bolted upright, her palms extended to halt him. "We don't have time for experiments of the boogidy-boogidy kind! I have a clock tick-tick-ticking away over my head, counting down the few short hours until this *thing* inside me takes over. What we need to do now-ish, if not sooner, is to figure out how to contain it—or more to the point, *me*."

"What I have in mind *will* work, I just need you to show the smallest iota of patience."

"Patience?" Ireland erupted with a sharp, abrasive laugh that bordered on manic. "I'm sorry, how many innocent people have *you* killed lately?"

"N-none, of course," Rip stammered.

"That's right, *none!*" Her anger quickly dissolved into a truer emotion that far eclipsed it, guilt ridden sorrow. It took two hard swallows for her to choke down the lump of emotion that lodged in her throat. "That blood is on *my* hands, so you don't really get to weigh-in on my emotional breakdowns, okay? You want to go hunt for some long-dead chick? That's fine. Just … help me figure out how to lock myself up before you go? *Please*?"

Rip's face crumbled in a blend of grief and compassion. He paused his pacing at the counter beside her, draping a comforting hand over hers. "Come with me to research this. I *promise* we will be back long before nightfall. Plenty of time to lock you up, only by then we will have the information that will make the need for such things unnecessary. You'll see."

An idea sparked, brightening Ireland's molasses eyes. "What about the talisman? The original one! Maybe if I wore it—"

Rip interrupted with an adamant shake of his head. "No. We don't know the effect wearing both talismans will have. It's far too risky."

"How is it risky?" Ireland's hands clenched into tight fists of frustration. "They're both meant to control the Horseman. So, what? I'd have too much control? I'm totally okay with that! I'll get a label maker and embrace the newfound OCD."

"For all we know the two talismans could cancel each other out. I'm afraid I can't allow this." Rip's hand hovered over the hem of his left coat pocket, protecting the treasure she longed for. "The Horseman—or *you* rather—had been storing your weapons downstairs in a hidden compartment at the bottom of the trunk. I took it upon myself to hide them, quite well I might add. Even if the darkness does claim you, you will not have the weaponry needed to harm anyone. So, you see, precautions have been taken. We are free to go."

"You know what? After everything—*ahem*, excuse me—that you've done for me, you have most definitely—" Her words cut off as a barking cough tore from Ireland's throat. "Excuse me, I think there's something lodged in my throat. Anyway, you have definitely earned my trust. If that is—*ahem*—what you think is best, then that is what we'll do."

Her declaration was punctuated by another coughing fit that violently shook through her lean frame.

"Are you okay?" Rip frowned. "Do you need a drink of water?"

169

Ireland had to clear her throat twice before she could gasp out a breathless answer. "Yes, please. Not sure what's happening."

"Your body is probably weakened from the lack of sleep due to your nightly outings." Rip opened a couple of cupboards before locating the glasses. He positioned one under the tap to fill it for her.

"Yeah, I'm sure that's it." Ireland rolled her jaw, which drooped slightly to the right. "It's so weird. Feels like I've had dental work done."

"That does *not* sound like a lack of sleep." Rip handed her the cup, his gaze searching her face.

"Thank you," Ireland murmured, raising the glass to her mouth. Water trickled from her sagging lips and splashed to the ground, soaking the front of her shirt in the process. Her eyes widened in panicked Os. "Wha dah heck? Rip! I can'h feel mah face! Wha's happenin'?"

"I … I don't know!" His entire body tensed, his limbs rigid as he struggled with the decision to help her or run screaming from the house.

The cup slipped from Ireland's fingers and crashed to the floor, water exploding everywhere. "Oh, Gawd! I fink ih's happenin'! I'm urning inwho dah howseman!" With frantic hands, Ireland slapped at her face and head. "I can'h feel mah head! Run, Rip! *Run!*"

Rip's frantic stare darted from Ireland to the door. He managed one step toward his escape before his eyes rolled back and he folded to the ground in a snoring heap.

Ireland wiped her chin with the back of her arm before leaning over her dozing friend to dig the talisman from his pocket. "I should probably feel bad for exploiting what is an *incredibly* unfortunate malady for you." She weighed the silver talisman on her fingertips, its thick chain dangling from her palm. "But that was just too darned easy."

Ireland patted his shoulder before rising to her feet with her prize in tow.

Not knowing how long Rip would be out, she took the talisman into her bedroom and locked the door behind her. As soon as the lock clicked into place, she wasted no time. Ducking her head, she looped the chain around her neck.

It started with a spark of heat. A warmth radiating from where the talisman rested against her skin. Quickly, it spread, casting tendrils of sizzling euphoria coursing through her veins. She raised one hand in front of her face and wiggled her fingers. An impromptu giggle bubbled up from her throat. She looked the same, yet beneath the surface everything felt different.

Stumbling over her feet, and finding that uproariously funny, Ireland moved through a cloud of happy to her closet. She hooked her hands in the hem of her T-shirt and yanked the damp garment over her head, dropping it unceremoniously to the floor. Humming a song she didn't even recognize, Ireland pushed her boring, regular ole clothes across the hanging bar in her search for one *particular* item. She found it way in the back, with the clothes she kept but never actually wore—until now. She hadn't slid on the fake leather vest since Halloween a few years back when she went as a biker chick. Nonetheless, shrugging it up her arms and coaxing the zipper up just enough to flaunt a generous amount of cleavage, she found it fit her mood perfectly.

Pausing in front of the mirror that hung over her dresser, Ireland applied a liberal coat of ruby red lipstick. Then, tousled her hair into a punky disarray and sprayed it in place. Shooting a playful wink to her reflection, she threw open the door and sashayed out—shoulders back, head held high. Snagging her purse from the counter, she stepped over Rip to strut right out the door.

Still humming that same strange little tune, Ireland bypassed her car and crossed straight into Noah's yard. She rapped softly on the door, growing more … *anxious* with each passing second. Her hand slid up the doorframe, until reaching the level where she could curl it behind her head and lean against her elbow.

The door cracked open. Noah peered out clad only in a pair of well-worn jeans and an unbuttoned shirt. Ireland's appreciative gaze lazily devoured his sculpted abs.

"Ireland?" Noah asked, visibly jolted by her appearance. "Is everything okay? What happened to your arm?"

"Everything is better than okay," she purred, taking a brazen step forward to loop her finger in the waistband of his jeans. "Remember those vices you mentioned?"

"Yeah?" He flinched back at the forward nature of her touch.

"I have a few I'd like to explore." With the toe of her boot, Ireland kicked the door shut behind her.

21

Ireland groaned and mashed her face deeper into the pillow as bright morning light beamed in through the blinds, stabbing her brain with a thousand tiny knives.

"Ya know, vices really aren't for everyone. Some people are better off sticking with a more *vanilla* existence."

Ireland spun at the sound of Noah's voice, the rapid motion making it mandatory for her to slap the butts of her hands against her temples until the room stopped spinning. Only when the tilt-o-whirl effect eased did she risk opening her clamped lids again ... and found herself staring straight down at her *extremely* bare chest.

"This is your house, your bed, and I am all kinds of naked," she stated, clinging to modesty long since lost by yanking the comforter up to shield herself.

"That would be at your insistence." Noah shrugged his suit jacket up his arms. After situating it into place, he thumbed the front buttons closed. "I tried my damnedest to keep you clothed. Even took you back out to the beer tent, hoping a public venue would curb that impulse. Right around the time they kicked us out, I figured that wasn't the case. So, I brought you back here. You stripped down, while I slept on the couch— safe from your persistently wandering hands. Which brings us to the fun question; what exactly were you on? Uppers? Downers? Viagra?"

"I ... don't remember." Ireland wiped the sleep from her eyes and tried to force her hazy brain to piece together the puzzle that was last night. "I was at the hospital yesterday. Maybe I had a reaction to the pain meds?"

"If that's the case, don't take them again," Noah suggested, one corner of his mouth tugging back in an impish half-grin. "They turn you into Courtney Love."

"Noted." Ireland huffed a wry laugh that aggravated her parched throat. "*Ahem*—I'm sorry if I embarrassed you, or me, or both of us."

The bed springs squeaked as Noah flopped down beside her, his arm playfully nudging hers. "My old Sunday school teacher thinks her time with me was a total waste, but other than that we're good."

"Again, so sorry." Ireland could barely force herself to meet the eyes of the beautiful man that would now, most likely, cross the street to avoid her.

"Ah, no worries." He shrugged, the warmth of his smile making her painfully aware she was sans pants. "We all do stupid crap we shouldn't sometimes."

"Oh yeah? What have you done lately that can even remotely compare with my barfly moment?"

Noah leaned back, pretending to peek around the comforter she clung to tightly. "I may have stolen a quick glimpse while I was tucking you in."

Ireland shoved him away, an abrupt laugh sneaking past her lips. "So, what's with the monkey suit? Did my antics from last night prompt you to join the CIA? Did I offend a government official?"

"I wish it was something cool like that." His tone went suddenly somber as he bent down to slide a pair of black loafers out from under the bed. "Today is Mason's funeral."

Tucking the blanket around herself, Ireland busied herself looking for her clothes in a pathetic attempt to distract from the knot of guilt that twisted in her gut. "His poor family. I can't even imagine what they're going through."

Because of me.

Noah rested the heel of his foot on the bed to tie his shoe, then switched to do the other. "It would be easier if they leaned on each other during this, but key members of the family have decided they will all be taking the 'lone wolf' approach to coping."

"What does that mean?" Ireland plucked her panties from the top of the lamp on the dresser and her pants off the floor. "And, side note, any idea where my bra ended up?"

"That would be on the antennae of my truck. Again, at your insistence."

"Of course it was," Ireland groaned, with an exasperated eye roll.

"As for the Fabulous Brunt Boys, my sister Cassie has been tight BFFs with Mason's stepmom, Analysia, since high school." Rising off the bed, Noah shook the legs of his trousers straight. "Cas called last night in one of her high-pitched tizzies that make my ears bleed. She can't make it into town for the funeral, but insisted—amidst very colorful language—that I *have* to be there for Ana. Apparently, the less than charming Mr. Brunt has banned her from riding in the car with the family to the cemetery and won't even let her be seated with them during the service. It's ridiculous. Just because she didn't carry the kid for nine months doesn't mean she won't mourn him."

"I met her once at the school." Ireland adjusted the comforter that had begun to slip. "She wanted a relationship with Mason. That may as well have been written on her face in Sharpie. Who knows, maybe with time he would've opened up to her enough for them to have some kind of relationship. Now that will never happen."

Because of me.

Guilt stabbed into her, causing more pain than any of the injuries she'd suffered trying to remove her tattoo. She swallowed hard to force down the rising lump of sorrow. Even then her voice came out a dry rattle. "Your sister's right. She needs a shoulder today."

"And a shoulder I shall be." Noah closed the distance between them in three strides. His palm brushed her cheek as he curled his fingertips around the back of her neck, tilting her face to his. "If you're available, I'd love to see you again tonight. But maybe a little *less* of you this time? I'm not sure how long I can keep up this whole 'gentleman' thing."

Ireland leaned into his touch, blinking away the anguish she felt certain had clouded her gaze. "I'd like that ... both parts of it."

176

"I look forward to it." Noah leaned in to brush a quick kiss to her forehead, allowing Ireland a moment to breathe in the fresh, smooth scent of his aftershave. A naughty twinkle warmed his hazel eyes to a brilliant aquamarine as he turned on his heel and strode for the door. Pausing at the threshold, he glanced back with one hand rested casually against the door jam. "Oh, I almost forgot, I took your necklace off and laid it on the nightstand. That chain is pretty long and I didn't want it strangling you in your sleep."

"My necklace?" Ireland frowned, her gaze flicking toward the table. Just like that it all came rushing back; faking out Rip, stealing the talisman and sliding it on in hopes of protecting the residents of Tarrytown ... from *her*. "Oh. *Oh no*! Noah, di—did I hurt anyone last night? Did I leave your sight for even a minute?"

Noah cocked his head, obviously surprised by her direct line of questioning. "No, we were together all night. There was a moment that you almost punched a girl that cut in front of you in line for the bathroom, but I was able to intervene before the earrings came off."

"Thank you." She clamped both hands over her heart, muttering the declaration to Noah and the universe in general.

Rip sat on the couch, his legs—clad in an old pair of her sweatpants—crossed at the ankles as he stared at her expectantly.

"You showered and helped yourself to my clothes."

"I did." Rip's mouth pinched tight, not even attempting to hide the fact that he was in a full snit. "It was mandatory after a pitcher of ale was spilled on me last night."

"Well, whatever the reason, I'm glad you made yourself at home." Ireland let her purse flop to the floor, which caused the bra she'd snagged off Noah's antennae to bounce out of it. Snatching the offending garment up, she quickly stuffed it in her back pocket. "Okay, look, I'm *truly* sorry for causing you to take the impromptu siesta."

"*Humph.*" Rip folded his arms over the *Blues Traveler* T-shirt he'd borrowed.

"And I will admit that you were *partially* right." Ireland nervously ran her fingers through her hair, which reeked of stale nicotine and bad choices. "The talisman *did* have unforeseen side effects. Namely, that it completely erased any and all inhibitions I may have."

"I know." Rip's bushy eyebrows rose to his hairline, his frown dripping with disapproval. "I woke just as you and the neighbor were driving off, and I gave chase. Tracked you all the way to that tent of debauchery. Thanks to you, I now know what twerking is, and deeply long for my *own* time when a flash of ankle was considered lewd."

Ireland's stare darted from the beige wall, to the coat closet door, to the rug under her feet, *anywhere* but at the man who had witnessed her Miley moment that she didn't know she was capable of. "Again, so sorry. If I could brain bleach that image from you, I absolutely would."

"You and me both," he grumbled.

"On a good note, I didn't kill anyone last night. Yay!"

Rip stared her down, refusing to utter a sound until she met his glare. "Do you agree with me now that it was a bad idea?"

"I do," Ireland admitted.

"Good." Slapping his hands to his knees, he rose to his feet. "Now, it is early in the day, we have *plenty* of time until the Horseman becomes an issue again. Would you *please* come with me to the library, so that we may research a more permanent solution to your possession?"

A deep-seeded yearning for freedom forced the words from her throat before Ireland could even consider them, "There's nothing I'd like more."

22

Ireland

"It's just too much." Rip yawned. His eyelids drooped, yearning to give in to sleep's persistent draw. "The stress is forcing my curse. I ... can't go on."

"You can and you will!" Ireland's fingers dug into his shoulders as she pivoted his upper body toward her and shook him awake. "You're stronger than this, I just need you to focus. *Come on!* Stick with me, buddy!"

"I'll ... I'll try." Once more, Rip forced his heavy eyes to focus on the glow of the screen. The way he struggled to lift his hand to the table made it seem that the bothersome limb weighed a ton. "Okay, this thing is called the mouse—I got that part. To move up, I click here. To move down, I click there. Then, when I find one of interest I click right on it to open the ... *drat*! What did you call it?"

"The link."

"Ah, yes. The link."

"See? You're getting it! I know it's a lot to take in, but you really are." She kept her tone light to hide her building annoyance that they had been there for two hours and had made exactly no progress. For a while she had been in the driver's seat behind the computer. However, considering she had no idea what they were looking for, and Rip's old man eyes had to be inches from the screen to actually read it, she came up with the wise idea for them to switch places. Now she wanted to thank herself for that stellar decision by high-fiving her forehead with the desk. Whoever invented the Internet really should have made it more user friendly for time-traveling hobos.

"I miss old-fashioned newspapers that coated my fingers with ink and made a wonderful crinkling sound with each page turned," Rip sighed sadly.

"Me too, Rip." Ireland gave him a comforting pat on the back. "Me too."

"Is there a way I can find articles with particular names in them?"

"Yeah, scoot." Ireland nudged him with her elbow and leaned over the keyboard. "What's the name?"

"Eleanora Tremaine."

"That's quite a mouthful," Ireland mused, her fingers clicking over the keys. Just as she hit send, a dull ache bloomed behind her right eye. "There you go."

Leaning back so Rip could read, she blinked hard in hopes that whatever it was would pass.

"Yes! Yes! This is good!" Rip clapped his happiness. "That's it, right there! Click on that!"

It was hard to tell by the way he looked from the mouse to the screen and back again if he was talking to her or actually expected the mouse to respond to his verbal command. Either way, Ireland scooted back to the edge of her seat and leaned in front of him to grab the mouse. The screen swam in and out of focus before her throbbing eyes, making it impossible for her to read the words.

"Am I on the right link?" she asked, squinting at the screen.

"No, it's ... here, let me try." Rip shooed her hand from the mouse. "Hah! I did it!"

"Good for you." Slumping back in her chair, Ireland pinched the bridge of her nose—right between her eyes—with her thumb and index finger. The pain had spread to both eyes; the incessant pressure causing her teeth to ache. "Leave it to me to get a sinus infection in the face of mortal danger."

"Huh, her daughter was her only relative and somehow she proceeded Eleanora in death. Never would've guessed that." Rip chuckled, his engrossed gaze not wavering from the screen. "Had you met Eleanora you would've gotten the humor in that. Is there paper? I need to jot down notes."

Ireland's stomach rolled angrily as her headache morphed from mild nuisance to a full-blown migraine. "Next to the computer," she mumbled, pressing the butts of her palms to her eyes to block out the light. "They usually have a stash here."

"Ah-ha!"

Pencil lead scratched over paper.

"Are you okay? You've gone all pale and pasty." Rip's tone, first heavy with concern, shifted noticeably toward open suspicion. "This isn't a repeat of yesterday's performance, is it?"

"No, I just have a—" Ireland's words morphed into an anguished shriek brought on by a piercing pain that settled between her eyes and burrowed deep. Her hands gripped the armrests in a white-knuckled grasp. A spasm jolted through the muscles along her spine, arching her forward with enough force to launch her from her seat. Her knees banged against the faded linoleum floor as she crumbled into a ball, gasping for breath or even a momentary reprieve from her torment.

That's when the storm hit.

Glass shattered, pelting deadly shards through the library caused by every window in the place exploding in. Tornado-force winds whipped through the building, reducing the front and rear doors to kindling as they tore from their splintered frames. Glass whirled through the air, slicing and dicing any flesh it could find. A chorus of frantic screams rang out, yet were barely audible over the freight train roar of the storm. Ravenous gusts sucked up whatever they could, making each new item a weapon in their deadly cyclone. Paper flapped from tables. Books flew from shelves, smashing into any bodies that mistakenly got in their way. A projectile pencil soared, end over end, before impaling itself deep in the eye of a boy that barely looked old enough to drive.

Ireland bit back her pain and slapped her palms to the floor, intending to push herself up and run. Instead, in a blink, she found herself plunged into pitch-black stillness. Everyone and everything around her vanished. Headache all but forgotten, she hesitantly rose to her feet. In the distance, a lone light flickered. Equal parts instinct and apprehension forced her lead feet forward. As she neared, a dentist-style chair took shape before her. A flannel-clad figure gripped the armrests with clawed hands, his gaze locked on the ceiling.

"Noah?" The word formed on Ireland's lips, yet the sound was gobbled up by vast emptiness that surrounded them.

He didn't look her way, didn't so much as flinch. Only when she inched closer did she see why. Small silver hooks had been fished through his upper and lower lids, forcing them open. Blood puddled at the corners of his eyes, trickling down his face in crimson slashes. Ireland's hand hovered over him, wanting to help—to free him—but not having the foggiest idea where to start. Slowly, his mouth began to move. Sneaking syllables passed barely twitching lips.

Tipping her ear to his mouth, she leaned closer.

"*Save her, save me. Save her, save me,*" Noah chanted in a detached whisper.

Ireland snapped upright. The words "save who" formed on her lips, but flapped away into oblivion.

The chair—and Noah—were gone.

Her frantic spin to locate him ended in an abrupt halt. A horrified gasp slipped from her parted lips as her trembling hand fluttered up to her mouth.

Amber hung before her, strung between two posts. Her hands and feet were splayed out wide, bound by thick leather straps. The gaping hole in her gut allowed her entrails to spill out and swing in the

184

nonexistent breeze. If this was who Noah meant for her to save, it was too late. No one could survive torture like that.

Or, so she thought.

Sluggishly, Amber's head lolled in Ireland's direction, revealing eyes clouded a deathly white. Rotting grey lips cracked into a grotesque smile lined with black gums and rotting teeth. A rattle reverberated from her chest, shuddering through her decomposing form in an almost sing-song melody. *"Save her, save me. Save her, save me."*

Save who? Ireland merely thinking the words caused them to erupt around her like the caw of thousands of taunting black crows.

Amber's head fell back, her shoulders shaking in a maniacal laugh that cracked and dissolved into an anguished scream. Before Ireland could clap her hands over her ears, her rotting friend vanished. In her place, a long hall with black and white checkered walls appeared. Its mirrored floor seeming to stretch on forever. The need to find an exit from this maddening labyrinth urged Ireland on. Her footsteps padded against their own image in a strange beat that held a warning all its own:

Another-did-rise-another-did-rise-another-did-rise.

With her heart hammering against her ribs, Ireland's hand closed around the knob of the first door she came to. The click of it opening echoed around her like a gunshot. Inside, a woman sat alone at a banquet-sized table. Ireland recognized the blonde ponytail immediately and dreaded what atrocity had claimed her.

Again, she could only think her response, *Ana? Are you okay?*

The pretty blonde glanced over her shoulder, her blue eyes wide and eager. "Save her, save me." She smiled, then returned to her task.

Her elbow rose as she pulled back, and slammed something hard against the table. She gave a muted yelp. Whatever had happened caused her body to quake at the impact.

Ireland crept around the table, a knot of terror twisting tight in her stomach. Blood *drip-drip-dripped* from the table in swollen drops. Two severed fingers lay on the table—still twitching. Ana positioned the blade of her butcher knife to rid herself of a third.

Ana, no!

Just as the blade scissored down, the scene stretched out before her, elongated like an effect in a funhouse mirror. It snapped back in to the form of a towering guillotine. Air whooshed over her skin as the gleaming blade fell, ridding the body it held captive of its head. It hit the ground with a wet squish. Sheer force of the strike causing it to roll— straight toward Ireland. Her frenzied back-pedal succeeded only in tangling her in her own legs as the floor rose to meet her. There was no escape but to watch in utter revulsion as the severed head rolled to a stop beside her. Bile rose in her throat as Rip's head landed slightly askew, his stare already fixed and vacant. One last reflexive sigh seeped through his parted lips, *"Save her, save me."*

Finally, Ireland found her voice. It returned in a blood-curdling scream that ripped from her core.

She woke with a start at the sound of it, finding herself flat on her back on the floor. As she panted out each ragged breath, her gaze flicked around the room for clues of what the hell had happened. She was back in the library, which seemed completely undisturbed—except for all the patrons that were gaping down at her in shocked silence. Two faces appeared over her, a very alive Rip, and the librarian whose creased brow was extenuated by her cat-frame glasses. Each took one of her arms and eased her to sitting.

"Are you okay, miss?" The librarian gently patted Ireland's back.

All Ireland could manage was a twitch of a nod.

Turning to Rip, the librarian muttered, "My niece is epileptic. She has seizures like this all the time. Should I get her some water?"

"No," Ireland gasped. Clearing her throat, she tried again. "I'm fine."

Relying heavily on Rip, she rose on wobbly legs. His stare, wide with alarm, caught her gaze and held it tight, silently inquiring many of the same questions she was asking herself.

"We need to go," she croaked. "*Now.*"

No sooner had the outside door banged shut behind them then Rip pounced, *"What in Heaven's name was that?* If that was another put on episode like yesterday it was *far* more convincing!"

Ireland held up one shaky hand to halt his tirade, a hot rush of tears flooding her eyes. Only by clenching her jaw to the point of pain did she prevent them from spilling over her red-rimmed lids. "It's the middle of the day, and I was surrounded by people. Even so, that *thing* managed to take me over completely. I could've—"All the horrific what-ifs swelled in her throat, lodging there in a constricting lump. Swallowing hard, she gulped them down. "Whatever is inside of me is getting stronger. Soon, the limitations we thought were on our side won't matter, and *no one* will be safe."

187

23

Ichabod

Thick clouds smothered moonlight's gleam before it could even think to penetrate night's effective blockade. Voices rose from the Old Dutch Church as the residents of the Hollow engaged in a heated debate over how best to protect their treasured town. Ichabod shifted in his saddle, readjusting the musket laid across his lap. In the distance he watched Irv's horseback silhouette meld into the darkness. Both men were engaging in yet another lap on their patrol. Irv's path took him passed the school house and round the shops and dwellings at the south end of town. Ichabod's designated area consisted of the church grounds and adjoining cemetery, across the Sleepy Hollow Bridge and back again. Each step of the journey he was forced to nudge and coax the stubborn mule—loaned to him by Constable DeMarr's stable hand—forward. A raven squawked overhead, taking to flight from its perch atop a headstone. That simple motion seemed amplified on the otherwise still night. Ichabod lulled side to side in the saddle, the mule's hooves squishing into the earth with each trudged step. Those same steps transformed into sharp clicks the moment they found the first plank board of the enclosed bridge. They had clacked across half its the length when a chill skittered down Ichabod's spine. Pulling back gently on the reins, he pivoted in his saddle, sure he'd heard something slosh through the muck behind him. Nothing but darkness trailed them.

"Perhaps the ground settled." The explanation rang hollow to Ichabod's own ears, however he clung to it just the same.

With the heels of his boots, and an encouraging cluck, he cued the mule onward. Two strides was as far as they made it before the sound returned. Closer now, more definite. His rising tension showed itself in the spasms that pulsated through his arm. Ichabod didn't have to turn to know there was someone behind him. He could feel the heat of their stare boring into his back. That inkling failed to lessen the shock of Ichabod's head slowly turning to find a looming figure astride a formidable ebony stallion. Their combined presence filled the entire entrance to the bridge. A cloak was fastened around the rider's neck. The space above it—vacant. The stallion anxiously pawed at the ground. Its rider raised one gloved hand, blood dripping from the leather. Glowing, flickering shadows danced across the bridge walls, cast out by one of Eleanora's macabre jack-o'-lanterns that the rider held high.

Ichabod's rational thought fought to be heard over the drumming of his heart. Something about the figure seemed off. His torso—too long to be believable. This was a ruse, all orchestrated by clever costuming. It had to be. Unfortunately, that did nothing to ease Ichabod's mind. People were dying bloody, horrible deaths in Sleepy Hollow. A Horseman spawned in legend being blamed for the crimes. Any twisted mind with a

189

deadly agenda could concoct a disguise that would free themselves of the blame.

"Whoever you are, I have no quarrel with you." Ichabod's sweat dampened hands tightened around the hilt of his musket.

"*Iccchhhaboddddd,*" a wraithlike voice rasped.

The stallion edged closer, its wide nostrils flaring, casting puffs of steamy breath into the night.

"Halt! No further!" Ichabod snapped his gun into position, pushing the butt in tight to his shoulder to thwart its loathsome quakes.

Stallion nor rider gave a moment's hesitation. Hooves thumped against creaking planks in the steady, rhythmic beat of a war drum.

Ruse or not, Ichabod couldn't afford to hesitate. Staring down the sight, he took aim. His finger closed around the trigger, applying the steady pressure needed. A mere beat before he could fire, his shoulder revolted, bucking hard enough to knock the musket from his sweat dampened hands. The well-sighted shot went rogue, firing as it slammed to the ground. Blood sprayed as the bullet skimmed his mule's front leg. A wall of grey fur and mane swelled before him, the mule rearing in panicked protest. Ichabod gripped the saddle horn tight, his feet slipping from the flapping stir-ups. Had the mule steadied, Ichabod may have stayed on. Instead, it bounced on its good leg, then arched back to paw at the air once more. Ichabod skidded from his saddle, his hip exploding in pain as he slammed to the ground. The mule took off at a full canter. The smattering of blood that had streamed from its leg was the only thing it left behind with its banished rider.

Biting back his anguish, Ichabod rose to his feet, inching away from the approaching "Horseman."

"*Iccchhhabbbooodddddd.*" His assailant rotated his wrist, one way then the other, allowing the sharp-angled shadows from the pumpkin's carved features to waltz and swirl around them.

One wrong step and Ichabod's back slammed into the sidewall of the bridge; all hopes of escape lost in the grain of the wood that held him trapped. A snort from the stallion's muzzle assaulted his face. Ichabod recoiled, pulling himself flat enough to the wood to feel its coarse texture through his thick wool coat.

His lip curled into a snarl. "Do your worst, demon."

He expected to hear metal hiss from leather; to watch the candlelight flicker off a gleaming blade. Of all the ways he anticipated meeting his end, never once did he entertain it being by gourd. *Until* … the cloaked figure arched back, catapulting the pumpkin straight for Ichabod's head. Bracing for the painful impact, the schoolmaster clamped his eyes shut. It hit with the force of poorly thrown punch, heat having been kind enough to soften the hard outer shell. Seeds and goo exploded in his face, showering him in a layer of their sludge. Ichabod slapped at his head, extinguishing his smoldering hair lit by the candle.

"Sleepy Hollow has no use for likes of you, Ichabod Crane." The so-called Horseman's ghostly tone vanished, giving way to one human in origin … and familiar. "It's time for you to move on."

Ichabod's eyes narrowed as he scraped pumpkin innards from his shoulder and flung them to the ground. "Brom?"

"Quite the ruse, wasn't it, scho—" Brom's arrogant boast cut off the moment Ichabod's hands closed around his boot-clad ankle and yanked him from his horse. The bridge beneath them shook from Brom's heft as he slammed to the plank boards. His cape fell askew, revealing two pillows tied to the sides of his head acting as makeshift shoulders.

The spasms in Ichabod's arm vanished, chased away by a blind rage. "If you are here, *where is Katrina*?"

For a moment, Brom's eyes widened to goose eggs at the anger he saw brewing within the mild-mannered teacher. Then, his usual sneer boomeranged itself back into place. "I told you once before, she is no concern of yours. Katrina is *spoken for.*"

Where Brom had size on his side, Ichabod had speed and agility. Before Brom could attempt to hoist himself off the ground, Ichabod snatched his fallen musket and lunged. Lodging the barrel to Brom's thick neck, he put his weight behind it to force the arrogant aristocrat back down. Brom's mouth opened and closed, gasping for breath. His face blooming from red to purple.

"*You were to keep her safe!*" Spittle foamed at the corners of Ichabod's mouth as he ranted, "*There is a killer on the loose, you incompetent fool!*"

"Soon … to … be … two." Brom forced the words out, his veins and tendons bulging.

Ichabod relaxed his hold, allowing Brom to gulp an eager breath. "Where is Katrina?" He spoke the words slow and clear, their underlying threat strongly implied.

"I called upon the Van Tassel's maid, Elizabeth," despite his watering eyes, the color quickly returned to Brom's face, "and asked her to escort Katrina back to Van Brunt Manor. She is perfectly safe. Think what you will of me, yet know I would never allow any harm to come to her."

"Whoever is taking lives in Sleepy Hollow is somehow connected to Katrina. They left a body in *her* room, killed *her* father. Even so, this very night *you* sent her off without a second thought, so you could satisfy your own vendetta." Ichabod leaned over Brom, positioning himself nose to nose with the man that had tried, and failed, to run him from Sleepy Hollow. "If she is harmed in *any* way, I *will* come back for you. Trust that you will wish the *actual* Horseman had gotten to you first."

Ichabod released his hold, allowing Brom to roll to his side, a deep scowl creasing his broad face. If Ichabod noticed, he couldn't be bothered to care. With resolute determination in his stride, he collected Brom's stallion. Seizing the reins, he slid his foot into a stir-up and hoisted himself astride. One firm kick to the horse's sides and they were galloping into the moonless night. Their set objective? The Van Brunt residence ... and Katrina.

24

Ireland

"Most people would hear my dream of the terrifyingly gruesome and would try to cheer me up. Maybe even buy me a cookie. Not you. You take me on a stroll through a cemetery. I haven't decided yet if that makes me love you or hate you."

"Want me to coddle you?" Rip held the gate at the cemetery entrance open and waved her in. "Stop killing people in your sleep."

Ireland winced like he'd slapped her. "Too mean, dude. Too mean."

Rip's shoulder rose and fell in a halfhearted 'what are ya gonna do' shrug, his gaze skimming the paper he clutched in his hand for what had to be the millionth time. "Have you given any more thought to what the message the Horseman inflicted upon you might mean? It had to be crucial for him to take such a drastic step."

"Not necessarily. He may have just wanted company on his mind trip to Serial Killer's Disneyland." Ireland hesitated at a grave, struggling to remember which way they buried people so she didn't walk on them.

Behind the marker? In front of it? Was it too much to ask for a 'this side up' sign? Finally, she opted for tiptoeing around the tombstone, allowing the deceased a wide berth.

Rip's beard bobbed as he gummed at the inside of his mouth. "In the vision each individual was being tortured in some way?"

Ireland nodded, all the while focusing on keeping a mental wall up to prevent those horrifying images from playing on repeat. "All four of you were tortured or killed."

Rip was so intently scouring the landscape for the rise of a mausoleum that he failed to see the wreath leaning against a grave marker until it ensnared his foot like a bear trap. Stumbling forward, he caught himself on the neighboring tombstone and shook his leg free. "And why, in the Hessians time, were people normally tortured? Ruling out the odd case of it being for the torturer's own amusement."

"You would know better than I would. Maybe they were viewed as a threat?" Ireland offered her best guess. "Or they had valuable information they wouldn't give up?"

Rip strode to the door of the first mausoleum they happened upon, dry grass crunching under his boots. Ireland doubted it to be the one they were looking for. The ornate angel carving over the door and elaborate vine stonework were still solid and intact. Time and the elements had yet to mar this structure.

Sure enough, Rip double checked his paper and walked on. "Besides myself, who were the other victims?"

Ireland counted them off on her fingers. "Other than you, there was my secretary, Amber, one of my victim's step-mom, Ana, and my neighbor, Noah. Maybe each of you have some sort of information that I need? Anything you've forgotten to tell me?"

Whether it was deliberate or not, Rip ignored the question, choosing instead to press the first knuckle of his fist to his lips in contemplation. "We were all tortured or killed in different ways. Which— unfortunately—may indicate that each person represents an entirely different meaning. We can rule nothing out."

Ireland paused for a beat, her glare boring a hole in the back of her fuzzy-haired friend. "Basically you're saying we still have *nothing* to go on after my trip down the rabbit hole?"

"In the simplest possible terms? Yes."

"Awesome," Ireland grumbled under her breath, punctuating the thought with a few of her favorite four-lettered words.

"There's still the hope Eleanora may hold the answers we need ..." Rip's voice trailed off, reduced to nothing more than a low buzz that faded into the background.

She'd forgotten. What kind of monster did it make her that she actually *forgot*? Ireland's shaking hand rose to stifle the anguished whimper that escaped her quivering lips. Truth, stripped bare to its very essence, stared back at her. Roughly fifty chairs had been lined up across the cemetery from where she stood, all centered around a steel grey casket. Atop it lay a beautiful spray of white lilies, roses, gladiolus, and daisies resting against a bed of greenery. Every chair was filled, with a standing room only crowd of mourners lined up behind them. Noah stood among them, and even he was having a difficult time holding back his sorrow at the loss of a life taken so young.

Ireland ground her teeth to the point of pain, then clenched them harder still. No matter what she did the remainder of her days, no amount of penance could ever redeem her of this. Her gaze wandered over each person in attendance, taking in their grief and allowing it to feed the all-encompassing guilt that swelled inside her. It had to be Mason's mother that sat in the front row, her flaxen hair pulled back in an elegant twist, the rest of her consumed ... broken by the loss of her child. Ireland guessed the handsomely regal gentleman beside her to be Mason's father. His dapper façade was battered by the open sobs that shook his shoulders as they tore from his chest. Family, friends, heartbroken teens; all leaning on each other. Be it through laced fingers or a much needed embrace.

All ... but one.

Ireland's sweeping gaze pulled up short, caught by the gripping stare of another. Ana wasn't dabbing her eyes or giving sorrowful nods to the pastor's message, like everybody else. Instead, her narrowed eyes were fixed on Ireland. A complex blend of emotions played across her face, jockeying for primary position. Recognition. Confusion. Blame. Contempt. Until finally one won out—abject, mind-blowing terror. Ana's pink glossed mouth swung open wide. Her blood curdling scream shattering the serenity of the somber event. Bodies swiveled in a wave of concerned bewilderment, turning just in time to see Ana's knees buckle beneath her.

Ireland's hand shot out, as if to catch her from twenty feet away. However, it was Noah, standing beside Ana, who swooped into a low lunge. The cradle of his arms caught her before she crashed to the ground. Even the pastor paused, rising up on tiptoe to see over the buzzing crowd what the ruckus could be.

Ana's warbled screams raged on as she raised one visibly shaking arm. All it took to condemn the guilty was one finger, pointed straight at Ireland. The crowd moved as one body, following her motion to its target.

Ireland held her breath in anticipation. Maybe here, at the final resting place for one of her victims, they could see her as the monster she truly was. Gulping down her trepidation, she braced herself for the fury they would unleash—that she deserved.

That same breath was expelled through slightly parted lips. Nothing but perplexed stares met her. Whatever infliction struck Ana, it had spread no farther.

"Is ... is she okay?" Ireland called out, cautiously closing the space between them.

Ana's cries grew frenzied. Her hands clawed at the ground. Scrapping for traction, for freedom.

"*Ireland, stop!*" Noah barked, his hand raised to halt her. He softened the sting of his tone with a look slathered in apology. "Whatever this is ... you just need to go."

Ireland's feet were rooted where she stood. The weight of so many sets of eyes cut into her, dissecting her to her very core. She could feel their judgmental stares weighing her, like a bothersome bur that needed to be plucked away and discarded. If they only knew the half of it, they'd string her up from the nearest tree. Suddenly, she found herself relating to Frankenstein's monster more than she ever thought possible.

"I-I'm so sorry for the disturbance." Ireland struggled to maintain what was left of her quickly crumbling composure. Her voice betraying her by cracking. "My deepest condolences, to all of you."

Spinning on her heel, she scurried off to find Rip without looking back. The sooner they could get out of this cemetery, the better.

Rip found her wandering, lost in her own tumultuous thoughts, over the rise of the second knoll. His cheeks were bright with color. His breath coming in short, excited pants.

"There you are! I located it! We must go now!" Only then did he notice her change of demeanor and lose a bit of his gusto. "What happened? Where did you venture off to?"

"I terrorized some nice people in their ultimate moment of weakness," Ireland stated, her voice hollow, matching the detachment of her stare.

Rip cocked his head in confusion before physically shaking off the words. "No time for such frivolousness! Come on!"

The mausoleum matched a standard storage shed in size. Its stone sides and decorative pillars worn and aged by time's artistry. Fingers of moss and ivy curled up the grey walls, adding the only touch of life to this home of the dead. The front roof peeked in ornately carved vining flowers that centered around a crucifix cut deep into the stone. Two names had been etched beneath.

"Termaine and Jameson," Ireland read. "I feel whatever we're about to do warrants a preemptive apology to them."

"They will just have to understand," Rip grunted through his teeth, struggling to force open the heavy iron door, "that ... *huuf* ... this is for ... the greater ... *hunh* ... good."

Throwing his shoulder into it, Rip yanked until every tendon in his scrawny arms bulged. Still he made exactly zero progress.

Ireland bit the inside of her cheek to stifle a wry laugh that threatened to escape, despite her somber mood. "Impressive display of strength, *Cal-El*. Mind if I give it a try?"

Rip's mouth screwed to the side. Nevertheless, he stepped away and waved her forward with a formal bow. "By all means. If you think you can do better."

Cold iron chilled her palm as Ireland gripped the handle. Her other hand braced against the unyielding stone structure. Stone dragged over stone, the door gradually sliding open. A dry breath of stagnate air sighed out at them.

"After you." Ireland turned her hand, palm out, her pretense of politeness thinly veiling her own unease.

"I loosened it for you," Rip huffed, before marching inside with his head held high.

Ireland's head swiveled, her anxious stare following him in, waiting for some big catastrophic event to befall him. A zombie jumping out and lunging for his flesh. A safe falling on his head. Something. The moment passed without incident. Hesitantly, she poked her head inside. A thick layer of dust covered the two coffins positioned on opposite sides of the room. Five urns, of various sizes and colors, lined the counter-height table pushed against the back wall. Rip took care, scooting each urn aside with delicate hands, before flopping his brown leather satchel down beside them. Without offering a word of explanation, he busied himself pulling the tools needed for his task out and arranging them on the table.

"Need some help?" Ireland asked and braved her first step within the mausoleum walls.

A shudder—sizzling and electric—entered through the ball of her foot, coursing through her body. Her heart jerked in an abrupt stutter-start. Its rhythm launched into overdrive, hammering against the wall of her chest with audible thumps.

Da-dun, da-dun, da-dun.

Sweat soaked her palm, which clung tight to the doorknob.

"Rip," she gasped, forcing the words through laboring lungs. It took all of her concentration and every ounce of willpower she had to keep her feet planted *exactly* where they were. If she let them move an inch—creep forward even a step—it would all be over in the bloodiest possible way. "You see that end urn? The big one?"

Rip, seemingly oblivious to her plight, barely glanced at it. "Yes. Why?"

Her nostrils flared. Her chest rising and falling with each ragged breath. "Because I'm going to need you to pick it up and smash it over my head."

Da-dun, da-dun, da-dun.

"Why would I—" Glancing over his shoulder, the light hearted chuckle died on his lips. "Ireland? What's happening, child?"

"I can't control it." Focusing on her breathing did little to distract from her scorching skin, which yearned to be sated. "There's something about this place. Please. Don't question it, and don't hesitate. I *think* I can hold him back, but you have to hurry. Do it. *Do it now!*"

Rip shook his head. Slowly at first, but quickly gaining speed and conviction. "No, I—I can't. Why would you ask me to do such a thing?"

Da-dun, da-dun, da-dun!

"Because all I wanna do right now is tear your head off and bathe in your blood!" Ireland snarled. She rotated her upper body just enough for her other hand to squeeze around the iron knob, in hopes of buying herself even a moment longer. "Don't make me live with the guilt of that, Rip! *Knock me out!*"

Rip's vibrating hands closed around the urn. As he padded toward her, with visible unease in each step, Ireland turned her face to the door and held it there. Not in fear of the pain to come, but because each centimeter closer he edged threatened her quickly slipping control.

T-shirt sleeves fell back, revealing even more of his pasty white skin. Rip arched the urn up over his head—and paused.

A red haze seeped in around the edges of her vision, its wisps licking, swirling, and dancing before her steadfast glare.

"*Rip, do it!*" A tremor, more demonic than human, tore from her tightening throat.

The last gap in that curtain of red knit itself together, extinguishing what remained of her restraint.

"I am so very sorry." Rip cringed, bringing the urn down hard ... just as her hands slipped free from the door.

25

Ireland

The scent of sandalwood and jasmine woke Ireland from her groggy slumber, a groan slipping past her lips. Dull, pulsating pain throbbed from the left side of her forehead. Her chin lolled to her chest. Noticing the thick coat of grey dust that covered her, a grimace crinkled her face. That same dust rocketed from her nose with a sudden sneeze. "*Ugh*, I have people dust in my nose."

"Shall I remind you that the urn was your idea?" Rip's elbow rose and fell, blending herbs in a wooden bowl with a matching crusher.

"Would you prefer I had killed you?" Ireland attempted to get to her feet, but couldn't seem to get them under her.

"I'm quite partial to the way it turned out." Rip banged the crusher against the side of the bowl, knocking the remaining ingredients off of it. "Then again, I'm not the one covered in the charred remains of a human corpse."

"Not to change the subject … because really, who *wouldn't* want to talk about the human remains caught in their teeth?" Ireland ran her tongue over her gritty top teeth and stifled the resulting dry heave. "But why did you tie my hands and feet together?"

Rip struck a match, lighting one candle, then another, before shaking it out. "For the same reason I put the talisman back around your neck. It seems the Hessian cannot be trusted in this space, and we have important work to do. Fortunately, I had some extra braided twine in my bag."

"That is fortunate," Ireland grumbled. Shifting to her side, she tried to find a position that was even remotely comfortable to sit in. "So, when the Horseman takes over completely, the talisman doesn't make me panty-twirling crazy? That's a nice change."

"*Mm-hmm*," Rip muttered, not even pretending to listen. He gripped the bowl in one hand while the other creaked open the lid of the coffin positioned across the room from where Ireland sat.

Curiosity getting the better of her, Ireland sat up a little straighter and craned her neck to see. "What does she look like? Is she super nasty?"

Rip tilted his head to consider the coffin's inhabitant. "Oddly enough, she looks strikingly similar to how I remember her."

"That's harsh."

In place of a response, Rip dipped two fingers into the bowl's concoction. His hand, sure and steady, reached in to mark the corpse. Taking a beat to wipe the remnants off his pants—*her* pants, actually— before bowing his head to mumble an inaudible chant.

"What's happening? Is it working?"

Narrow shoulders sagged in annoyance. Rip turned his head just enough to shoot her a sideways glare.

"Easy to be snippy when you're not the one tied up in the corner," Ireland grumbled and slouched against the wall, the cold stone wall scratching the back of her arms. "I'd pantomime zipping my lips closed, but I'm not bendy enough to do that with my toes."

Rip's chest swelled in a deep breath meant to squash his annoyance before he resumed his chant.

Ireland sat. Watching. Waiting. Wishing for a better seat for the show. Her mouth opened to request a progress report when a deep, ghastly moan cut her off.

"It worked!" Rip's yellow-rimmed eyes widened with an excitement. "Eleanora, you have crucial information that we need—"

A reverberating rasp—the very voice of death—resonated from the open coffin.

"*'Fore the Horseman steps foot in this place,*

The veil shall weaken to show his true face."

"*What?*" Ireland snapped, recoiling at the memory of her strong desire to tear Rip limb from limb. "*That's* why I went all *Cuckoo's Nest* when I walked in here? Someone should really put up a sign."

Bones snapped. Dried tendons crackled. One bone arm rose from within the coffin to point to the wall by the door. Carved in the stone was a replica of the Horseman's talisman, crossed out with a big X.

"Sure, put it *inside* the door," she scoffed with an exaggerated roll of her eyes.

206

"Eleanora," Rip's stern tone guided his long dead associate back to his desired conversational path. "My dear friend has been infected with the Horseman—*Ichabod's*—essence. We need to know how to help her before she can hurt anyone ... else."

Ireland's jaw swung open. Prickles of icy reality seeping through her veins. "The Horseman ... is *Ichabod*? Your friend, that you claimed was the most heroic man you ever knew, is *inside me*? Making me do these horrible things? After ... *everything*, you didn't think to tell me that?"

"What he became does *not* represent who he was," Rip snapped, the firmness of his tone offering no trace of apology. "The beast took him over. You, of all people, should understand that."

"We *will* be discussing this further, later on." She glared daggers into the back of the man she'd come to count on.

"And I shall anxiously count the seconds until then."

Eleanora's chilling groan interrupted, eternity's oblivion blocking her from the rising tension in the room.

"Four were present at Ichabod's end,

the quartet required as he rises again."

Ireland's head snapped toward the coffin, her glower crumbling under building intrigue. "Four? Just like in my dream! Cryptic limerick be damned, we might be on to something."

"Each spirit shall select a host,

chosen by blood or one they relate to most.

To break the curse and free your friend,

save his returned love 'fore she meets her end."

Rip winced, rapidly blinking in shock. "Katrina didn't die. At least not of anything other than old age or extravagant living. Ichabod gave his life for her and she betrayed him by marrying that Neanderthal, Brom. Although, from what I've read, guilt shadowed her days. Late in life she insisted people call her Elizabeth. As if a simple name change could somehow undo what had happened."

"'*Tis not what happened at all,*" the long dead Eleanora croaked.

"*While another did rise, Katrina did fall.*"

Those simple words acted as the shatterpoint that sent the wall Ireland constructed in her mind crumbling. That one sentence, plucked from her vision, echoed in her head.

Another did rise. Another did rise. Another did rise.

Her bound hands rose to her head, massaging her temples that were suddenly pounding.

"If what you say is true," Rip stroked the length of his beard, "we must find the body Katrina inhabits, and ... what?"

"*Embrace the legend, shoulder the cloak,*

Let the beast within ye be awoke.

Yet beware, prepare for the flood,

With the power comes lust for blood."

Rip's hands closed around the edge of the coffin, his upper body anxiously leaning in. "And if we do this, and save Katrina, this will all be over? We will have beaten the Hessian?"

"*Ichabod shall rest and relinquish control,*

But for this prize there is a toll."

The unearthly tremor from the casket grew weak, losing ground to death's heavy hand. The ebb and flow of her words peaked at a whisper then faded to the barely audible.

"The Horseman is unending, his presence ... shan't lessen.

If ... you break ... the curse, you become ... the legend."

Eleanora's waning spirit gave out, leaving Rip and Ireland to stare in stunned silence.

26

Ireland

"You invited," Rip gummed at the inside of his mouth, choosing his words carefully, "a *guest* over, and didn't feel that merited a conversation?"

Amber stood just inside the doorway. Her ever present smile stayed firmly in place even while confusion creased her forehead.

"Ireland invited me," she offered in cheerful explanation.

The sun was sinking low in the sky. The threat it presented caused Ireland's skin to twitch, a fresh sheen of sweat beading across her brow.

"Oh, are we telling each other things now?" Her rebuttal sounded harsher than she intended even to *her* ears. Instead of attempting to soften it, she thrust out her chin and pressed on, "Because, I got a different memo."

A hot rush of red filled Rip's cheeks. "You are greatly exaggerating a small oversight in the midst of a much more dire—"

"*Small oversight?*" Ireland's hands clenched into fists at her sides; her fingernails digging half-moons into her palms. "The guy that's basically stalking me is a close personal buddy of yours, and you didn't think that deserved a mention?"

"I brought *Trivial Pursuit!*" Amber injected, shoving forward the box that had been tucked under her arm.

Rip's hand smoothed the front of his borrowed T-shirt, like he was forcing his couth into place. "Amber, is it?"

Frizzy curls bobbed around her face with her exuberant nod.

"Why don't you set up this game of yours, while Ireland and I have a quick chat in the kitchen?"

"No problem!" Amber gushed, shrugging her purse strap off her shoulder and letting it flop to the floor. "I'm pink!"

Rip looked from Amber to Ireland and back again. Shaking his head, his lips pressed in a thin line of incomprehension.

"Uh … the game pieces. Pink's my favorite." Her eyebrows rose and her mouth curled to the side, as if she knew she was being awkward and hoped they'd ignore it.

Lucky for her, her hosts were distracted enough to disregard the norms of social conduct for the moment.

"Pink it is," Rip said with a forced smile. His hand tightened around Ireland's clammy forearm to drag her toward the kitchen.

"Pardon my uncle," Ireland called before her head disappeared around the doorjamb. "He's at the old and crotchety phase of his senility."

Rip didn't release his hold until they'd rounded the breakfast nook into the kitchen. His hand falling to his side when he spun on her. "*Why?* Why *her?* Why *now?* In spite of everything! *Why?*"

"So, the question you're asking is why?"

"Do *not* be glib!" Rip hissed through his stained teeth, stabbing a finger in her direction.

Ireland felt her nostrils flare and took a breath to claim control over her raging emotions.

"Because," she explained in the calmest tone she could muster, "Noah is her cousin, and he's a Van Tassel. I'm guessing she's got a blood tie to Katrina in her somewhere, too. Going by what Eleanora said, we're dealing with a residual haunt. I've watched enough ghost hunting shows to know that. If Katrina *did* hitch a ride inside Amber, then it's up to us to keep her safe from whatever is after her."

Rip's gaunt shoulders sagged with sadness. Compassion softened the stern lines of his face. "Not whatever, Ireland. *You.* The thing hunting her this night will be *you.* Hence you inviting her to *your* house to socialize with *you* being the worst of possible ideas."

Ireland let those words hang heavy in the air for a moment, batting them around in her mind before she strode straight for the fridge. Rising up on tiptoe, she dug a bottle of coconut flavored rum out of the cupboard above it. Tonight, unscrewing the top from the bottle would suffice as her mixer.

"Did your plan extend any farther than luring that poor girl to what could be her eminent doom?"

She slammed the bottle back, chugging a healthy swig before wiping her mouth on the back of her hand. "There was no plan! I have no idea what I'm doing! All I know is that some time tonight the Horseman *will* ride. I can already ... *feel* him, slithering around inside of me. Everybody has a part to play in this, and I was cast as the villain. It's who I am now because I-I don't know how to stop it!"

Rip took a cautious step closer, his hand raised as if to comfort her. Ireland shot him a warning glare that such an act would *not* be well received. "Eleanora advised you of what must be done. Shoulder the cloak, remember?"

"And willingly become a monster? What if this is a self-fulfilling prophecy? I do this and become the—*thing* that hunts and kills you all?" Tears welled behind her eyes. The hard blinks she attempted did nothing to prevent them from sliding down her cheeks unchecked. "I ... *can't*."

"You *will* become the Horseman tonight, Ireland. You're right about that." Rip's hands curled like he wanted to grab her and shake her—a move that could prove deadly in her vulnerable state. "Do it under your own terms and you might just be able to control it."

"*Might*," Ireland pointedly emphasized that crucial word. "Or, I *might* slaughter an entire town."

Rip spun on his heel, the palm of his hand connecting with the countertop in a loud crack. "*There* is *no other way!*"

"*There has to be!*" The intensity of Ireland's resolve easily matched his.

"I-is everything okay in there?" Amber called.

"Fine." Rip spun back toward her, the look on his face making it clear it was anything *but*. "You think on that, then. Ponder how best to avoid killing the lovely young lady in the next room. I'm going to go keep her company with a board game." He closed the distance between them with one wide step, his determined glare locking with hers and holding firm. "However, you need to realize one crucial detail. If you make *one* move to hurt her, *I will stop you myself*."

Without glancing back, he stormed from the room.

Ireland stared out the kitchen window, admiring the skyline painted with twilight's violet pallet.

"No, you won't," she murmured sadly and tipped the bottle to her lips once more.

The sun relented, giving its final bow while gesturing forth the threat of night that galloped in with unspeakable intent. Ireland slammed back another tangy gulp of rum, her skin suddenly humming. She tried to reassure herself that the rum was to blame, not some dark and sinister atrocity within her that was anxiously scratching and clawing its way to the surface. Unfortunately, she wasn't drunk enough to buy that line of logic ... yet.

For a minute, she batted around the idea of grabbing her keys and bolting for the door; slamming the accelerator to the floor and not letting up until she crossed at least two state lines.

What was that saying? she asked herself. *Run like the devil himself was chasing me?*

Only in this case he would be riding shotgun. Any place she went, any cute little burg that caught her fancy, would have the fury of the

Hessian unleashed on them. No one was safe anywhere near her. Unless ... there actually was a glimmer of fact in Eleanora's instructions.

This reverie into life and death was set against the oddly mundane soundtrack of casual banter from the next room. A none too subtle reminder that even as everything crumbled around her, the world spun on.

"How is this played?" Rip was considerate enough to force polite interest despite the growing tension in the house.

"*You've never played?*" Amber gasped. "How is that possible?"

Become the monster—without losing myself in it. Was such a thing possible? Ireland pondered.

"Games in my day involved kicking cans or dropping handkerchiefs."

"Oh, stop!" the adorable secretary laughed. "You're not that old!"

I've never considered myself a person of strong institution. After all, it only took a handsome face and sexy swagger from Brantley to alter the entire path I'd laid out for my future. That being the case, could I really call forth energy of that magnitude and somehow manage to hold it at bay?

"Huh," Rip huffed, clearly impressed. "I didn't expect you to get those references at all. It seems you're far more than a pretty face."

Ireland's head snapped to the side, one eyebrow hitched. *Is Rip making a play for Amber? Everything that's going on and his decrepit ass is trying to hook up?*

She *had* to have heard wrong, because it *really* sounded like Amber encouraged him with a coy giggle. "Well, a game of pure trivia *is* my favorite for a reason."

"By all means, m'lady," Rip practically purred.

Ireland stifled her threatening dry heave with a tip of the bottle. She was not nearly drunk enough for this kind of crap.

"Share your pleasure by teaching me how to play. Help grow my ... *mind*."

It was a good thing she didn't know where the Horseman's sword was. She would've run herself through right then and there.

"I would love to," Amber agreed with an audible smile. "It's fairly simple. You roll your dice and move clockwise that number of spaces. Whatever color you land on you have to answer a question for the category. If you answer right, you get to go again. Here, I'll go first and show you."

Ireland tipped her head back against the fridge door, reveling in the cool relief it offered her feverish skin. She heard the dice thunk against the board and Amber click her piece the necessary number of spaces.

"Yellow, history! That's a favorite of mine! Now take one of the cards from the box and ask me the yellow question."

Rip cleared his throat as he slid the card from the box. "What did Walter Raleigh's wife carry in her purse for twenty-nine years after his execution?"

"I remember this only because I found it insanely icky ... his head."

A pause as Rip checked the answer. "How disturbingly grotesque, yet oddly fitting."

"What?"

"Nothing, my dear. You go again."

Ireland rolled the bottle of rum over her forehead, hoping for cooling relief but finding none there.

More incessant clicking. "Entertainment."

Was it anxiety causing Ireland's heart to hammer in her chest or something far more ominous? If she wasn't going to follow Eleanora's advice, she was going to need to find a way to lock herself up—and soon.

"Who was the first non-human to win an Academy Award?"

Fingernails drummed against the coffee table, somehow managing to keep time with the pulsating in Ireland's temples. "Hmm, I suspect that Mr. Disney was behind whoever it was. I know *Snow White* was his first full-length feature, but ... I'm going to go with the mouse that started it all, Mickey."

"You got it!" Rip's tone bubbled with awe. "How do you know all of these things?"

Moving on legs that wobbled and threatened to buckle beneath her, Ireland crossed to the sink, and her stomach slammed into the counter as she turned the faucet on full flow. Dipping her head, she sucked water directly from it. Thirst somewhat quenched, she turned her head this way and that, soaking her head in search of even a moment's relief.

Amber's voice dropped to a whisper, like she was revealing a glimpse of her soul to what she probably thought was a grungy old hippie.

"I've always been a big reader. Only not fiction novels, like most people. Medical journals, non-fiction memoires, law books, more often than not I have my nose buried in a book."

Ireland turned the water off and wrung the extra water from her hair.

"I've never been more than a casual reader," Rip admitted. "The services I—"

"Provided paid only in salves and a burning sensation over the chamber pot," Amber boldly finished for him.

"Wh-where did you get those words?" All amusement and playfulness drained from Rip's tone, leaving behind a haunted echo.

"I am so sorry! I don't know what came over me!" Amber sounded on the verge of tears; her voice rising and falling in an unsteady quake. "I would *never* say such a thing! *Wait!* Where are you going?"

Ireland's head swiveled as Rip stumbled into the dining room, his pale skin ashen.

"She's not Katrina," he mumbled, the whites of his eyes bulging.

"How do you—"

Gradually, his head turned toward her. Terror had slashed its markings deep into the creases of his face. "The day I came to Sleepy Hollow, Irving spoke those very same words to me. No one but he could have possibly known that. We've made a horrible miscalculation, Ireland. Wh—where is *our* Katrina?"

Somewhere deep within her the beast chuckled maliciously.

Ireland ran her trembling hands over her face, fighting to think over the warning sirens blaring in her head. "Mason's wake, it was going to be at the Van Brunt manor. Noah and Ana are there with about half of Tarrytown."

"Ireland, if the Hessian goes after them there the body count will be higher than you can possibly imagine! You can't—"

One finger snapped up to silence him. "Get Amber out of here, *now!*"

The rasp of Eleanora's words booming through her mind, Ireland shoved herself from the counter and lurched for the basement stairs.

Break the curse, become the legend.

27

Ichabod

Ichabod leaned into the stallion's wide gait, the pair galloping toward the regal Van Brunt estate at breakneck speeds. His leg swung over the stallion's back before it halted, his boots skidding across the gravel and kicking up a cloud of dust. The moment he secured his footing, he rushed across the grounds. The planks of the porch squeaked their protest under his weight as he bolted toward the front door that hung open like the hungry jaws of a beast.

Families like the Van Brunt's prided themselves on maintaining a staff of servants to cater to their every whim. Be that as it may, the house was eerily vacant. No lamps were lit. Not a whisper of sound broke the ominous silence. The muffled clomp of Ichabod's cautious steps echoed through the foyer like a trumpet blast. His head snapped in one direction then the other as he crept, searching the darkness for a clue to Katrina's whereabouts. To his right, two rooms away, a soft light beckoned. Moving on the balls of his feet, he slunk through the doorway to the neighboring dining room. One step inside and his heart leapt into his throat. Two men stood statue still on either side of the door wall.

"A thousand apologies—" Ichabod's hands rose in a gesture of truce.

The men, dressed in standard servant attire, didn't move or acknowledge his entry with so much as a blink. Ichabod slunk closer with caution to inspect the suspiciously tolerant fellow on his right. At first glance he seemed utterly fine—other than the milky white voids where his eyes had been. Ichabod waved his hand in front of the boy's face, expecting a flinch or a blink. Nothing registered past the haunting fog in his eyes.

"I am going to take this as an ominously bad sign," Ichabod muttered before continuing his quest deeper into the bowels of the house.

"How will the world remember Ichabod Crane?" a feminine voice, with a trace of malice as sharp as a dagger's edge, asked from somewhere in the darkness. "As a noble man that rushed headlong into danger to save the woman he was never meant to be with? Or, perhaps as the coward that ran to save himself? We shall soon see."

Long shadows danced across the walls, cast by the small fire crackling and hissing in the sitting room fireplace before him. Inside the door, just like the last, two servants stood like stationary sentries.

"If I were to place a wager on it," the faceless voice continued, "I would guess history will not remember you at all. You will be nothing more than a snagged flaw in the intricate tapestry of life—easily overlooked due to the threads surrounding you that are far more important and impressive with their painstakingly perfect weavings."

His only plan, to follow the light, turned out to be a sufficient one. Stepping farther into the room, he spotted Katrina seated in a wingback chair with her hands and feet bound by a thick, braided rope. The golden tresses, which curtained most of her face, parted just enough for him to see the blood trail that zigzagged down her face.

His heart lurched in a panicked stutter-beat. Without hesitation, he sprang to her aid. His goal was extinguished painfully short of completion by the two servants that broke from their stoic stillness to block his passage.

"You could still make it out of this alive. I suggest you not force my hand." She emerged from the darkest corner of the room, taking shape as she stepped into the light. Conservative uniform, tight-pulled bun, lines from a none-too gentle-existence already marring her young face; the girl could have been lovely had life showed her a kinder hand.

"Elizabeth?" Ichabod gasped, his face a question mark.

The Van Tassel's house maid pursed her thin lips, her head bobbing in an impressed nod. "You recognize me? There are some I have crossed paths with every day since I was a child that would fail in that same regard. After all, of what consequence am I?"

Ichabod's gaze flicked over to Katrina, who had yet to stir. "I am beginning to think quite a large one."

A smile, malicious and deadly as the maw of ravenous crocodile, curled across her face. "You *are* a fast learner, Schoolmaster."

A low moan seeped from Katrina's lips, causing a flood of thanks to overcome Ichabod. He had never been more grateful for anything than to see her head loll to the side, her heavy lids fight to open.

"Oh good, you are awake," Elizabeth said with that same hungry grin. "Now the real fun can begin."

"Elizabeth?" Katrina murmured, struggling for the awareness that eluded her obviously foggy mind. "You must release me. The Horseman ... c-could be here at any moment."

Elizabeth crossed her arms over her chest, drumming her fingers against them. "Be thankful you are beautiful, because it seems you were not blessed generously with cognitive reasoning."

Finally, Katrina's cornflower blue eyes found their focus in the troubled gaze of the man she had confessed her love to. "Ichabod? What is happening?"

Ichabod fought to keep his expression neutral, not wanting to panic her further. "I believe we have found the puppet master that has been yanking at the Horseman's strings."

"A second point awarded to the schoolmaster!" Elizabeth laughed and jubilantly clapped her hands. "You really are too clever for our sweet, yet obtuse, Katrina."

"My father achieved peace with that murderous ghoul!" Katrina raged, struggling against her restraints. "Why would you risk upsetting that?"

Ichabod didn't see Elizabeth move, nonetheless the next instant she stood by Katrina's side. Pinching Katrina's chin in her chapped hand, she bore down with a murderous glare. "You think that man such a hero?" Metal hissed from leather, and a pearl handled dagger emerged from the sheath tied around Elizabeth's waist.

Every fiber of Ichabod's being tensed. The twitch of his shoulder making that strain visible.

"Every success he ever had in this town was owed to his manipulations of the Hessian. Perhaps it is time you learned the *truth* about your precious father, princess." Elizabeth rolled the opalescent handle between her fingers, letting the light from the licking flames glisten off the polished blade.

Katrina clamped her lips shut to muffle a whimper that escaped.

With deliberate nonchalance, Elizabeth brought the very tip of the dagger to Katrina's cheek, pressing hard enough to dimple the flesh without piercing it. Ichabod lunged to Katrina's aid, a protective inferno erupting inside of him potent enough to heat an entire city. All it took was a flicked glance from Elizabeth for her mindless servants to seize his arms and deny him passage. Try as he might, he couldn't free himself from their herculean holds.

"You were born with the luxury of a pedigree; the golden child of Baltus and his lovely wife, Mariella Van Tassel." Elizabeth used more force than necessary to tip Katrina's head to the side. Leaning in, she whispered against her ear, "Even as the sickness grew within your mother, your father kept the secrets of his betrayal from her. She died never knowing that for years her doting husband had been quenching his most vile of desires in the servants' quarters with *my mother.*"

Elizabeth applied pressure to the blade, slicing a crimson trail across Katrina's porcelain cheek. Tears streaked down Katrina's face, mingling with the blood and dripping from her chin in diluted droplets. While terror screamed from her stare, all that eeked passed her lips was a muted yelp.

"Katrina!" Ichabod shouted, his heart hammering in the hollow of his chest.

"I was conceived in the shadows, one floor beneath where you slept in your finely-crafted crib, wetting your nappies. In those same shadows is where I learned all I needed to unravel our twisted family ... *sister.*" Elizabeth hissed the last word, a viper releasing her venom. "You were sent away, always shielded from the darkness father dabbled with. I was allowed to linger; an invisible being with no identity worth mention. A ghost before my time. There, I watched ... and learned."

Flipping her wrist, she shifted the blade to Katrina's other cheek. Luminescent skin split in a second eruption of red with the drag of her blade.

Ichabod threw his body forward, yanking for freedom from his captors with every ounce of his strength. "*Leave her be*! Do *not* harm another hair on her head!"

Elizabeth straightened her spine and cocked her head as though to consider his plea, the dagger dangling from her fingers. "Absolutely. I would have it no other way."

Her gaze locked with Ichabod's, a manic smile spreading across her face as she turned the blade on herself. She drew it down one cheek, then the other, reveling in the slashes like a lover's seductive caress.

Katrina spun away from the gruesome spectacle, her eyes squeezed shut. Locks of fair blonde stuck in her wounds, the seeping blood staining them pink.

Gore streaked Elizabeth's beaming face like crimson tears. "I *did* have to overcome the obstacle presented by not having the bond with the Horseman that Baltus did. Even that was easily remedied with a little Wiccan education—a fact I'm sure you can appreciate, Schoolmaster. All it took was a sacrifice, a kill for a kill. I offer up a soul to him and he claims a life of my choosing. After which he politely returns to whatever hellish dimension claims him."

"The maid's wounds." Slowly, Ichabod was putting the pieces together. The familial picture it formed made Greek tragedy seem tame. "The rest were killed with one fatal strike. Her death was brutal. She'd been hacked apart."

"*She deserved it!*" Elizabeth shrieked, the tendons in her neck bulging. "She was pathetic, waiting her entire life for Baltus! When Mariella died, she expected her day had come. That he would come to her, and the two of them would finally be together."

Katrina's angelic face crumbled at the horror of such a revelation. "She was your ... *mother?*"

Elizabeth spun on her heel to pace the length of the room; this turn of topic setting the off-kilter maid on edge. "*And she deserved to die!* When Baltus took Selena as his second wife, Mother reached the decision that her own daughter would never be restricted by the confines of love as she was. She insisted making my own choices about such matters would only weaken me—make me like *her*. She met with Baltus behind

226

closed doors. There, the two orchestrated an arrangement to marry me off to that idiot stable-boy, Daniel. He was nothing more than a man-child aspiring no farther than raking up manure. Yet, our father was thrilled to hand me off to him just to free himself of the burden and obligation he felt toward me."

Tears tinged with blood dotted Katrina's gown with pink. "That is why you ordered the Horseman to kill Daniel? So the two of you would not be wed?"

"Do not dare judge me!" Elizabeth stomped the remaining distance between them to jab the point of her blade against Katrina's throat. "Men like Brom Van Brunt pant after you, yet you cast them to the wayside! What makes you better than me? The same blood pumps through our veins! Be that as it may, *you* get your pick while *I* get handed off like an old sow!"

"What of the others?" Ichabod interjected, mostly to divert the blade from Katrina's flesh. "The Horseman has been called at least thrice. Who else have you sacrificed?"

His mission proved successful when she pulled back to face him. The tip of her index finger pressed to the point of the dagger as she slowly turned the hilt. "Silly boy, do not you know? Servants are a status symbol in this town. Fortunately for me, no one notices if a few go missing."

A glimmer of something sinister flashed across her face as she walked toward him. Desire? Amusement? Savagery? It was gone before he could adhere a label to it.

Positioning herself body skimming close, her warm breath teased across his earlobe. "I bet you think you are clever, coercing all of my

227

secrets from me. However, there is one crucial flaw to your plan ... I have yet to decide if you are going to make it out of this house alive."

Ichabod threw himself forward against the hold of his imprisoners, ignoring the stabs of pain that radiated from his overextended shoulders. "Do what you will with me, witch, but let Katrina go!"

"Oh, sweet boy. Katrina's fate has already been decided. The only question now is, what of you?" The back of her hand, rough and coarse from daily chores, brushed his jawline. "I could take it all away. A few simple herbs, the right incantation, and the pain of knowing—and losing—Katrina could be wiped from your mind completely. You could leave here. Try for your fresh start in a town not bogged down by its own curse. Say the word, Ichabod, and you will be free from Sleepy Hollow."

"Ichabod, go." Katrina's hair fell in her face, matting with tears and blood. "If you have ever loved me at all, take this opportunity and run!"

"No! I will not leave you!" Ichabod's exclamation burst breathlessly from his chest, as if the nearing midnight hour was somehow sucking the oxygen from the room in her greedy hunger for another life to be offered up.

Elizabeth paused, her head inclined to consider him. A casual lift of her shoulder and she was off, striding back to Katrina. Her chin dipped just enough to shoot Ichabod a coy smile over her shoulder. "Let us see if we can shake your resolve, shall we?"

The air sizzled with a palpable tension. Elizabeth pulled back her dagger wielding arm. Her devilish smile widened as Katrina flinched and squirmed to free herself. Ichabod sucked air through his tightly clenched jaw. The blade sliced through the air—and severed the ropes around Katrina's wrist.

Katrina's gaze searched her newly-discovered sister's face. "You are … *freeing* me?"

"In a matter of speaking." Elizabeth arched one brow, her face a mask of indifference.

Before Katrina could question the motives of such an act, Elizabeth seized her hand. Forcing her palm skyward, she dragged the blade from thumb to pinkie. Layers of skin burst open in a gush of red. Adrenalin pumped through Ichabod's veins, and Katrina's anguished scream rang in his ears. He threw his weight into the larger of his two captors, hoping the other would lose his hold. Unfortunately, his valiant effort gained him no ground.

Once again, Elizabeth duplicated Katrina's wound on her own body. "The future holds so much promise for Katrina Van Tassel. Her marriage to Brom Van Brunt will be the wisest possible choice. One that will make both families infinitely wealthier." Her face folded in mock sadness as she clasped her bleeding hand with Katrina's. "It is really quite a shame you will miss it."

Ichabod's jaw fell slack, awed by the light that surged from Katrina's pores, enveloping her in a halo of white. Her goodness and purity emerged as its own separate entity … but it wasn't alone. Darkness hatched from beneath Elizabeth's skin, wriggling out of her like an infestation of smoky spiders. Their vastly different auras seemed to repel each other. Live tendrils of darkness and light swirled and roiled in an intricate waltz, the two sides never crossing or joining. That hungry, black aura snaked its way inside Katrina, taking the optical route. Her peaches and cream complexion faded to a dull grey pallor. As the white light entered Elizabeth, her fumbling hand relinquished control of the dagger to Katrina.

"*Katrina! Quickly—*" Ichabod's exclamation cut off. Before his very eyes, Katrina's features sharpened, the cornflower hue of her eyes sinking to a deep sea blue.

"Ich-Ichabod? What's happening?" While it was Elizabeth that stuttered the words, the voice undeniably belonged to Katrina.

His heat lurched into his throat. He had to choke down a swallow to croak around it, "Ka—Katrina?"

Before he could press for even one answer to his surfeit of questions, Katrina's body rose from the chair she'd been confined in. She pitched forward, thrusting the dragger deep into the maid's core.

Raw, chapped hands covered the wound, an endless flow of red seeping and bubbling between her fingers. A high-pitched wheeze escaped her parted lips as her legs crumbled beneath her. Impending darkness dimmed the light in her eyes, yet her gaze sought out Ichabod's face.

He knew. Without a shadow of a doubt, he knew. The spirit of *Katrina* lay dying before him. Somehow, they had switched.

"Ichabod," she gasped, "*run.*"

"She is not wrong." Elizabeth cut her still bound hand free. Tilting her chin one way then the other, she admired her reflection in the dagger's blade. "The blood sacrifice has been paid. My noble Hessian is on his way, galloping closer by the second."

She wore the face of the woman he loved, nevertheless all he felt as he glared at her was revulsion, loathing, and a thirst for vengeance. "We could still save her. Set me free, let me tend to her."

Elizabeth's nose crinkled at Katrina's now still form. "I fear we may be too late."

She bent, as though to check Katrina's pulse. Then, weaving her fingers into Katrina's tied hair, wrenched her head back and slit her throat.

"Yes, we are most definitely too late." Elizabeth let Katrina's head thump to the floor as she rose to her feet, wiping the blade with the folds of gown.

All Ichabod could do was stare. The simple act of breathing was an anguishing task now that he'd watched his future die before him while he stood impotent to help.

"Release him," Elizabeth ordered with a casual flick of her wrist.

Ichabod's hands fell to his sides: twitching, shaking. Longing to wrap around that swan-like neck she'd stolen and wring the life from it. He lumbered forward in a threatening step, his nostrils flaring with each heaved breath.

"Ah," Elizabeth halted his advance with one finger. "Tick-tock, Ichabod. The Horseman is on his way."

"Let him come," the schoolmaster growled through his teeth. "Let him claim my head while I rejoice over your lifeless body. I have nothing else to live for."

Her lower lip protruded slightly. "That is heartbreaking, truly. However, I never said the Horseman was coming for *you*. How are those friends of yours?" A curtain of blonde cascaded over her shoulder as she cocked her head, tapping her chin with one elegant finger. "What are their names? I believe one is Rip and the other Irving?"

Ice cold fear injected itself in his veins. "*No.*"

"You can be the avenger to your fallen love, or save your friends. Which will it be?"

28

Ireland

The bloodcurdling scream tore from her throat, strangling her from within. Her watering eyes bulged, her tongue swollen in her mouth. The drumming of her pulse resonated in her ears like the whirring blades of an industrial fan. The basement swam out of focus a moment before the floor rose to meet her. If any pain accompanied her knees slamming down on unyielding cement, it didn't register. She could comprehend nothing beyond ... *them.*

"I-I couldn't have. I couldn't—" Ireland's attempt to console herself in the face of true gruesomeness transformed into a choked sob, purging forth her sins.

The bare bulb swung, casting shadows over the ground that seemed to mock her with their illusion of a doubled body count. Noah. Ana. Hanging limply from the floorboards overhead. Their fixed stares cloudy. Their heads craned to the side in an unnatural angle caused by tightly wrapped nooses. Hollowed voids gaped from their chest cavities where their hearts had been ripped out, showering the front of their funeral attire with gore. Their feet dangled, clomping against each other with each sway of the rope.

Ireland's head turned, following a muted thump. The paint cans were gone from the shelf. In their place sat two Mason jars … holding the still beating hearts of Noah and Ana. Something within her snapped, pushed to the brink then nudged over the precipice. The shake of her head started slow, quickly building in speed and intensity, until she was snapping it side-to-side in a frantic denial of the horror before her.

"*No. No. Nooooo!*" Bellowing until her lungs ached, she crumbled to the ground. Her legs drew into her chest, curling her into a tight ball while her torrents of tears soaked the ground.

Overhead, the ropes creaked their malicious giggles.

Rip banged down the stairs behind her. "Ireland! What is it, child? What's happening?" he asked, easing her trembling frame from the ground and gathering her in his arms.

"It's my fault. All my fault." Her fingers curled in a white-knuckled grasp around his shirt sleeve, drawing strength from him just to breathe.

Rip pulled back, cradling her face in leathery hands. "What is your fault?"

"Them!" She jabbed her thumb over her shoulder, sparing herself another glimpse of what the monster within her was truly capable of.

Rip took his time before answering, choosing his words carefully. "Ireland, there's nothing there."

"How can you say that? They're hanging right—" She spun toward … *nothing*. Her claim trailed off, lost in the sea of her tumultuous thoughts.

"If I were to wager a guess, I'd say the Hessian knows of your plan. He's pulling out every parlor trick in his arsenal to prevent you from stealing away his control," Rip theorized while guiding her up onto wobbly legs. Once she achieved steady footing, he pivoted her toward the hidden cubby with his hands on her shoulders. "You mustn't let him. Amber has been sent home. You have nothing else to concern yourself with than claiming the cloak that is rightfully yours."

A confining casket of unease smothered Ireland, forcing her gaze to flick back to Rip.

"Whatever you see," Rip murmured. Ireland tried to reassure herself the razor blade that suddenly appeared in his hand wasn't real. Even as he dragged it gradually across one cheek, spilling blood from earlobe to mouth, then shifted the blade to do the other side. "Whatever you hear, no matter how real it seems, keep going!"

Ireland clamped her eyes shut tight just as the ghoulish image of Rip punctuated his thought by slitting his own throat.

"Ireland?"

One lid pried itself open to peek. Rip stood staring, eyebrows raised in expectation. Not a scratch or drop of blood on him.

"I'm going," she gulped, wiping her sweaty palms on the legs of her faded black jeans. "The Horseman just decided to widen your smile in the ickiest possible way."

"My smile?" He patted his face with frantic hands, searching every inch for flaws. "*What happened to my face?*"

And then he was gone. Bounding up the stairs two at a time, most likely in search of a mirror.

"Three quarters of your face is covered by hair, but by all means run off and leave me to my threatening sanity," Ireland grumbled under her breath, each of her tentative steps drawing her that much closer to her uncertain fate.

Dust rained down from the crumbling wall under the pressure of her hand. Ducking her head, she glanced inside. Her cheeks puffed, exhaling a breath she hadn't realized she'd been holding. She had anticipated a ghoulish nightmare inside orchestrated just for her. After all, the Horseman could root around inside her brain. He had to have stumbled across a few phobias he could use to make her squirm. But no. In an even more off putting turn of events, the room was eerily, deliberately, silent.

"It may be time to reevaluate your life when bodies hanging from the ceiling is less jarring than an empty room." Rock scrapped across her back, snagging her fitted tee, as she stooped under the wrecked wall to creep inside.

Then ... that damned proverbial other shoe dropped.

The floor came alive beneath her feet. Snakes, of every size and color, flooded the room ankle deep.

"It's not real." Ireland stared straight ahead, doing all she could to ignore the writhing body of motion beneath her while she forced one stubborn foot forward.

It wasn't real. *Nothing* had slithered underneath the cuff of her pants, tickling over her skin with deadly intent. The walls were *not* reverberating with a menacing hiss, as though any minute more of the legless demons would spew forth from any available crack in the foundation.

"You ... are not ... going to—*mhmm* ... have a ... panic attack." Her words were broken. Forced from her mouth in pained whimpers each time she lifted her foot and set it back down in the reptilian sea. "Get to ... the trunk ... grab the damned cloak ... *ahhh-haaa*!" Her pattern of avoidance got exponentially more difficult following the strike of an ornery rattlesnake that *wasn't really there*. Biting the inside of her cheek hard enough to taste a rush of coopery warmth, she pushed on. "Then, I'm gonna ... run from this ... pit, and enjoy ... the full-blown ... girlie, hissy fit ... *I have earned*!"

The second her hand thumped down on the trunk, the snakes vanished. Granted, her skin still crawled, but there was a good chance that would now be a permanent affliction. She wasn't foolish enough to think the ringleader of terror had retreated. Nope, this was intermission. The decapitated showgirls were probably stretching for the big finale. Her hands curled around the lid. Bracing herself with a steadying breath, she lifted it open. It creaked its stubborn protest until relenting and flopping back against its hinges.

Bile scorched its way up the back of her throat, threatening to spew the remnants of her lunch down the front of her. Outwardly, the trunk was only about two foot by three foot in size. What loomed before her was an endless abyss of suffering. Mouths hanging open, locked forever in their final scream. Fixed eyes gaping at the brutality of their end. Ireland gazed down into the depths of despair, which was basically a walking tour through the history of the Horseman. Each severed head a placard commemorating yet another kill. Right on top, where their impact would have the juiciest potency, rested Mason and Victor's heads. Her own victims.

Impulse one was to give in to the guilt that ate at her. Cower to the ground, legs drawn tight to her chest, until the world crumbled around her. Then, the tide of crazy rescinded, allowing the sands of rational thought to sift through. There was no giving up. Doing so meant willingly allowing more people to die—by *her* hand.

That left only one—*awful, icky, sweet baby Jesus I hate my life*—option.

Averting her eyes, Ireland plunged her hand straight down into the sea of heads. It entered with a sickening slurp, lost in a slow cooker of death and rot. Slime coated her skin with a dense, clammy film. Exposed, jutting vertebrates, hacked by the Hessian's blade, raked over her flesh, threatening to break the skin like a dulled pocketknife. Something small—and uncomfortably bug-like—wriggled beneath the tips of her finger. Ireland readjusted to a new spot. Maggots, real or hallucination induced, would set her gag-flex on a go for launch countdown. Tucking her nose into her shoulder, she concentrated on breathing through her mouth. It seemed the Horseman had found the button to push in her brain to add aroma-vision to his performances.

He'd proven how quickly he mastered veiling reality for her benefit, but he couldn't *actually* alter it. The cloak was there. It *had* to be. She rotated her hand at the wrist; skimming, searching, rooting for that one beacon of hope. Fabric, thick and coarse, rubbed against the knuckle of her thumb. Ireland turned her hand, causing the mountain of heads to shift. Mason's face lolled to the side; his parted lips mere inches from her face. The proximity of a lover, longing for a kiss. Revulsion skittered down her spine. Her hand closed around what she prayed to be the cloak and yanked it free. She anticipated an avalanche of heads. Instead, they blinked from sight. A clear indicator, without even having to look, that she had scored her desired cargo.

Black, benign fabric hung from her extended arms, the coarse wool fibers scratching against the sides of her fingers as her thumbs rubbed over it. Swallowing hard, she forced down the lump of trepidation rising like a fishing bobber in her throat, and swung the cloak around her shoulders. A garment closed away for centuries should've smelled musty. However, as the air moved beneath it, she caught whiffs of pine, spicy autumn air, and the unmistakable scent of equine. Her hand hovered over the clasp before securing it in place. Gnawing on her lower lip, she flicked her gaze toward the stairs. Should she warn Rip? Tell him to hide until she could steer the beast outside? Something about that idea struck her as almost laughable. Like she would snap the cloak around her and instantly become a matador to the supernatural. Physically shaking off the thought, she fastened the cloak over her breast bone.

Ireland filled her lungs to capacity and exhaled slowly—a deep sea diver preparing to plunge to the depths. Her pulse drummed each passing second in her temples as she waited for the change to take hold.

A slow green haze to seep in with leisurely laps.

A jolt of DNA altering gamma radiation.

A friggin' lady in gold lamé asking if she was the keymaster.

Something!

"Come on, dammit!" Thumbing the button free, she flipped the fabric out behind her and refastened it, as if its metaphysical powers needed a jump start.

Still nothing.

"Wha-what does this mean?" Rip stammered from his crouched position outside the cubby.

Ireland turned with a jerk. In her distraction of impending mortal peril, she hadn't even noticed he came back. "It means the dead aren't nearly as wise and all-knowing as we give them credit for. It means our last chance has failed. Most importantly, it means the Horseman can continue to use me as his little butt-monkey and there isn't *a damned thing I can do about it!*"

Just like that, it all became too much. The cloak too heavy. The room too constricting. Rip's stare too demanding.

"I have to go. I have to get out of here." The thick tread of her boots clomped across the floor, kicking up puffs of dust with each step. Bending, she swatted Rip out of the way and ducked through.

"Ireland, wait!" He side-stepped in front of her to block her traveling tirade. "Maybe we could revisit your idea to lock yourself up?"

His tone, dripping of compassion, only fueled her rage. She was a monster undeserving of pity or kindness. "There isn't time to test stupid theories now!"

His cheeks reddened at the sharp slap of her words and she rejoiced in it. *Yes! Hate me! Fear me! Run from me you stupid, sleepy bastard!*

"There's only one option left, and I need you out of my way so I can do it!"

Rip trailed her march up the stairs and through the kitchen, allowing a lag time between them so as not to smother her. "You tried hurting yourself before." His words came soft, measured. "You know that's not an option."

Ireland paused at the breakfast nook. Glancing back over her shoulder, she felt her mask of bravery crack. He shouldn't worry for her. Of her, but never for her.

"I'm not going to hurt myself." Her chin betrayed her by quivering, tarnishing her attempt to reassure him. "I'm going to drive as fast and as far away from here as I can. Praying I can get a safe distance before my internal bomb goes off and *he* takes over."

She left Rip floundering for a way to talk her down, scooped her keys off the counter, and darted out the door.

One breath of crisp autumn air.

One boot stomping over the concrete landing.

One beam from the fat-bellied moon illuminating the thick weave of her cloak.

And everything changed.

29

Ireland

Ireland's body instinctively moved with the stallion's gait. Tipping her chin slightly, she kept herself safely cloaked in the shadows of her hood.

Another red tinged flash. Rip's body splayed across her front stoop. One of his arms dangling off the concrete.

Ireland dug her heels into Regen's sides and gave him a little slack in the reins. He pulled back slightly to collect himself before bolting forward in a fresh burst of speed.

Rip shouldn't have been there. Not for the change. Not until she'd contained it. She racked her brain, trying to remember if she'd *actually* hurt him.

It had started like a scene stolen straight from a retro noir film. Lightning flashing overhead. Dried leaves whirling around her, caught in the same powerful gust that rippled beneath her cloak, whipping the heavy fabric out in a sharp *snap*. In the distance, heavy hoof beats thundered closer. *Had* it been an actual film, that's the moment a smoke machine would have belched dense black wisps to curl and snake between her legs. Someone in a cramped little booth would crunch a bag of potato chips over a microphone, adding gruesome bone crunching effects to her transformation. However, this was reality, and reality is often a cruel bitch that prides herself on the pain within the details.

The skin on Ireland's face pulled, tightened. Like an animal hide left to dry in the sun. The rises of her cheek bones and chin jutted out, only a paper thin veil of flesh whispering over them. A howling wind whistled over newly exposed bone, triggering a deep ache that stabbed into her marrow. Her mouth watered, the taste metallic. She could feel her gums—parching, burning, receding—from her teeth.

Her own desiccation had distracted her from the explosion across the street. The neighbor's shed doors blasted open in a shower of kindling. The sword—believed by Rip to be well-hidden—emerged from within, pinwheeling straight for her. In an automatic, jerk reaction, her hand raised. The hilt slapped into her waiting grasp. Ireland flipped it in her hand, with the practiced grace of someone who had spent their adolescence in fencing lessons and *not* shop lifting lipsticks, and slid it into the scabbard that had materialized on her right hip. Its counterpart erupted from a shallow mulch grave in the flower bed of the tri-level house two doors down. The axe flew, end over end, making a full loop around her before she caught it and holstered it in the leather loop on her hip.

The steady drum of hoof beats grew deafening before darkness birthed forth a magnificent equine frame from within its cloak of shadows. Ireland stumbled down the stairs and across the yard to greet him. She knew the curve of his face even before laying eyes on the ebony stallion. Knew how he responded to each subtle cue before climbing on to his back. The feel of his hot breath warmed her palm as he nudged her with his velvet muzzle, filling a void within her she didn't know she carried. Like a lost limb reattached on a grateful amputee.

Staring into the deep onyx pools of his wide eyes, she let her hands wander over the contours and valleys of his face. *"Regenboog,"* she read off the engraved silver plate on the side of his bridle. "Is that your name?"

He gave a soft whinny in response, waves of glossy back mane falling between his perked ears.

"I wonder what it means." She scratch his forehead between his eyes. "Gunpowder? Thunder? Vengeance, maybe? That'd be cool."

"Actually," Rip interjected, cautiously stepping out onto the stoop. "It's Dutch for Rainbow; a name that breeds fear in the hearts of no one. Maybe shorten it to Regen? That's slightly better."

Ireland's head snapped around at the sound of his voice. Her narrowed gaze took Rip in through the gauze-like effect of a three martini buzz. The tips of her fingers hovered over the hilt of her sword, anxiously drumming against steel.

The thump of his pulse, beneath the wiry tendons of his neck, hummed her a sweet siren song. Tempting her with seductive whispers of exactly where to strike to release the headiest gush of intoxicating crimson.

Reading the look on her alarming new face, Rip took a nervous step back. His hand fumbled with the doorknob. "Ireland? It's me, Rip. You know me."

Her head cocked playfully, a malicious grin lifting the corners of her mouth. Of course she knew him. Centuries ago she'd been ordered to kill him; a bothersome task she'd never successfully crossed off her to-do list. Until now. She stalked forward, light and easy, on the balls of her feet. Assuming the role of a predatory cat working up an appetite by playing with its food.

That's where her memory got fuzzy. Did he pass out? Did she actually draw her sword? Spiriting into the night astride Regen, Ireland still couldn't remember. The next clear recollection she had found her standing over his slumped form, shocked into submission by the reflection staring back at her from the glass door. She had turned her head one way, then the other, examining her skin, the pale hue of luminescent moonlight, which whispered over the jutting bones of her face in a delicate veil. Dark brown eyes had warmed to melted gold, the color swirling and roiling within the black hollows of her sunken sockets. Sapphire veins scrolled across her cheeks and brow in a pattern as intricate as hand-woven lace. Raising one trembling hand, she brushed the tips of her fingers against formerly rosy lips now kissed by the blue hue of death. In the change she once feared, she found a tragic beauty. One strikingly similar to the sugar skull image inked on her arm.

Disfigured as her features were, Ireland could still find herself within the monster façade. No longer was she lost deep within herself as the Hessian took hold. She had fought for her foothold and secured one.

245

Yet, the victory was not hers alone. Ichabod's essence, battered from lifetimes cuffed to the epitome of evil, had wriggled out of hiding. She could feel him, in the thudding of her heart and the odd twitching of her arm, pushing her onward. His motive? Not self-preservation, or even to aid another soul fallen victim to the Horseman. No, there was only one thing that could spur the schoolmaster, long since beaten into obedience, into assuming a defensive stance once more.

Katrina.

Somewhere, lost beneath the fallen blanket of night, danger loomed for her risen spirit, the threat coming from a force so malevolent it made the Horseman seem tame.

Covering her hand with her cloak, Ireland dug into Rip's pocket to retrieve her fail safe—the talisman. Then she spun on her heel, sprinting to Regen's side in three wide strides. The talisman disappeared inside the black leather saddle pouch, landing with a muffled *plunk.* Before another wasted second could pass, she slid her boot into Regen's stir-up for the first—and millionth—time. The feel of settling into the padding of his saddle could only be described as comfortably terrifying.

Steam wafted from his flared nostrils. Bouncing twice on his front legs, he threw himself into a rear, hooves pawing at the moon. Ireland clenched her thighs, holding the reins in a white-knuckled grasp to keep her hold. No sooner did his hooves smack to the ground, than he launched them forward in a mission completely uncharacteristic to the Hessian—*a rescue.*

30

Ichabod

Ichabod forced his lead feet forward, gaining speed and determination with each step. Within the eye of his emotional storm he found the peace of a concrete certainty. Leaves crunched under his boots as he stepped off the Van Brunt porch. Without breaking stride, he closed his hand around the handle of an ax stuck in a chopping block and yanked it free. First, he would save his friends. Then, he would come back and bury the filthy axe blade deep into the skull of the devil that killed his love.

Brom's stallion raised his head, a mouthful of grass grinding between his teeth. The untethered horse didn't run or shy away. Instead, it arched its thick neck and clomped to meet Ichabod.

The schoolmaster's hand lingered over the horse's soft muzzle for a beat before he hurled himself into the saddle. Driving his heels in hard, he spurred them both toward the inevitable.

The duo galloped into town, following the sounds of a scuffle that led them to the cemetery behind the Old Dutch Church. Rip and Irv—his brother's in war—were already engaged in a heated battle with an entity whose very existence defied all laws of science and rational thought. The two were backed up to a fence. The Horseman drew closer with taunting steps, his axe and sword whirling before him. Interweaving blades of terror. Irv's frantic hands scrambled to break off a fence post. He handed the first off to Rip, before claiming one for himself.

Even as they blocked the swings with the posts, Ichabod entertained the idea of this all being yet another ruse like that staged by Brom. Granted this Horseman, in his tattered and filthy military garb, had a much more convincing disguise. Yet this still all ventured too far into the realms of the unbelievable. Be that as it may, fact or fiction was irrelevant. Whoever, or whatever, it was planned to harm his friends. That he would not stand for. Ichabod flung his leg over the horse's head and slid from the saddle. His knees bent to absorb the shock. As soon as his boots sank into the grass, wet with dew, he plunged himself forward to dive headlong into the mix.

Rip, drenched with sweat that made his hair stick to his forehead, noticed Ichabod's intent just as he pulled back the axe. "Ichabod, no! *Run!*"

Holding the axe firm in a tight, two handed grip, Ichabod threw his weight into the strike. The blade sunk into the valley between the headless beast's shoulder and neck. Brown mire, like old blood, coursed from the wound.

There was no way to determine if the creature felt the slash in the slightest. However, his obvious displeasure became evident in the elbow he let fly at Ichabod's face. The schoolmaster's head whipped back, pain exploding from his surely shattered nose. Black spots danced before his eyes, his nose gushing like a primed spigot. He needed a moment to collect himself, but unfortunately such a pause would not be found.

Ichabod backpedalled as the long dead soldier spun on him. His feet tangled beneath him. The ground rose to meet him as consciousness—that fickle strumpet—threatened to forsake him. He had the foresight to shield himself behind the axe, as the Hessian swung his sword down for the death blow. Gleaming steel caught in the solid wood handle and held. Both man and monster pushed against each other, matching one another's strength in their fight for the upper hand.

Gaping at the headless corpse over him, the truth behind the legend made itself grossly real. Sludge oozed from the stump of the ghoul's severed spine as he leaned forward, pressing the blade of his sword down hard against the axe handle.

Rip and Irv flew to their brother's defense, smashing the fence posts against the Horseman's back, enraged cries screaming from their parted lips.

Time slowed.

The world crystalized into pristine focus.

The beast had been called to kill his friends. If they distracted him, averted his attentions for even a moment, he would eagerly complete his task. Ichabod couldn't kill what was already dead, but that wasn't really the point, was it? He didn't need to best the beast, only to stop it from hurting those he cared about. There was only one way to do that. The Horseman had been summoned to collect a head. He wouldn't rest until that twisted goal had been achieved.

For his friends, for the memory of his beloved Katrina, Ichabod relaxed his hold on the axe. It thumped against his chest before sliding into the grass beside him, announcing his surrender. His gaze flicked past the Horseman, who arched back, his sword brandished in both hands over the exposed neck stump. Ichabod's stare locked with that of his friends. In that moment, he offered them all he had left to give; a look of serenity and acceptance that he genuinely prayed would bring them peace.

Then, shutting his eyes, he accepted the swing of the blade.

31

Ireland

While cars lined both sides of the Van Brunt's long, circle drive, no movement could be detected from within the lavish estate. No soft murmurs of respectably somber voices cracked the smothering stillness of the night. Ireland kicked her leg over Regen's head, dismounting as he slowed to a walk. While a post-funeral gathering was—by no means—a hootenanny, this marked silence dripped with ominous intent.

Ireland eased herself up the two steps onto the red-brick lined porch. Black rocking chairs—that perfectly matched the paint of the door—creaked in the night breeze from either side of the entryway. Glass crunched under her boot. Ireland glanced up. The bulb from the Colonial-style fixture overhead had been smashed. Her sweat dampened palm closed around the doorknob. Finding it unlocked, she slipped inside and closed it softly behind her. The only light came from a dimmed crystal chandelier that hung from the foyer's cathedral ceiling. Cringing at the squeak of her boots over polished marble tiles, she paused. Her head snapped one way then the other, searching for movement within the darkness. The beat of her heart drummed an anxious chorus against her ribs.

Smacking the back of her hand over her mouth, she stifled a gasp.

A winding staircase, the kind you'd expect to see Rita Hayworth sashay down, sat at the opposite side of the opulent foyer. The most influential of Tarrytown residents lined both sides of the staircase, positioned shoulder to shoulder. They each stared straight ahead, still as the dead. The color was drained from their eyes, leaving them chalky white. Ireland's gaze followed the path of people up to a door at the top of the stairs. It slid open as if cued, the soft light within gently beckoning.

Ireland shook her head, expelling an exasperated breath through puffed cheeks. That couldn't have been more of a blatant trap if a neon sign dropped from the ceiling to announce it. Leaning back, she cast her gaze out the visible length of the house in either direction; her hope being to find another way upstairs that might give her even the slightest edge.

"Where's a grappling hook when you really need one?" she grumbled in a dry, cadaverous rasp that sounded frighteningly foreign to her own ears.

Seeing no other option, she edged her way up the stairs. It only took two steps before she came to the conclusion that the blank stares were far too Madame Tussauds-ish for her comfort. She opted, instead, to fix her gaze straight ahead. Her hand closed over the hilt of her sword, poised and ready.

Sinking into the lush, thick weaved carpet, Ireland stepped into a professionally decorated sitting room the size of her entire house. More of the statue-still minions lined the walls, their very presence making the hair on the back of her neck rise. Gulping back her mounting trepidation, she crept further into the room. Her weight balanced on the balls of her feet.

"How will the world remember Ichabod Crane?" Ireland immediately recognized the voice as Ana's, however the sharp edge in it was new. "As a noble man that rushed headlong into danger to save the woman he was never meant to be with? Or, perhaps as the coward that ran to save himself? We shall soon see."

Deep within her, Ireland felt Ichabod tense at the words. A red haze of hate tinted the edges of her vision, seeping in like a low lying fog.

Let's attempt a rational course of action, Ireland mentally soothed him. *One of us still has the option to make it out of here alive.*

"If I were to place a wager on it," Ana continued from her concealed vantage point. "I would guess history will not remember you at all. You will be nothing more than a snagged flaw in the intricate tapestry of life—easily overlooked due to the threads surrounding you that are far more important and impressive with their painstakingly perfect weavings."

The room opened up ahead, jutting out to the left in a separate space. Judging by the fully stocked bar, crackling fireplace, and poker table, Ireland took a wry guess it *wasn't* a knitting room. There, in one of the high-backed leather chairs, Noah sat slumped over. His hands and feet were tied, his head hung slack. Between the disheveled locks of hair that fell across his forehead, a bloody gash was visible.

Ireland lurched forward to free him. The motion was immediately halted by two formerly immobile white-eyed guests that stumbled

253

toward her in a state of third-party manipulation. Their arms swung, in a haphazard homage to Frankenstein's monster, hungry fingers curling for a hold. Ireland's sword hissed from its sheathe. She barely had time to flip it, the blade balanced between her palms, before her body launched into an attack she didn't know herself capable of. The blunt end of the handle connected dead center with one man's forehead. The woman was taken out with a potent knee to the gut, elbow to the head, combo.

"You could still make it out of this alive. I suggest you not force my hand," Ana purred, her shape emerging from the darkened corner behind the bar. While she still wore the demure black dress from the funeral, the look that curled across her face was anything but weak. Her smile could only be described as predatory.

Somewhere in the blackest recesses of her mind, Ichabod shrieked one word that resounded with a maddening echo.

"Elizabeth?" Ireland tried out the taste of the name on her lips, gauging the reaction it prompted.

"You recognized me?" she stated, her lips pressed together in a thin line as her head bobbed in an impressed nod. "There are some I have crossed paths with every day since I was a child that would fail in that same regard. After all, of what consequence am I?"

Concealed beneath her cloak, Ireland hitched one brow. "That's funny coming from you. If you weren't possessed, you'd probably appreciate the irony."

Ana's head suddenly jerked, this way and that, like an old VHS tape fast-forwarding while stuck on play. "You *are* a fast learner,

Schoolmaster." She finally settled into a deadly smirk with the passing of the unnerving episode.

"That was interesting." Ireland opted to sheath her sword and take out the next two incoming mindless drones by grabbing them by the scruff of their shirts and knocking their heads together. "I'm guessing that's what happens when the loop of events goes off script."

Her query was overshadowed by the low moan that escaped Noah's parted lips. His head lolled to the side, heavy lids fighting to open.

"Oh good, you are awake," Ana said with a little clap, bouncing on her toes like an excited child. "Now the real fun can begin."

"*What the hell, Ana?*" Noah fought against his restraints. Growing irritation wiping away the haze from his injury. "Why am I tied to a chair, and more importantly, why did you hit me with a *three-hundred dollar bottle of Scotch?*"

Ana folded her arms over her chest, drumming her fingers against her arms. "Be thankful you are beautiful, because it seems you were not blessed generously with cognitive reasoning."

"Not so much in the way of an answer, but hey, I'm a flexible guy." Noah's brow knit in tight, beads of sweat dotting his forehead. "I know you're under a lot of stress, so how about if you untie these ropes and this will be a fun 'remember when' story between friends?"

Once more, Ana seized in a series of violent twitches. Ireland took a brazen step in Noah's direction, planning to take advantage of the distraction and free him, when a harsh hammer of reality nailed her foot to the floor. The monster within her was—quite literally—on display. All her deep, dark secrets were scrawled across her bony face in an elaborate calligraphy that would show her for *exactly* what she was—*a killer*. The sanctuary of anonymity held too tempting a pull. The floor betrayed her by announcing her tentative step back with a shrill squeak. Noah's head snapped in her direction.

Dammit.

"Hey! Could you give me a hand here? The lady and I seem to be having a dispute as to what constitutes appropriate conduct in the face of deep mourning. If you could just—" Ireland felt the heat of Noah's gaze as it traveled the length of her; the unconscious bodies riddled across the floor, the weapons hung at her hips, and—the jewel in the crown of his unease—the onyx cape that concealed her face and head in shadow.

She wanted to reassure him, unfortunately there was no time. Every second that ticked by led them closer to conclusion of this tale in which Noah would die—just as Katrina had.

The best she could offer was raising her index finger in front of the shadow of her hood. *"Shhhhhhh."*

Only after watching his skin blanch did she consider how creepy that gesture probably looked.

So many nuances to consider ...

"Is this a joke?" Strands of sandy blond tangled in Noah's lashes as his nervous gaze flicked from Ireland to Ana and back again. "Because after everything that's happened lately, the Horseman thing is all kinds of unfunny."

Again, Elizabeth's spirit forced Ana into a herky-jerky fit. She settled back into real-time directly in front of Noah, with his chin clasped tight in her strained grasp. "You think that man such a hero?" Ana's image waved, like steam off of hot asphalt. For a moment the shade of her hair darkened, her features sharpening. She solidified back to herself, a dagger materializing in her hand. "Every success he ever had in this town was owed to his manipulations of the Hessian. Perhaps it is time you learned the *truth* about your precious father, princess."

Ireland moved with cautious side-steps, her fingers itching for the reassurance of her axe. Her attention was so intently focused on Ana's gleaming blade, drawing dangerously close to Noah's face, that she missed the scuffs and shuffles idling up behind her. Hands closed around her upper arms in unyielding vise grips. She fought against the hold of the white-eyed brigade, panic rising in her throat with the harsh scorch of bile. Despite her attempts, and the plethora of power that lay dormant at her novice feet, she was incapable to do anything but watch as Ana pressed the point of the dagger into Noah's cheek hard enough to dimple the skin.

"You were born with the luxury of a pedigree," Ana raved, giving the handle of the dagger the slightest of turns. "The golden child of Baltus and his lovely wife, Mariella Van Tassel."

"You know what?" Noah muttered through forced fish lips. "Put down the knife and I'll even let that princess comment go."

Noah's interruption sped Ana forward in time. She sliced his cheek in a blurred burst of speed before he could even yelp at the coursing crimson trail.

A volcano of hate erupted in the spirit of the Horseman. Seething. Bubbling. Foaming with spite that flipped the axe into her waiting grasp. It moved as an extension of herself driven by sheer force of will. Maybe later she would mull over how that happened. Now, there wasn't time. A flick of her wrist sent the axe boomeranging around the outer rim of the room. Air whistled past it as it soared. She controlled it the same as she would her own limbs, adjusting each strike to make it purposely non-fatal. One after the next, bodies collapsed to the ground. The axe taking out each of the white-eyed wall-flowers with its flat edge before they could be called into action.

Ireland didn't wait for the last of the outer cuff to go down before turning on her captors. Metal whispered from leather at the same moment she threw herself forward. The heel of her sword winged back in a potent strike, slamming between the eyes of the man on her left—that she recognized as the bank manager of the Tarrytown Credit Union. His grip loosened a moment before he toppled straight back, the floor quaking beneath the thud of his weight.

The sword flipped itself in midair, settling comfortably into her free hand. Pressing the flat of the blade to her shoulder, she lined up her shot like a wicked game of nine ball. "Sorry, Mr. Van Brunt," she murmured, placing his face from the cemetery. "For a great many things."

With no further explanation, she pounded the hilt into his temple hard enough to send him crumbling to the ground.

Ireland spun on Ana, the longing for bloody vengeance pumping through her in an endorphin bolstering rhythm she yearned to lose herself in. Her attempt at a cleansing breath came out shaky and ragged.

"I bet you think you are clever," Ana wet her lips with the tip of her tongue, sashaying coolly to Ireland's side. Amusement twinkled in her eyes like stars against the navy cape of night. "Coercing all of my secrets from me. However there is one flaw to your plan … I have yet to decide if you are going to make it out of this house alive."

"I've already decided," Ireland muttered, her teeth clenched to the point of pain, "that *you* won't be."

Ana's head spastically jerked in another precarious time skip.

"Ichabod, go!" Noah screamed, blood streaming from his face and raining down on his dress shirt. He jerked at his own words, blinking hard in visible confusion. "Wh—what … did I just say?"

Ireland's vision swam out of focus, blurring Ana's face with Ichabod's memory of Elizabeth peering at him with a complete lack of comprehension. "Is it love that roots you here? Or the fear of being made to look like a coward? Let's see if we can shake your resolve, shall we?"

Ana pivoted on her heel. Something about that subtle motion, or what he knew followed it, caused Ichabod's spirit to coil—tight, tense, ready to strike. The venom of his apprehension spread through Ireland, contaminating her thoughts with a thirst for violence. Flipping her sword in the air, she let the hilt find its home in the valley of her grasp before closing her fingers around it.

Noah pulled back as Ana neared, like he was hoping to disappear through the back of the chair. "Stay away from me with that thing, you crazy bitch!"

Ireland muttered an expletive under her breath as Ana sped into another chancy time loop. Time stabilized with Noah screaming. Ana dragged her blade over his upturned palm. Layers of tissue split. Blood pooled in the wound, seeping over the edges and spilling to the floor.

The sands in their hour glass of opportunity were quickly draining. Each reality hiccup whisked them a few chapters closer to the bloody conclusion of this tale. Noah's frantic gaze locked on Ireland, panic building behind his eyes. She watched, in slow motion, as the plea formed on his lips. Her hand raising to halt him. The axe simultaneously settling into the dip beside her thumb.

"Please, whoever you are ..."

Ana moved, skipping through the present in a ghostly blur. Ireland didn't want to tear her gaze from the glint of the dagger, unfortunately she was out of options. Filling her lungs, she uttered a silent prayer ... and closed her eyes. Ichabod had been here before. Only he knew what truly happened, making him the *only* one that could stop it.

You wanna save, Katrina? Ireland internally goaded the hitchhiker inside of her. *So,* save her, *dammit!*

Deep within her, a constricting knot of tension unraveled. Its fraying threads spreading, filling every inch of her. Her fingers adjusted on the handle of the axe, under someone else's will. Behind her lids, her eyes flickered—back and forth—spastically scouring Ichabod's memory for the moment. The opportunity. Commandeering control of Ireland's functions, it was Ichabod that lunged. The downward swing of his sword knocked the dagger from Ana's hand a second before she thrust in for the death blow. Spinning with the momentum, *he* threw the axe overhand. The blade caught the hem of her dress, pinning her, as it embedded itself in the drywall.

Noah collapsed to his knees, blood from his wounds staining a circle of gore in the beige carpet, but he was safe. That should've been enough. And yet ... the sword sizzled in Ireland's hand.

Whispering.

Goading.

Seducing her to *finish this*.

Ireland tilted her head, peering up at Ana from within the shadows of her hood. The pretty blonde foamed at the mouth, her body convulsing as the spirit within her fought to maintain even a finger-hold of control. For the moment *she* was still in there.

Elizabeth.

The warped soul that forced Ichabod to watch the woman he loved die. The vile filth that unleashed a curse that had ruined so many lives. Ireland couldn't tell if her hand moved under her own will or Ichabod's, and—if she was truly honest with herself—she really didn't care. She watched with a voyeuristic thrill as Ana's throat bobbed in a gulp beneath her blade. A little pressure, that's all it would take.

"Ichabod?"

Ireland's—*no*—Ichabod's long-dead heart leapt within his chest. The spirit of his love called to him in a sweet serenade that made all the anguish and sorrow since he'd last heard her voice fade into oblivion. Shelled in the body of his ancestor, he sheathed his sword and slowly turned. For a moment reality flickered, the image of a young man crouched on the floor being cloaked by the glowing radiance of *his Katrina.*

Apprehensive that the fates would yank her from him once more, Ichabod wasted no time. He held his breath as he closed the space between them, taking a knee at her side. Only when his tentative hands brushed her cheeks could he exhale, the tip of his finger catching a stray tear that slipped free. Her face tipped up to his, lips parting in a long awaited invitation. Their mouths met in an explosion of passion that erased the centuries they'd lost, while penning a vow for a fresh forever.

32

Ireland

His hands traveled the length of her back. The tips of her fingers brushed along the strong line of his jaw. Where Ichabod ended and Ireland began failed to matter. The same could be said for Noah and Katrina. Technicalities like that were of little consequence. The world could implode around them and still would fail to tear them apart. Not this time. Not again.

Cold, like throwing off a blanket, shocked through Ireland. She countered it by arching her back, pressing closer to Noah's warmth. With this chill came a calming peace, certainty of the most hopeful kind. Katrina and Ichabod had moved on, *together*. Ireland knew it, she felt the shift within her. Instead of untangling herself from Noah's embrace, she sought his tenderness to compensate for the sudden solitude in her core.

Only when Noah's wandering hand pushed back her hood, tangling in her short hair, did she hesitate. It took every ounce of willpower she had to pull back, her trembling lips hovering over his. The

Hessian's features were still carved on her face, reminding her of their presence with the icy prickles that sparked over exposed bone.

A groan snapped Ireland's head around. Behind them, Ana began to stir. A blaring reminder for Ireland that a none too hasty retreat would soon be mandatory. When Elizabeth's spirit lost its hold all those she'd been controlling had fallen to the ground, unconscious. Being there when they came to was *not* an option.

First, a quick good-bye. Her upper body swiveled back toward Noah, praying the spell hadn't broken for him ... not yet. She found her answer in the conflicting emotions that played across his face. Confusion. Anger. Disgust. Fear. It was the long shot contender, disbelief, which settled into the creases of his forehead and secured the primary position.

His mouth gaped open in shock. "Ireland?" he gasped.

Even if she *did* have time to explain, words failed her.

"I–I can't," she stammered, rising to her feet.

She made it a half-stride toward the door, when Noah's calloused hand closed around her wrist. "I can't let you leave." He shifted onto his hip, pulling one foot under him. His body language screamed the message that if she tried to bolt he would be right behind her. "I have some pretty major questions—the least of which being why the hell you suddenly look like the Grim Reaper's punk cousin. Before I can let you take one more step, there's a lengthy conversation that needs to happen."

Ireland's shimmering gold irises flicked nervously around the room. "And I promise that conversation will happen. I will tell you absolutely everything. Most of which will probably convince you I've gone totally bat-shit. But right now, I *have* to go. And you have to let me."

Sprawled bodies began to rouse, coming to with the noisy, gracelessness of the mindless zombies they played the part of.

Noah tightened his grasp, the pressure from his fingers marring her flesh with white divots. "I'm not letting you out of this room until you assure me you had *nothing* to do with Mason's death. And you better be pretty friggin' convincing about it, because I'm feeling awfully skeptical."

Ireland's head cocked, the pleading of her eyes canceled out by her harsh new appearance.

"Noah, please?" Desperation setting in, she yanked her hood back into place—as if that could somehow save her.

"Dammit, Ireland! I need a little truth right now!"

Her free hand itched for the hilt of her sword, encouraged by a sinister voice hissing, *Cut off his hand.*

Ireland's head snapped violently to the side. "No!" she barked. "I'm not going to hurt him!"

Noah winced, though his grip held firm.

"Ireland," his said, his words coming calm and measured, "just talk to me, *please.*"

The bank manager she'd knocked out rolled to his side. With his back to them, he cradled his head in both hands.

Time had officially run out.

"I'm sorry." Genuine sorrow made the words catch in her throat.

Gritting her teeth, she raised one heavy treaded boot. What was meant as a shove to the chest was set off course by lackluster aim. Her boot connected with his chin, wrenching his head back with a painful twist.

"Oh, *shit*! Sorry!" Ireland's hands fluttered like nervous little hummingbirds that didn't know where to land. "I'll ... pay for the dental work."

Villains don't apologize, the low growl corrected. *Now, run. Save yourself.*

Whoever he was, he had a point.

Ireland bolted for the door, her cloak snapping behind her. Sidestepping fallen bodies, she maneuvered the stairs like a high-impact obstacle course. Pausing in the foyer, she eyed the front door, choosing instead to veer to the left. The guests would beeline for the front door the second they woke up, she internally reasoned as she shimmied around the formal dining table to the French doors. Going out the back might buy her a few crucial seconds.

No sooner did the sliding door shush shut behind her, thrusting her into the harsh chill of night, than a soft whisper threatened to thwart her escape.

"Ichabod? Is that you?"

Ireland spun to find Rip staring at her with a look of hopeful expectation. Visible need etched across his face.

"He's gone, Rip. I'm sorry." Guilt twanged the strings of her heart as his face fell.

"The pull of the loop was too strong," he mumbled, almost to himself, and cast his gaze to the ground. "I had to come. Thought maybe I'd finally get that chance at good-bye."

"You were at a safe distance. He would've wanted that for you more." Ireland gave his arm a comforting squeeze, the only solace she could offer. "Now, I need you to get home. Pack us a couple bags of essentials. We may need to take an extended holiday from Sleepy Hollow. "

Rip sniffled and wiped at his nose with the back of his hand. "Figured as much."

"Hey, Rip?" she called to his back in a hushed whisper, before he could step from the paved patio.

He glanced back over a deflated shoulder.

"I'm glad I didn't accidentally kill you tonight."

Rip graced her with a tight smile before fading into the darkness.

Porcelain skin gleamed with an ethereal luminescence as Ireland tipped her head to the three-quarter moon. Pursing her blue-hued lips, she whistled one quick blast. Hoof beats thundered closer, announcing the shadow that emerged from the tree line at the back of the Van Brunt property. Regen's soulful black eyes locked on her—his totem. He stormed straight for her with the unstoppable force of a freight train.

Ireland crossed the yard to meet him, leaves crunching under her boots. Throwing one arm around his thick neck, she breathed in his scent while her other hand scuffed along the soft fuzz of his muzzle. "You have no idea how happy I am to see you."

Regen snorted his response, his nose nudging her ribs.

"Rumors of your headlessness have been greatly exaggerated." Noah's statement was punctuated by the door sliding into its latch behind him.

Throw the axe! Embed it between his eyes! That same psychotic voice giggled.

"Whoa! Easy, Dexter." Ireland winced, laying her palm to Regen's side to steady herself. "Let's try a little thing called communication."

Noah's hands rose to halt her crazy. "Okay, who the hell are you talking to when you do that? Because that is all kinds of creepy. And, trust me, after tonight, I know creepy."

"You … can't hear that?" Ireland's eyes narrowed; her stomach rising in her throat, her breath quickening to fend off an impending panic attack.

Ichabod was gone. He had been the buffer between her and the essence of the Hessian. Now the beast, and all his vile charms, belonged to her … *alone.*

More than anything, Ireland wanted to canter off into the night. To let the wind whip over her skin, lashing away reality and freeing her mind to process *any* of this. Unfortunately, Noah's tense posture made it obvious he didn't come out here for a goodnight hug.

Begrudgingly, she let her hands fall limp at her sides. A gesture that *would've* seemed innocent had it not been for the weapons slung at her hips. "So, is this the part where the noble citizen challenges the monster that ravaged the hapless town?"

Noah stepped down from the cement stair, inching his way closer. "I haven't decided yet. Right now it's pretty much up to you."

Hack him to bits!

Ireland swallowed hard to keep her internal battle in check. *You really need a hug and a cookie, don't you?*

Long bangs fell into her eyes that she flicked aside, her gaze drifting down the long driveway. "What do you want to know, that isn't blaringly obvious?"

He scuffed the heel of his foot forward in a deliberate step made to look casual. "First off, you're what? Like three hundred years old?"

"Twenty-four," Ireland corrected, with a humorless scoff. "But, thanks. I'll look into a better moisturizer."

Noah chewed on his lower lip, which was still blushed red from their brief interlude. "How does that work if you've been killing people in this town for centuries?"

"I haven't. There's been more than one Horseman. It's a curse that gets handed down to unfortunate folks like myself."

Regen nudged her back, whinnying his growing impatience. Ireland's hand wandered over her shoulder to scratch his face.

"Like the Dread Pirate Roberts, only bloodier." Noah shook his head, rubbing a hand over the back of his neck.

"Kind of, yeah." Another time, another situation, and she would've rewarded that reference with a smile.

Hazel eyes, which shone a brilliant jade in the moonlight, peered up at her from under a lowered brow. "How long has it been you?"

That wasn't his real question. They both knew that. He was skirting the issue of body count.

Ireland's hand paused mid-stroke and flattened against Regen's face, drawing strength from his might. His body stilled beneath her touch, as if he knew exactly what she needed. "From what I can tell, it started when I came to Sleepy Hollow. As soon as I learned the truth, I did

269

everything I could to gain control of it. Tonight, I did just that. I claimed what's inside of me. It won't rule me anymore."

You think that's true, little girl?

"My cousin, Vic, Mason, hell-even your own ex, those were all *your* doing?" His jaw tightened as he crammed his balled fists into the pockets of his slacks.

"I know it sounds crazy, but all of those things happened while I was sleeping. I didn't know what I was doing."

Even I don't buy that line of rubbish, and I was there.

Can you not *help?*

"I know it sounds like a cop out, but it's true." Ireland's attempt at assertiveness sounded weak even to her.

Noah's gaze locked with hers. "Why would I believe that?"

Truth was all she had left.

Squaring her shoulders, she let both hands fall to her sides. "Because I could've killed everyone inside that house tonight. And I didn't. Not a day will go by that I won't wrestle with the guilt of what I've done. But that fact only adds weight to my words when I say it *won't* happen again."

Noah chewed on her proclamation, digesting it, as he tapped the heel of one shoe on the toe of its counterpart. "That's easy to say, and maybe you even believe it. But what kind of assurance does that give me that if I let you leave here tonight any future blood you spill won't be on *my* hands?"

Words and explanation failing her, Ireland spun, taking the two steps back to Regen's side.

"Ireland, don't try it." Noah took a threatening step forward, his tone taking on an Arctic chill.

Raising one hand to steady him, Ireland covered the other with the hem of her cloak before she dug into her saddle bag. Plucking the silver chain from the thick-woven fabric with her thumb and index finger, she unbuttoned her cloak and let it fall to her feet. She focused on her breathing—in through her nose, out through her mouth—as she approached Noah with cautious strides. Warm sensation returned to her features. Each beat of her heart rushing the blood through her veins and shaking the Horseman's pull. By the time she stood face-to-face with Noah, she had reverted to the girl he'd first met that threw her coffee at him.

In the house behind them she could hear the murmur of voices and shuffling movements. At least now, if anyone peeked outside, her appearance would be less jarring.

She held the necklace out and waited the beat for him to extend his hand. The metal chain pooled in his palm, followed by a soft *tink* as the clasp thumped against the medallion. "This is the talisman of the Horseman. If I ever lose control, all you have to do is slip it around my neck. If the medallion is touching my skin it *will* shut me down. Consider it your fail safe. One I feel confident handing over to you, because *that* is how sure I am that I can be trusted."

Ireland turned away, leaving Noah staring down at his new token. Regen trotted forward to meet her, just as she bent to retrieve her cloak, and angled his body to offer her the stir-up. Without hesitation she slid her foot in and hoisted herself astride.

Noah squinted into the moonlight at her silhouette. "And if I don't believe this? If I think you're nothing but a cold-blooded killer that belongs behind bars? Then what?" There was no threat in the question, just a genuine inquiry.

"Then, I guess you're going to have to catch me first."

A light nudge from her heels was the only cue Regen needed to bolt forward, seeking refuge for them both in the concealing shadows of the night.

33

Ichabod

"That was the last you saw of the Horseman?"

China clinked as Irv set his tea cup on its matching saucer. "Far from it." He dabbed the corners of his mouth with the edge of his napkin, buying himself time to attain the right words. "The best I can deduce, the Horseman needed a specific head to allow his spirit to move on. One belonging to a person that died a hero's death, as the first Hessian did."

"One soul put to rest, while another is forced to wander in its place." Rip's bloodshot eyes filled with tears he attempted to sniff away.

"Death walks, and talks, and occasionally whisks you in a gruesome waltz." The dark-haired fellow to Rip's right twitched, his eyes wide and manic.

"Too true, friend," Rip agreed, scooting a bit farther from the eccentric stranger.

"We watched Ichabod rise," Irv rushed the words out as if longing to be free of them. "His head … gone. The last of his life blood still pulsating from the stump of his neck. He climbed onto the back of the Horseman's raven-hued steed and the two disappeared into the night."

"As I suspected." Across the table, four figures sat cloaked in plum robes with gold embroidery around their cuffs and hoods. It was the hefty man, directly across from Irv, that steepled his fingers and tipped his concealed head to the colleague to his left. "Were you able to procure the talisman?"

The second man gave a brief nod. A thin, frail hand rose to deposit a necklace onto the table. It settled with the soft clink of metal on metal.

"This was formed from metal procured from a gate that protects a synagogue in Jerusalem." The spokesman for the mysterious band plucked the medallion from the table and turned it over between his thick, swollen fingers. "It was then blessed and enchanted by the purest and most potent monks, mediums, and shaman in the farthest reaches of our world. This talisman *will* control the Hessian. The will of he who possesses it will prevent your friend from rising and claiming lives—"

A slow burn began in Rip, spreading through him like a rash that reddened his face and coated his skin with a sheen of sweat. "You did not acquire a possession such as that in a day's time. You have *had* it! *Known* what it could do! You could have stepped in! Could have saved him … could have saved *all* of them!"

The man raised his hand to steady Rip's rant, his sleeve sliding further up to reveal two small age spots on the side of his forearm. "I understand your dismay, and you have my deepest of sympathies. However, as regrettable as it is, we could not save Ichabod Crane. The former Horseman's essence had been submerged in the perils of darkness for far too long. The talisman would not have had the same pull on him. By implementing it now, we can—for lack of a better term—inoculate Ichabod's spirit before it can be completely corrupted. Yet, our work must not end there. The truth of what happened here must be concealed."

"It may be too late for that." Irv rubbed his chin, his jaw clenched tight. "Rumors have surfaced in the Hollow that the Horseman can be controlled. I have no doubt that some may already be attempting to deduce how."

"Then we must act quickly!" The spokesman jolted the room by slapping his palm against the table. His chin jerked toward the soft-spoken man with the bushy mustache drumming his fingers on the edge of the table. "Mr. Hawthorne has connections within the literary community. I propose we conceal the facts in plain sight. Create our own bit of folk lore and legend that will steer people from a truth that could result in genocide. Mr. Irving, could I trust you to pen such a work?"

"I am a scholar, *sir*," Irv spat, infuriation morphing his face from red to purple. "I thrive off the pursuit of knowledge and the power that comes with an excess of information. Yet, you invite us here, by elaborate hand-scrolled invitation, and coax us to spread deliberate falsehoods? What possible motivation could you have in this? If you have *facts* to back these uproariously preposterous claims of yours, please, *speak!*"

Silence stifled the room. The cloaked figure at the far end of the table rose to his feet. His chair squeaked across the wood floor as it pushed from the table. Pivoting his upper body, he faced Irv and drew back his hood.

Rip threw himself back in his chair, his hand seizing his friend's arm. Irv's mouth opened and shut—a fish on dry land flung into a world where everything it thought it knew was wiped away.

"That one is lively," the manic-looking fellow beside Rip giggled, "has not even begun to reek."

What they were seeing delved into fantastical realms of the impossible. Even so, the old man—with the eerily familiar face—spoke in a recognizable cadence desiccated by time, "All at this table have been touched by the very darkest of magicks."

At the other end of the table, the mustached man scoffed in obvious disdain. Still, he said nothing.

"Each of your unique situations could be unleashed on this world, with the impact of unstoppable plagues against mankind," the man continued, his gaze flicking to Irv's face, in particular, with interest. "This is not a threat, or a possibility, but an absolute certainty that has been foreseen."

"By ... *you*?" Irv croaked, finally finding his voice. His earlier arguments replaced by slack-jawed astonishment.

The old man's mouth twitched in an almost smile. Whether intentional or not, he avoided the question. "The other two gentlemen have already given their compliance."

"*I wish I could write as mysterious as a cat,*" Rip's increasingly odd neighbor mused, gazing wistfully into the flickering flames atop the candelabra.

"It falls now to the two of you." Hands ravaged by arthritic knots curled around the armrests as the elderly man eased himself back to sitting. "What say you, gents? Will you join the brotherhood of our cause?"

Irv's lingering points of concession were lost in the overloaded labyrinth of his mind. The most he could muster was jerking his chin in agreement.

"Very good," the spokesman said with audible pleasure. "There is one more favor we must ask. This one falling to you alone, Mr. Van Winkle."

"Me?" Rip snorted, deeply longing for a pull from the flask hidden beneath his coat. "What possible good am I?"

"For this particular task, you are actually quite the treasure," the barrel-chested figure corrected. "Your ... lackadaisical existence making you the perfect candidate."

Rip leaned forward in his seat. Cradling his head in his hands, he internally vowed to drain the flask bone dry the second he stepped foot from that stuffy room. "Planning to feed me to the Horseman, are you? Letting him quench his thirst for violence with this glorified drifter no one will miss?"

"You depreciate your worth. A new, and decidedly undesirable, trait in you." The old man steadied himself with a hand on the table as he turned to address Rip directly. "The role we have for you is an imperative one. Another Crane will come to Sleepy Hollow. With your guidance she will change everything the world will come to know of the Hessian. Until then, we need you to keep the talisman safe and prevent Ichabod from harming anyone."

Rip rubbed a hand over the bristly stubble of his growing beard. "And when is this prodigal Crane set to arrive?"

The spokesman's index finger flicked in a subtle gesture to the older man's hood. Quickly, the fuzzy haired man replaced it. "The wait will be a lengthy one. Fortunately for you, we know of a way to make it breeze by in what will feel like a blink."

Rip gulped, his mind seeing sinister smiles beneath the shadowed voids of those hoods. Casting a nervous glance to Irv, he hoped his studious friend would offer some valid argument that would free him of this yolk. Instead, all Irv offered was a resolute nod of encouragement.

Epilogue

Ireland

"It feels like we're running."

"We aren't running."

"I didn't say we *were* running. I said it *feels* like we're running. And this does, in fact, have a very definite fleeing vibe to it."

Rip slapped a hand over his eyes, then slowly dragged it down his face and over his beard. "Twenty minutes. That is how long we have been having this exact same argument. Is there *any* chance we can agree to disagree on the terms of our travels and achieve some sort of peace?"

Ireland's grip tightened on the steering wheel, faux leather squeaking beneath her hands. "Probably not! You made me look like a liar!"

"How exactly did I do that, when *you* were the one that told *me* to pack our bags?" Rip shifted in the passenger seat, turning his upper body toward her in genuine, slightly irritable, interest.

"You weren't there! You didn't see how things went with Noah!" Her hand flipped from the steering wheel as if that erratic gesture could somehow demonstrate her point. "I had this big, bold moment where I told him I could be trusted. After which, *despite what I said to you*, I fully intended to take a firm stand *at home* to show him I meant it and have nothing to hide! Now, because of you, I have a poorly packed weekender in the backseat and look like I'm oozing guilt!"

"Well, you did recently slaughter two innocent people," Rip pointed out, crossing his arms over his chest.

Ireland's chin dipped to shoot him a sideways glare. "In what world is that considered helping?"

"Didn't know I was supposed to be trying to." One narrow shoulder rose and fell casually. "But the truth of the matter is that things have escalated far faster than we could've possibly imagined. You *are* the Hessian now and somewhere out there is a person, or persons, that had the foresight to pull the right strings to get that talisman inked onto your flesh. Which means someone out there knows you can be controlled. Now we *could* sit idly by, cross our fingers, and hope for the best—a method that *used* to be my tried and true. However, to save you from going on another unintended killing spree, I suggest we take a more proactive approach. The tattoo came from a shop in Manhattan, that's as good a place as any to start looking for answers."

Ireland's narrowed gaze flicked from the road to Rip, and back again. "You've known about my tattoo from the beginning of all this, and yet tonight, after everything that's happened, you *insist* we drop everything and go investigate? Why do I feel there's more to this than you're telling me?"

Rip clung to the dashboard as the car swerved between the lanes. "Because you're an infuriatingly suspicious girl that drives with the bouncing skill of a metronome?"

"Nope, try again!" Ireland jerked the wheel in another rapid lane change.

"*We had to break the curse first!*" he yelled, finding his sense of urgency in that second swerve. "Only then would you be fit to travel and *safe* to be around others! We succeeded at that! There wasn't an ideal time to pursue this until *now!*"

Ireland steadied the wheel. The nasty pill of rational thought Rip administered dissolving bitterly on her tongue.

That would've been the end of it, had Rip not felt the need to get one last jab in. "Now could you *please* focus on the road, or should I brace myself for further infantile tantrums?"

Blatant disrespect! Cut off his tongue and feed it to him!

Ireland's shoulders sagged. "Way to go, you woke up my little friend," she grumbled. "Do you think I'll ever get used to his endless spewing of hate and violence?"

Rip twisted the end of his beard around his index finger. "Eventually you'll learn to tune it out, or it'll drive you slowly mad. One or the other."

Shove his head out the window and drive through a narrow overpass!

"That's a comforting thought." Even she was a bit unsure of which of them she'd answered.

Rip bobbed his head, pleased with himself for helping. "We don't need to make the entire lengthy voyage tonight." He stifled a yawn behind his hand. "Perhaps we could find an inn? Continue our quest in the morning?"

"Nice of you to volunteer me to fund this exhibition, Frodo." Ireland smirked, flicking her bangs from her eyes.

"My apologies. I was thinking of your comfort as much as my own. We can press on if you'd like."

He's not sorry! Slice his throat! Let his body rot in a ditch!

"*No!*" Rip's eyes widened at the sharp bite of Ireland's tone. Clearing her throat, she attempted to imitate normal. "We can absolutely stop somewhere, not a problem at all."

Even better! Take your time and slash him into small flushable bits!

"*Hey!* Let's listen to some music! The louder the better!" Ireland stabbed the radio on, cranking the volume. Finding static on the first station, she hit the search button. It settled on a deep, raspy voice that filled the car with the audible equivalent of warm molasses. Instantly, she recoiled. "Ugh, no."

She was about to tap the search button again when ….

What is this drivel that assaults my ears?

Her finger hovered over the button. Waiting. Testing. "This would be the music of one Kenneth Rogers in which he soulfully explains to his female companion—or his, *lady*—that he is her knight in shining armor and he loves her. You like?"

"I do!" Rip beamed, swaying side-to-side, blissful in his misconception she was talking to him.

282

Turn it off you vile sorceress! End me of this torment!

"Yeah, I don't think I'm gonna." Ireland demonstrated that point further by securing her hands precisely at the two and ten o'clock positions.

I shall return! Make no mistake of that!

Then, *finally*, silence.

"This is much nicer than the music from my day," Rip said, humming along to the tune. "Significantly less accordion. Do you listen to it often?"

"I do now." Despite the horrific night, a slow smile curled across her lips. "Matter of fact, I think this is my new favorite song."

Ireland perched on the edge of the hotel bed with one leg curled under her and the other dangling off the side. A soft knock at the door tore her gaze from her laptop. "For the last time, Rip, we are not sharing a room. Go to sleep you skeevy, old perv!"

Silence restored, she clicked the mouse and dragged another overly sappy country song from her purchased folder onto her iPod. Another knock sounded, more insistent this time, just as she highlighted another selection.

"Oh, for crying out loud!" Throwing herself off the bed, she stomped to the door and yanked it open with more force than necessary. "It seems redundant for me to have to say I am the *wrong* person to tick off, yet—"

Her rant trailed off. Replaced by her jaw swinging wide at the well-muscled frame casting a long shadow through her room. His name slipped from her lips as a breathless whisper, "Noah?"

"I can't imagine the reception would've been any warmer if you knew it was me." His gaze rose slowly, peering up at her from under his brow. The look of a naughty boy that had stayed out long after the street lights came on.

"I wouldn't have rolled out the red carpet, that's for sure." Tossing her hair back, she tried to distract from the rosy flush that warmed her cheeks at the sudden *painful* awareness of her tank top/boy-short pajama combo. "What are you doing here?"

"I followed you." Leaning his shoulder against the doorframe, his gazed flicked passed her into the room. "Spent most of the drive right behind you. Heck, I even waved a couple of times. It's actually kind of alarming how unaware of your surroundings you are when you drive."

Ireland scowled and glanced over her shoulder. "What are you looking at?"

"Checking to see where your 'uncle' or that gigantic horse are hiding. Seems a small room for the whole family."

"Rip is most likely snoring away next door at an octave that can make the human ear bleed. And Regen, honestly, I have no idea where he goes. Maybe he haunts a hay field until I need him. Plus," she tagged on, pointedly hitching one brow, "they know I can handle myself."

"I saw you in action. You don't have to tell me." Pushing himself off the door, Noah took a brazen step into the room.

Ireland planted her feet, refusing to give an inch. "What do you want, Noah?" Sweat dampened her palms, but she refused to give him the satisfaction of seeing her wipe it away.

For a moment he said nothing, just stared, his hazel eyes gleaming flecks of warm amber in the room's dim light. His tongue flicked across his lower lip while he searched for the right words. A simple gesture that caused tingles of heat to spread through her chest.

When explanation failed him, he dug into his pocket. Presenting her with his closed fist. "This belongs with you."

Ireland forced her stare to his slowly opening hand. "My talisman? Why would you give that back?"

"The night you spent at my house, you had it on. You were trying to control—whatever it is inside you."

Ireland's lips parted, yet bobbing her head was the closest she could come to forming a thought.

"Tonight, you saved me without hurting anyone and it had *nothing* to do with this thing." Metal clinked in his palm as he thrust his hand in her direction. "I believe you, Ireland, and I *trust you* enough to give this back."

Her brows knitting together tight, she took a tentative step back. "I don't want it."

Suspicion etched deep lines across his forehead. "Why?"

"I—I have control," she stammered in explanation. "I know that. Even so, it doesn't change the fact that I *have* hurt people. And I *never* want that to happen again." Blinking hard, she held back the sudden wash of tears that threatened. "I need someone I can trust to hold that for me.

So that if the worst were to happen—if the monster ever gets free—they can stop it."

Noah's features softened. With a brief nod of understanding, he returned the talisman to his pocket. "I think I'm the right guy for that job."

"I figured." Her gaze flicked around the room. Settling on the bed, the tacky curtains, anywhere but at him. "You've seen the monster. You know it needs to be stopped."

"*No.*" The firm, uncompromising rise of his tone snapped her head around. "I mean, yes—obviously—but that's not why I'm agreeing to this."

"Thanks for clearing that up," Ireland muttered, pulling down the drifting hem of her fitted tank.

Noah raked his fingers through his hair, leaving it a disheveled mess. "I remember *everything.*" The words exploded from his mouth, tripping over his tongue as they rushed to be free. "I remember how they—*we*—felt about each other. How Ichabod and Katrina struggled, and ached for just a few more seconds together. And I ... I don't want to have to live with that same loss."

Ireland's hands tightened into fists at her sides, hope building within her that she tried to extinguish before getting burned. "I'm going to need you to spell out what it is you're trying to say in small words, because I feel a bout of dense coming on."

"I'm saying that there was a reason Ichabod and Katrina chose each of us and blood had nothing to do with it!" Noah rubbed his hand vigorously over the late-day stumble on his chin, finding a less anxious tone beneath a deep, cleansing breath. "There's something undeniable between us, Ireland, and it's been there since the moment you threw scalding coffee at me. Tonight, for one amazing minute, I experienced the perfection that could be *us*. It's the same connection Ichabod and Katrina had. When they lost that, it *wrecked* them! Their own deaths paled in comparison! Well, I'll be damned if I'm going to go through that. From now on, I want it to be you and me," a half-smile tugged at the corner of his mouth, most likely at the sudden realization he should give the lady a choice in the matter, "if you'll have me?"

Ireland's gaze scoured his face, her heart thudding in her chest. Still, her feet stayed planted, maintaining a safe enough distance for a clear head. "And if I say yes? Then what?"

Desired brewed in his eyes, sparking flares of bold citrine. Taking another step into the room, he kicked the door shut with the side of his boot. The curl of one finger gesturing her to him. "Then, come here."

Ireland stared out into the night, the tips of her fingers fiddling with the edge of the thick polyester curtain. The moon illuminated the scarcely filled parking lot with the potency of a lighthouse beam. She should have been sleeping, like Noah was. His hair ruffled and his handsome features mashed into the mattress. The sheet slipping down to expose his bare back, while selfishly hiding the perfect curve that lay just beneath it. Unfortunately, that blissful state of calm eluded her.

The *need* swelled within in her, building in intensity from the moment her head hit the pillow. Not for blood, or violence—thankfully.

But an anxious itch beneath her skin, longing for the moonlight's kiss as she raced through the darkness with the wind whipping around her. Gnawing on her lower lip, she dropped the curtain and went searching for her jeans. Even as she wriggled into them, she braced herself for the possibility that it wouldn't work. After all, she'd left the Hollow and hadn't felt Regen's presence since. Even so, the tremble of her hands proved she had to try.

"Going for a ride?" Noah mumbled, his voice low and gruff.

Retrieving her cloak from the back of the green paisley-print upholstered chair, she flung it over her arm. "That was the plan, but I can stay …" Her sentence trailed off, primarily because she wasn't sure there was an ounce of truth behind it.

Noah propped himself up on one elbow, his free hand grinding the sleep from his eyes. "If we try to stifle what you are, it'll fester and build out of control. Do what you need to do. But … *uh* …"

"What?"

"Put my mind at ease by leaving the weapons here?"

Ireland yanked the door open, smiling at him through night's veil of anonymity. "My sword is in the closet, the axe is in the back hatch of my car."

"Then, go." Scooting further down on the mattress, he flopped back on the pillows. "Conquer the night, make great haste, or whatever the hell you plan to do at this hour."

"Be back soon," she promised before clicking the door shut.

Her cloak came alive in the breeze, curling and snapping in giddy anticipation as she fastened it around her shoulders. Shifting her weight nervously from one foot to the other, she filled her lungs, then stepped under the moon's glowing reach. The familiar twinge came quick. Skin tightening, glossing over bone. Nerves, raw and exposed, becoming abnormally attuned to her surroundings.

The victorious moment of awakening was tragically tarnished by two mini-explosions. One raining toothpick-sized kindling across her boots as her sword burst through the closed door, finding its own way into its sheath. The second, by the axe blasting through safety glass. Ireland caught it in midair, shaking her head in dismay at the shards of glass that tinkled to the ground.

Noah's face appeared through the bowling ball-sized hole in the door, any traces of sleep chased away.

Curtains parted as other guests peeked out at the ruckus.

Ireland raised her hood to cover the flaming red blush of her skull. "We're gonna need to call maintenance, and a body shop."

In the distance, hoof beats thundered closer, moving in fast.

"You're footing the bill for this, Destructo-Girl." Noah scooted across the bed to snatch the phone from its cradle.

"I can't be bothered with such things!" she crowed with mock conviction.

Gravel kicked up under his hooves as Regen skidded to a stop in front of her, offering his nose in greeting.

She granted him a loving pat before hoisting herself into the saddle. "For, I am an enigma! A creature of the night!"

"Just remember who's holding your wallet and car keys, creature of the night," Noah called, his grin audible.

Ireland cued Regen forward, infectious laughter bubbling in her chest. She reveled in the sensation of his muscles pulling back for a beat before exploding forward, the lurch taking her breath away. Leaning into his gait, she let herself fall into the rhythm of his wide strides. The world whipping past in a blur of shapes and colors—at least for her.

Regen, on the other hand, saw everything. Each leaf that fluttered to the ground. Every stick that cracked beneath his hooves. His head twitched at a flash of black, finding a raven perched high atop the glowing neon of the hotel sign.

The stallion's ears perked as the raven's chest swelled to release one, lone caw, "*Nevermore.*"

The Adventure Continues

with

Raven,

Legends Saga Book 2
by

Stacey Rourke

releasing

Fall 2014

About the Author

RONE Award Winner for Best YA Paranormal Work of 2012l
Young Adult and Teen Reader voted Author of the Year 2012
Turning Pages Magazine Winner for Best Teen Book & Best YA Book
of 2013

Stacey lives in Michigan with her husband, two beautiful daughters, and two giant dogs. She loves to travel, has an unhealthy shoe addiction, and considers herself blessed to make a career out of talking to the imaginary people that live in her head. She is currently hard at work on the continuations of the Legends Saga as well as other literary projects.

Visit her at:
 www.staceyrourke.com
 diaryofasemi-crazyauthor.blogspot.com
 Facebook at http://www.facebook.com/pages/Stacey-Rourke/
 or on Twitter @Rourkewrites.

Also by Stacey Rourke:
The Gryphon Series;
The Conduit
Embrace
Sacrifice
Ascension

Nonfiction Work:
I'm Not Crazy, I'm on Lupron; a Journey through Infertility